Muddy Hearts

A Raleigh Cheramie Mystery

Jessica Tastet

Muddy Hearts
Copyright 2017 Jessica Tastet

Cover Design by Ashley Comeaux-Foret
Formatting by Polgarus Studio

ISBN 978-0-9986173-2-9
ISBN 978-0-9986173-3-6

For my Nanny Sue,
I can't imagine what my life would be like
without your support. Thank you.

Chapter One

"I'm not going to do the horizontal Hokey Pokey with him if that's what you think," Madison said, grabbing a cardboard box from the trunk of her silver coupe. "I just think he has a nice ass."

Raleigh Cheramie stiffened her back against the shudder inching up her spine. Raleigh willingly admitted to some prudish tendencies, but they were talking about the stuffy TV studio manager's derriere. With the three years he had over their father, not to mention the annoyance of him being their boss, his bottom did not fall anywhere on Raleigh's radar.

"Besides," Madison said, shrugging. "He likes blondes. He's been salivating over Aryanna since the show began."

Aryanna was one of the contestants on Barbeaux Bayou's newest craze, *Barbeaux Hearts*. This travesty was the small Louisiana Bayou town's attempt at joining the world of reality television. The show itself was primitive at best, but Madison's "baby" of an idea had hit it off with the locals, and its popularity had spilled over into the neighboring towns as fast as the Louisiana weather changed.

Raleigh was happy for her sister, as she was supposed to be. And that held no sarcasm in her head. At least not much anymore after she'd repeated it to herself for the umpteenth time. She had some serious questions about the whole karma thing not working the way it should since Madison had caused her fair share of trouble in their small town, most notably her recent scandalous sex party business, but maybe Madison had some escape-karma-biting-you-in-the-ass card that Raleigh didn't have enough karma points to achieve.

One of the Cheramie sisters should be so lucky.

From Madison's car trunk, Raleigh grabbed the last cardboard box overflowing with donated candle lanterns for the show's weekly shindig. "I thought you were dating the guy with the dog?"

"The guy" was this long, shaggy haired man with an overgrown beard who always wore t-shirts with weird sayings that required explanations. Never had a more mismatched couple been made, but Raleigh kept judgments to herself because heaven knew her personal life wasn't above scrutiny.

Trailing behind Madison, Raleigh noticed Mike's white Jeep parked in its usual spot at the entrance of the station. Raleigh and Mike, *Barbeaux Gazette's* reporters, worked most days of the week, but Raleigh had also agreed to assist Madison in producing her reality show. And since most of the show filmed on weekends, Raleigh couldn't remember when her last day off had been. Perhaps three weeks ago when she'd volunteered to take Me'Maw to the doctor's office. It had taken all afternoon with the blood work, and it had almost felt like a vacation.

Madison's button nose scrunched up in disgust as she scanned her badge in near the door. "He thought he was dating the old me. You know, man's fantasy version, complete with costumes and role playing. I'm just too tired after work to pretend that he's like *pain perdu* in bed, when he's really just plain sliced bread on his best day."

As the supposed dating expert on her reality show, she should know to steer her own dating efforts towards another town where no one knew her past. Everyone knew everything there was to know about you in Barbeaux Bayou... sometimes even before you knew it. Cousin Jolie had found out that Will was going to propose marriage from Ms. Maude who'd seen Will buy the ring as she'd been getting her new glasses from Lens Perfect, next door to Bayou Jewelry. By the time Will had walked down to Phil's hardware clutching the jewelry box proudly in his hand, Ms. Maude had called half their neighborhood, including Cousin Jolie's dad, who Will had planned to talk to that night at dinner. If Madison wanted to date, she should date in another state.

Raleigh kicked the door open and the dark, cool interior swallowed them. On Sundays no one worked in the front offices. Raleigh glanced towards the direction of the cubbyholes, but Mike's usual light didn't shine in the darkness. He must be somewhere in the mix of backstage workings where the actual production took place on the weekend. Madison and Raleigh placed the boxes down in the large recording studio, and then crossed toward the light shining from the small window in the door of the editing room.

As they approached, the gray door swung open, and Francois's head emerged. "Finally," he grumbled.

Not one for pleasantries, Francois spent most of his time mumbling under his breath these days about greedy people and shoving it all up their you know what. Raleigh tried to chalk his attitude up to stress. Besides from two talk shows, a fitness show, and a cooking show, the BBTL (Barbeaux Bayou television) studio did not usually spend much effort on local programming. Francois had grown lazy over the last fifteen years. A reality television series had proven a bit much for him. Sure, they'd hired a few camera guys right out of college to help out, but their lack of budget meant some creativity with filming, and Francois wasn't much for creativity. Or work. Or effort. He had attitude to spare though.

"Footage ready?" Madison said, putting the box down.

Francois shrugged. "It's your job to tell me, remember?"

Madison rolled her eyes. "After twelve episodes, I know, I get it."

Raleigh pressed her lips firmly together to avoid her emerging smile. Madison and Francois hadn't exactly hit it off. In fact, Francois's laziness and stone age habits grated on Madison's impatience and short-temper. There'd been a screaming match between the two just last week when Madison accused him of stealing a granola bar. Of course, it had really been over the not so easily resolved difference in editing styles for the show. Raleigh considered watching someone get under Madison's thick skin a perk of this job. Heaven knew that Madison had done more than her fair share of this to Raleigh since she was born.

Raleigh followed Madison and Francois into the editing room where a row of flat-screen television screens rested on top of tables with several dilapidated chairs scattered across the room. On the left screen, a pretty blonde with a sprinkling of freckles was frozen in a more flattering way than the usual terror-filled widened eyes look she managed every time the camera focused her way. Clara Boudreaux's shyness hadn't brought her popularity or proved attractive on the shallow matchmaking show, even though she'd shown potential in her audition.

"How did Clara's interview go?" Madison asked, sliding into a chair on the computer to the right. With her hand on the mouse, she popped open several video files at once, images splaying across the screens.

"Better today." Francois shook his head. "But she's still the wallflower of the group, and I've noticed she doesn't get as flustered one on one with the camera."

Raleigh leaned over and clicked the play button on Clara's screen. Clara's pale oval face became animated, but her eyes didn't meet the screen or look directly at anyone beyond the screen.

"I don't think it's fair that some of these girls… well, some of them… I really shouldn't say anything, I suppose."

Raleigh groaned. Editing Clara into the hour episode was impossible most weeks because she gave them nothing usable. This was just more of the same.

Francois grinned. "Wait."

Clara's brown eyes finally looked directly into the camera, right at the three of them in the editing room. An uncomfortable oddness came over Raleigh. Even after twelve weeks, it still felt strange having the people she spent her time with stare back at her from a television screen.

"I know who I want when this show ends. I've always known. But this show will end and all these women will stop acting like sluts for the camera, and then he'll notice me. That's what happens to two-bit hoes when they are seen for what they are. They will lose out."

"Oh my," Raleigh said, bracing herself on the back of the nearest chair. Clara had another side to her, and it had not learned to just say *bless your heart* like any normal southern girl.

Madison smiled. "Well, won't that add a bit of hot sauce to this week's menu."

Raleigh frowned. Frankly, more hot sauce wasn't what they needed. A fire hose to cool this crazed bunch down would be better served.

"Make notes." Francois handed Madison a clipboard. "I'm going out for a smoke."

Madison nodded as she clicked to replay the clip back.

Raleigh didn't care for that focused look in Madison's eyes. This show had been like dumping live crawfish in a boiling pot and only turning the stove to simmer so you could watch them swim around a bit before they died. Trouble had simmered from the introduction mixer, and Madison had enjoyed stirring the pot and watching them swim. On national television that might be what people wanted, but Madison and Raleigh lived in a small town. Raleigh had just bought a house, and she didn't want to be chased out by a lynch mob when the show ended because the crawfish rebelled.

"Madison." Raleigh sighed. She knew talking sense into Madison was impossible, but she still tried, on a daily basis. "I think that may be going too far. Do we want to show a brawl on television?"

Madison smiled that perfect teeth smile, the smile that Raleigh now referred to as the television smile. When Madison was fourteen, Raleigh called it the evil smile.

"It's exactly what we want." Madison jotted down a few words on the clipboard. "Everyone is watching now, from Barbeaux to Houma. If we could get New Orleans to notice, we'd be set. It's the only way to get a second season."

"I know you don't want to hear this again, but we live here with these people."

Nodding, Madison ignored her and continued scribbling. Deon Soignet came onto Madison's screen, his cocky grin and warm honey eyes playing for the camera. As one of the standout contestants with the female demographics, Deon garnered much air time that Raleigh didn't believe he deserved, but to be fair, he was the father of her close friend Sheri's son, and a horrible one at that. After only two months sobriety, he was using the show to gain sympathy for his upcoming custody hearing, at least in the court of public opinion. The man was a sleaze bag. At auditions, Madison had believed him perfect for the camera though.

"I need a good woman so my son can have a good role model, you know." He smiled, his face the picture of sincerity. Even that dimple on his right cheek perfectly fitting the image. "I'm not sure which one would be a better mother though. I'm hoping for a little help from the audience in deciding." He winked at the screen. Raleigh could vomit. Shawn had a perfectly fantastic mother, and he didn't need one of these desperate women to screw him up.

Madison tapped her pencil on the clipboard. "I wish he'd shut up about that already. He already gets the sympathy vote from the audience. He can stop going on and on about it." She glanced at Raleigh, one eyebrow raised. "Maybe you can talk to him?"

"Me?" Raleigh narrowed her eyes. "You may want to rethink that."

"Oh, all right." Madison groaned. "I will. You can work more with Clara and get her to come out of her shell during the challenges. She'll still be single when the show is over if she continues shying away from the camera."

"Maybe we should find out who the guy is that she obviously wants and see if we can get that on screen."

Madison nodded. "You do that and then maybe at one of the next challenges we can try to get some sparks to fly. The finale is in less than three weeks. We need as many matches as possible."

Madison chewed on her lip, staring at the television screen. Madison's dream was to start a matchmaking business, and she wanted this to be the start of it. Apparently, some random comment Raleigh had made months ago had sparked a fire in that brain of Madison's, and she'd pursued it like a mother bear with a lost cub. Within two weeks, Madison had put a proposal together for this show and had worked her way into Nolan Delacroix's, the owner of the station's, good graces, and had the green light to push ahead with a miniscule budget that Madison had spent the next two weeks tripling by gaining sponsors. In the midst of this, she'd outlined the business that would pick up where the show's season left off in a few weeks.

Madison's finest quality was determination, and Raleigh had to give that to her. Raleigh had never thought the former stripper, ex-whore house owner had it in her to go legit, but Madison had put everything she'd learned into this new venture.

But Raleigh also knew that Madison was worried that the show wouldn't be enough to propel the business forward. She needed the grand finale, a huge Mardi Gras ball, to leave a lasting impression, but the contestants' matches were lukewarm. Not too many sparks flying.

Raleigh wasn't sure that this planned lasting impression was the right impression either. The older residents of Barbeaux Bayou didn't like certain risqué scenes like last week's tops-off side show with two contestants who'd snuck off to the woods during the live taping. Madison's show had put Barbeaux Bayou in the spotlight, but the question became what were they spotlighting.

The door of the editing room swung open, and Francois stumbled in clutching his stomach.

Raleigh sprang away from her chair and from him, as he looked a little green. She hesitated moving in to aid him, unclear what was wrong.

Madison had turned at the interruption. "Well, what's wrong with you?" Madison snapped.

"Out...outside." His body trembled. He clutched his stomach tighter as he doubled over. "So much blood."

Blood. Raleigh's first thought this morning was that she'd managed three weeks without a dead body, and it had been nice not to see death. Looking at Francois, she recognized the look of death. That grim set around the mouth. The pasty flesh. The twitch around the jaw that fought the urge to hurl. Oh, no. That look. Wait. Mike hadn't come find her yet. She rushed past Francois, her heart thundering with the thought of a missing Mike among the offices.

Raleigh flung the back doors of the studio open where they'd had a social mixer just last night and where she also knew the smokers went to have their nicotine fix. She registered Madison stumbling out after her as her eyes searched the area where lights were still strung up and picnic tables were still scattered around the area. Pirogues had held ice and beer only last night, though now they stood resting against the trees of the tree line.

After a moment of frantic, unfocused searching, Raleigh settled on a crumpled body in a clear patch just before the tree line. A lump of blue fabric and lumps of brown and maroon jutted out, indicating something besides the trees and grass at least. Raleigh sprinted toward the body. Even with the setting sun, thirty feet away she could see that it wasn't Mike's sun bleached hair attached to a mess of a body. She slowed some so that she skidded to a stop five feet from the mangled remains.

Blood seeped from rips and mangled tears. Revulsion shuddered through her as she realized the body appeared chewed up and spit out.

Except for one cut across his cheek, Deon Soignet looked like he had only minutes ago on the screen, except for those lifeless eyes staring up at them.

The now familiar electrical tingling in her skull jolted her from her frozen stance.

She'd seen a dead body before. For heaven's sake she was Raleigh Cheramie, traiteur to the dead, after all. Her grandmother was Barbeaux's leading expert on everything that ailed its people. The living people that was. Raleigh's curse was the ailments of the dead.

She connected to the dead as they were dying to spend their last moments with the spirit before it moved on, and she'd basically became a hotline for Barbeaux's dead over the last few months as word had gotten out about what she could do. Gretchen Melancon had forgotten to tell her son that she'd left her savings in the mattress in the guest room last month before she died, so of course, Raleigh had connected with her as she was leaving her body during a heart attack. People didn't even have to like Raleigh to connect to her and curse her with experiencing their death.

Except Deon lay mangled before her, and he didn't like her.

She looked up at the orange and golden sky waiting for it to fall in on her because obviously the world had to be ending if she hadn't had to experience this horrible death. Someone up there wasn't usually that generous.

The clouds were still and the sky beautiful. Nothing would be falling in on her today, but Deon's last moments had slipped away with him, as well as any clues as to what had mutilated him.

Chapter Two

A stiff wind ruffled through the trees whistling eerily through the rustling leaves. Raleigh shivered. The overgrown trees and shrubbery grew wild and took on a sinister shadow now that a dead body rested only ten feet from the edge.

"What do we do?" Madison whispered, clutching Raleigh's arm.

Well, usually when Raleigh found a dead body by connecting to it, she came armed with Mike or Cousin Joey or Max or anyone really to stand between her and the dead body. It was always enough having the dead person in her head, so a barrier between her and the body served as a buffer.

The back metal door swung open, and Raleigh turned to see Francois clutching the doorframe. "I've called it in, and the police are on their way."

Francoise made no move toward them. Raleigh looked back toward the body, and then her flesh rose. Something had chewed Deon up like a dog's bone. Something might still be out here among the overgrown evergreen bushes and pine trees.

"Don't touch anything or get any closer," Raleigh said, scanning the area, wondering if they should wait back by the building with Francois. "We may destroy evidence."

"It's Deon." Madison released Raleigh and stepped back.

Raleigh nodded. That blue fishing angler shirt was the same one from the video earlier, which meant his death happened sometime between the video and Francois's smoke break— about a three hour stretch. Raleigh had been home, trying to wrestle some clean clothes from the growing laundry pile. Why hadn't Deon contacted her? By now, everyone in town knew she could connect with the dead.

True, Deon didn't like her much. As Sheri's closest friend, it came with the territory. But in the last two months, eight Barbeaux residents had died during drug overdoses or car accidents, and all eight had reached out to her. She didn't get all the natural causes deaths, but she took that as a plus. But this would have been horrendous to experience and just the thing Deon would have wanted to share, so why hadn't he?

Animal attacks may be different though.

Madison's voice pulled her back from her pondering thoughts.

"What will happen to the show?" Madison asked, her voice had returned to normal.

Looking into Madison's heart shaped face, arched eyebrows framed by her long dark hair, Raleigh could see Madison's seriousness. Raleigh pressed her lips together tightly to avoid criticizing. Madison had asked her not to do that anymore, but she made it difficult.

"I'm sure the show will be fine," Raleigh said, rethinking the working with the little sister agreement yet again. "A break won't kill the show."

Madison shook her head. "I can't believe this is happening to me."

Raleigh couldn't help the eye roll. To her? Raleigh must have missed the part where Madison had been mauled by some wild animal.

Shrill sirens interrupted the quiet and relief tingled in Raleigh's toes. The idea that an animal lurked within the reach of the trees had her on edge, and police with guns would be reassuring right about now since her Paw's shot gun was back at the house. Within moments, activity burst around them as officers approached from the side parking lot. Officers came running and Madison and Raleigh were pushed back by a short woman officer who kept saying, "Now, now."

Raleigh didn't find it soothing and felt herself wanting to stand her ground instead, but she'd been trying to keep her temper in check so that Max's job wouldn't be in jeopardy. And as she thought this, Max Pyles, lead detective and boyfriend, strolled onto the scene.

His baby blue shirt hugged his biceps and his dark hair already had a lick sticking up on the side. She had to give him credit for the straight line of his lips. At least he wasn't frowning.

A young, heavy chested deputy stopped him fifteen feet away from her. Raleigh thought his name was Peter or Jim or something old school, not reflecting the new trendy names of the age. He was not much over twenty and his dad had worked at the hardware store since he was a boy and had probably expected Peter or Jim Bob to work there as well. Raleigh couldn't hear what they said, but moments later Max closed the distance between them.

"Are you okay?" He stopped within professional distance, but his crossed arms gave his anxiety away.

Raleigh nodded.

"I'm not." Madison groaned. "I can't believe he's dead."

Her tone revealed her frustration far more than her concern. A stab of guilt hit Raleigh. Deon wasn't the nicest guy, but someone should feel remorse for the man's death.

"What happened?" Max asked. His eyes met Raleigh's, and the expectation creased the corners. Usually, the connections left her disconnected from the people around her, but the lack of one now left her feeling weighted to the surface, pulled down into the earth.

"I don't know." Raleigh shook her head. "There wasn't a connection this time. Francois came inside to tell us about the body."

Max's eyebrows furrowed as he studied her with that deep thinking gaze she'd come to recognize. Everyone had grown accustomed to her freaky-deeky talent. Even she had come to expect it.

"That's unusual these days."

Madison rubbed her arms, turning away from the view of Deon's body. "Poor thing probably didn't have time to think of Raleigh. Did you see the body?"

"Not up close yet." Max glanced back. "I've heard about it though."

Raleigh glanced in the direction again. Deon must have been attacked by an animal. But what animal? Barbeaux Bayou might have wild animals, the occasional black bear, coyote, wild dog, a bob cat maybe, but they'd never walked out the Delacroix building and seen an animal. Too much traffic noise. She supposed if an animal got hungry enough it would come this close, but those animals didn't attack humans. They might attack a small dog when hunger struck, but they'd left Deon and not carried their food off. None of this added up.

Madison said, "Scary to think we have animals that live around here that could do that to a person."

"Do you think someone was involved?" Max asked, his voice quiet, eyes softened.

"Huh?" Madison's head snapped away from studying the tree line. "Who would do such a thing?"

Max shrugged, avoiding direct eye contact as he scanned the area. After only six months of dating, most of it at crime scenes, Raleigh recognized this as his theories already forming. The nonchalance of the move revealed a thought building before he'd examined the body. Had Raleigh missed some sign of foul play? Max must be working from his own instincts because everyone around them buzzed with the words "animal attack".

Maybe she'd missed something though. The bite marks had been extremely distracting. With a connection to his death, she would have been certain. Raleigh couldn't believe she was the same person who only six months ago wanted to give this gift back to whatever God that had cursed her with it. Had she finally accepted that she was the traiteur to the dead?

If she had, it would be sure to snow in South Louisiana.

Max uncrossed his arms and took a step back from them. "I'm going to take a look at the crime scene. I will probably be here several hours."

Raleigh nodded, biting down on her lip without saying anything sarcastic, her specialty. They'd had dinner plans, but that wouldn't be happening now. It was the drawback of dating someone completely dedicated to his job and his son. They'd waited until Sunday night so Max could spend as much time with Mark as possible before he left for a Mardi Gras vacation with his mom and her new husband.

It all meant that the time they spent together as a couple dwindled as things always came up.

Max offered that understanding look before walking toward Deon's mutilated body.

"I need a shot of tequila." Madison released a deep breath. "Have any in your desk? I'm all out."

Not a hint of sarcasm touched Madison's porcelain beauty. You could take the girl off the bar top but not completely out of the bar room.

The door behind them opened, and a panic-driven Aryanna tumbled out, her momentum driving her through the small crowd gathered by the doors. Raleigh had to step to the side as Aryanna's shoulder collided with her own.

"It is true? Is it Deon?" Aryanna pitched her voice several octaves higher than usual.

Madison grabbed her by the arm as an officer stepped their way to contain her. "You don't want to see this."

Aryanna jerked away from Madison's grasp. "But is it Deon? Please tell me it isn't Deon." Her tone pleaded now, and she wrapped her arms around herself.

Raleigh sidestepped and blocked the view of the scene. "I'm afraid so."

Aryanna's face crumpled. She leaned forward, hands covering her face. "No!"

The two had paired up for the last audience match, but the filming hadn't caught more than a few sparks. No epic love story Raleigh could foresee. In fact, Raleigh hadn't thought of any of the ladies when she'd thought of Deon's death. He hadn't really paid consistent attention to one lady, just slight attention to all.

Sobs shook Aryanna's body though as she pushed against Madison, attempting to break away from the police line to get at Deon's body.

Madison and Raleigh exchanged a what-the-hell-is-wrong-with-this-woman look, and Raleigh clutched Aryanna's forearms to restrain her. In the middle of Aryanna's meltdown, Mike arrived and a male presence snapped Aryanna right out of it. She took a tissue someone in the crowd handed her and had the tears wiped away in seconds.

Mike's surfer blonde hair lay disheveled as usual on Sunday, but in that way that made it even sexier. His black t-shirt and jeans meant he'd worked construction today. Nate had probably just dropped him off, and that's why his Jeep was parked out front. He picked up old construction jobs on weekends sometimes, and it kept him lean and built as well. Remembering this could have saved Raleigh from all that panic earlier.

Aryanna glanced up at Mike, and then back down at her new running shoes. She mumbled, "We were supposed to be together. After the show. God, why is this happening?"

Aryanna forced deep breaths as if she couldn't breathe properly, and Raleigh tried not to roll her eyes. It was difficult to feel sorry for the dead when he had been such a douche bag in life. Paw would advise church with Me'Maw right about now to cleanse herself of these mean thoughts.

Mike nodded his head to her. She didn't see any sympathy in his eyes either. They could fill up Me'Maw's pew.

"I didn't realize the two of you were that close." Raleigh said, focusing on Aryanna's reaction. How much drama had Aryanna caused behind the scenes? Raleigh hadn't noticed much of it. As part of the show's agreement, the contestants had agreed to disclose everything involving the show on camera. Since it was Barbeaux, the cameras didn't follow the contestants around at all times, but during scheduled filming, cameras couldn't be avoided. It wasn't an agreement Raleigh would have signed herself, but she hadn't agreed to go on a reality television show either.

Aryanna pulled away. "I need to go. Someone I need to see."

Mike stepped toward her. "Are you sure you will be alright?"

Aryanna nodded, pulling her shoulders up. "I need to get out of here." She turned, sprinting back through the *Gazette*'s Sunday crowd, disappearing behind the metal door.

"That was weird, right?" Madison asked.

Mike nodded. "You may want to mention that to Max."

"It was an animal attack," Madison said. "Will they even investigate?"

Raleigh remembered Max's question and wondered if he knew something they didn't. "They will have to determine what animal and find it, I suppose."

Madison threw her hands up. "I guess I'll start making phone calls. All the contestants will need to know."

Raleigh looked to Mike. "I'll call Sheri."

Madison put her hands on her hips and frowned. "Well, she should be happy."

"Sheri will not be happy to tell Shawn that his father is dead no matter how much of an ass Deon was." Mike's voice was reproachful, although his expression didn't change.

Madison shrugged before hurrying back into the building into the safety of her office.

Mike grunted. "I hate to say it, but this couldn't have happened to a better person."

"Seems like a horrible way to die though."

"I know." Mike nodded. "The problem is all the people this will affect. Be gentle when you break the news to her."

Raleigh squeezed his arm and walked toward the building, dreading the call.

She didn't want to call from her own cubicle. If it went badly, she'd always think of it when she sat in her chair at a lost for that elusive word or sentence in her next story. She might create permanent writer's block.

Lance Sander's office was unlocked so she slipped inside. Not well liked over his poor office humor, Lance kept himself tucked away much of the day after offending this or that person until he'd decide to apologize with a dessert from a local bakery. Even with Raleigh's Twix obsession, the sweets didn't make up for his lack of a censor.

Raleigh took a deep breath and dialed Sheri's number, knowing she'd be at home on Sunday, one of her few days off from the salon.

"I was just about to call you," Sheri answered. "I need a favor. It's really a Me'Maw favor because, well, I know you don't cook, darlin'."

Raleigh's chest throbbed at the good cheer in Sheri's voice.

"Sheri," Raleigh began. Her thoughts felt dry. "I have some bad news."

"Bad news?" Sheri repeated. The good spirits not quite gone from her voice.

"Deon's dead," Raleigh said. Her throat felt as though it was closing. "He was murdered."

"He can't be. I just saw…" Sheri stuttered and then stopped.

The line grew quiet.

A moment later, she continued, her voice thick. "What am I going to tell Shawn?"

"I'm so sorry."

"I'm not," Sheri said. The happiness had gone. Replaced with something else. Conviction? Satisfaction? Raleigh couldn't place it. "But what do I tell my son?"

"Sheri, you're going to have to tell him the truth because it's all this town is going to be talking about."

Sobs came softly into the phone.

Chapter Three

A snapping sound startled Raleigh from a dream of chocolate raining down, drenching her as she ran through her Papa's garden trying to save his okra from drowning. For a moment, the disorientation between the dream and the noise raced through her, panic locking her to her bed.

Aunt Clarice's antique lamp took form in the darkness on the nightstand and Raleigh clicked it on.

It was probably nothing. Living in an old house caused many creaks and cracks Raleigh could never explain. It was like living with houseguests she didn't have to share her food, umm candy, with.

Creeeeeaaaak.

This noise came from the staircase. The third step still creaked, and although Raleigh had moved in nearly four months ago, she still hadn't gotten around to it or the leaky faucet or even the loose back railing. Figuring out how to turn on the lawn mower had taken a few weeks and a few lessons from Paw. The to-do list would eventually get checked off.

It was nothing, she was sure.

But Raleigh would not be able to sleep unless she got up and went to check on the creaky stair.

Dammit.

Out of bed, Raleigh crept towards the staircase and peered down. No one stood on the steps. Streetlight poured in through the front French doors and illuminated the front entrance.

Raleigh turned to go back upstairs, telling herself that she was being silly. It was just an old house. But then she heard a movement. A rustle really of fabric in the stillness of the creaky house.

She stopped mid-turn and listened. Silence. It didn't come again, but she knew she'd have to go downstairs and inspect now or she'd never get back to sleep.

At the bottom of the foyer, Raleigh looked towards the living room and could see Madison's cheek and black hair sticking out of the mounds of black faux fur throw blanket Raleigh kept on the sofa.

"Madison!" Raleigh hissed, relieved and angry all at the same time.

Swinging up to a seated position, Madison woke, her panic stretching across her forehead.

"You scared me," Raleigh said, feeling guilty now as Madison clutched her chest, trying to catch her breath. "I heard a noise down here and I thought someone was in the house."

"I swear I was sleeping," Madison said, looking around disoriented. "I lost my keys to Mom's house. Didn't want to wake them when I got back so late, so I came in here with your hide-a-key, but I didn't hear anything."

Sleeping as hard as Madison had been, she probably hadn't made the noise. It must have been the creaking old house after all. That and her own paranoia. Now Raleigh felt guilty for waking Madison up.

"Sorry for scaring you."

"Sure it wasn't one of your ghost friends?" Madison asked, kneading her forehead with her thumb and forefinger.

Raleigh shrugged. Unless she'd missed something in the torrential downpour of chocolate and her Paw's okra, no dead visitors tonight in her dreams. Deon hadn't visited earlier either, and Raleigh still wasn't sure how she felt about that one yet.

Madison nibbled on her bottom lip. "Uncle Camille hasn't really said anything about the dead during our training sessions."

Raleigh didn't respond. Me'Maw had trained her son to be the next family traiteur, as family tradition called for a female to train a male and a male to train a female. Raleigh should have been the next logical choice in the family since her visits with the dead already made her traiteur to the dead, but Uncle Camille held a grudge and had chosen Madison to pass the traditions onto as a result. Unable to save Uncle Camille's daughter Claudia, Raleigh's punishment had been to watch her sister, who didn't want the gift, to be trained. But since Uncle Camille's cancer wouldn't be healed by the folk remedies he'd sought out, Raleigh remained quiet so that the family traditions didn't die with him.

"Well, anyway," Madison said, lying back down. "You might want to get some sleep. Delacroix says we will be continuing production tomorrow."

"Really? Not even a one day delay?"

Madison shook her head. "The big finale is the Mardi Gras ball and parade, and he doesn't want it delayed. So tomorrow night we will have Cajun dance lessons as originally planned. He wants some kind of tribute on this week's episode, but that's it."

"You know maybe if you helped me clean out that guest room you could stop sleeping on the sofa." Raleigh turned to go. "The two-step and the jig tomorrow it is. See you in the morning Madison."

In the morning Raleigh woke up just as tired as she was when she went to sleep, but the alarm wouldn't stop beeping and it had fallen behind the nightstand, and she couldn't find it to make it stop. The doorbell rang just as she stumbled to the bottom of the stairs, and Mike stood outside the door, a cup of coffee in one hand and a Twix bar in the other.

She took the Twix bar from him without a word as he sipped from the paper coffee cup.

"I know how much you love Mondays." He at least kept his goofy grin to a minimum as he said it, although his blond hair and fresh shaven face spoke of his morning nature.

Raleigh peered into the living room and saw that Madison had evacuated her position on the sofa. Mom and Dad woke up at the crack of dawn, so she could get in early and crawl into her own bed and sleep until noon. After all, the show's events didn't get started until the afternoon. Raleigh had to work at the *Barbeaux Gazette* in the morning and then begin the show's agenda before crawling into bed at some indecent hour.

Raleigh ripped the shiny package open and sunk her teeth into the chocolate and tiny bursts of feel-good positivity burst through her. Like an addiction, the cocoa buzzed through her, tingling her senses awake.

It would all work out. The show filmed for two more weeks, and then Raleigh could sleep. She might even stay in bed the entire weekend.

"The councilman still on for ten o'clock?" Raleigh asked, placing her Twix on the coffee table and pulling the blanket off the sofa where Madison had left it unfolded.

"Yep," Mike said, playing with a ceramic elephant that once belonged to Aunt Clarice that Raleigh had always liked. Madison must have put it on the coffee table last night. Raleigh kept putting it on a shelf, but it kept finding its way to the coffee table one way or another.

The two were set to interview Councilman Ed Toups about new tax proposals to pay for the new bridge and pumping station. The tax had caused quite a stir with people who didn't feel this was the right time in the economy to be taking more money from people. Several people had written letters to the editor, and their editor David wanted yet another story since there was an interest.

"Let's try and get a jump start on the Deon story. I'm sure David will have it lead tomorrow's edition."

The Barbeaux Gazette issued a Tuesday, Thursday, and Sunday edition. News wasn't in a hurry just like anything else on the bayou, so people would be getting their news the old-fashioned way until tomorrow's paper. Oh, how the gossip would be flying. Raleigh could imagine the front porch conversations, phone calls, and even social media for those who'd advanced to modern communication.

"Last night they asked us to hold our questions until this morning." Mike placed the elephant down. "I heard someone say to call in old man Byce. He's that animal expert down at the university. I don't think they know what they are dealing with yet, so maybe by this afternoon they will know something."

Raleigh motioned for Mike to go. "Over lunch with Max, I'll see what I can find out. Officially and unofficially."

Mike chuckled. She knew he wasn't judging her though. Dating for a story was usually his area of expertise.

Raleigh followed Mike out the front door, stopping to check under the dying potted ivy plant if Madison had returned her hide-a-key. Locking herself out of her own house occurred on a regular basis since her keys always ended up in strange places. Just last week, she'd searched for an hour only to discover them in the freezer.

Right out front at the white picket fence gate, Mike had parked his Jeep. The three-foot fence closed off her front yard to Cheramie Lane, but not in any way that would block neighbors from watching her trying to push a lawn mower around those corners. To her right, a gravel driveway led to a carport where she parked. Raleigh kept telling Mike to park in the driveway, but he preferred leaving his Jeep on the side of a narrow road with the bad drivers of the lane. Not many Cheramies lived on Cheramie Lane anymore. She'd bought Aunt Clarice's house from her grandparents, but most of the empty houses had been sold recently to people outside the family, something that Paw ranted about afternoons on the porch. Uncle Camille's house would have to be dealt with at some point, and that was just a depressing thought to have on a Monday morning.

"Why, hello neighbor." A cheery voice called from across the street as Raleigh pulled the latch on the door of the Jeep. "I wondered when I might see some sign of life on this street."

Raleigh peered around the corner of the windshield to see a lithe, blonde striding toward Mike, who stood on the street by the driver's side door. With an easy smile and a slight tilt to her head, the woman held herself in that flirtatious manner Raleigh could never pull off and if she'd try it would look like she'd developed a twitch.

"It's nice to meet you," Mike said. He stuck his hand out, and she held hers out as if expecting him to kiss it. Mike hesitated a moment with her hand in his, but he released it after gently shaking it. In the meantime, Raleigh couldn't help but notice that the new neighbor wasn't wearing a bra, the evidence visible through her thin gauzy teal shirt. And now that she'd noticed, Raleigh couldn't not notice.

Mike looked back at Raleigh, and Raleigh stepped forward. "Raleigh is your actual neighbor though."

"How lovely." The young lady's acorn eyes slid right over Raleigh. "And you're just visiting… your… sister?"

Mike chuckled. Raleigh met his eyes and frowned. *Sister?* Could she be more obvious?

"Raleigh is my oldest friend," Mike said, turning back toward the young, nameless blonde.

Friend. The word sat like a heavy meal in her stomach. She wanted to pretend to be his girlfriend right now to protect Mike from this woman's nefarious motives. Being this overt didn't speak well for her intentions, and Mike did have a history of attracting crazy. That stinging jealousy burning in her cheeks was just a sense of protection. It couldn't be anything else, Raleigh assured herself.

"Fantastic." Her eyes flickered a moment over Raleigh with more interest. "I'm Amber. Maw Margaret was my great-grandmother, and I'm going to stay in the house—well, at least until Uncle Philip decides what he wants to do with it."

She glanced back toward the green weatherboard siding house. Ms. Margaret's old swing hung beneath the trees, unmoving since her death. Raleigh hadn't liked the old woman much, but she'd softened up that vicious tongue toward the end. Raleigh had tried to save her, had thought it might be possible to get her help for her stroke in time, but she'd passed a few days later in the hospital.

"It was nice meeting you, Amber," Raleigh said, looking to Mike. Mike's gaze studied Amber. Raleigh wondered if he'd also noticed she wasn't wearing a bra. "But we are heading into work, and we are running a little late."

Amber tilted her head and pursed her lips. "That's fine. The stars say we will have many more opportunities to get to know each other, and I certainly look forward to it."

Mike nodded toward her in good-bye. Raleigh puzzled over her words a moment, wondering if she should question what she meant, but then she walked back around and slid into the passenger seat.

Raleigh waited until they were pulling out of the driveway before speaking. "Was that a little weird, or was it just me?"

"Oh, I don't know. She seems nice."

Raleigh glanced at him, but his eyes remained focused on the road. "I didn't think she was your type."

Mike chuckled, swinging his Jeep onto the highway. "My mother claims that I will never make her a grandmother if I keep waiting around for my type."

"Oh." Raleigh swallowed. Children? Always the one to go on no more than one or two dates per woman, Mike didn't really think in terms of long term. Maybe that was changing. The idea made her uncomfortable. She wasn't ready for things to change between the two of them. And she knew a permanent woman would change the dynamic.

"Don't worry," Mike said, glancing toward her with his signature dimpled grin. "My type still includes a nose for trouble."

Raleigh couldn't help but laugh, feeling with a little more relief than she should for someone involved with someone else.

Chapter Four

The voices and dishes clattered relentlessly in the noonday crescendo that was Donny's Po-Boys. From the outside, its façade crumbled, but on the inside Barbeaux residents knew its food could win any contest. Max dumped catsup onto his red plastic basket of fries, and Raleigh scooted forward in the booth seating so she could hear him over the lunch rush.

"Most of the bites were surface wounds, really," Max said, shoving a fry in his mouth. His eyes took on that far away look, and Raleigh knew his thoughts were with last night's crime scene.

"But?"

Max wiped his hand on a thick white paper napkin. He raised his hands to demonstrate a blocking motion. "Deon raised his hands to protect his face, and the teeth caught the wrist and it tore through the veins. If he would have been found sooner, he may not have bled out. We figure he must have lost consciousness at some point during the attack so he couldn't seek help. We have questions we don't have answers to yet though."

"So we are definitely looking at an animal then? No bullets or stab wounds involved." Raleigh asked reaching over and snatching one of his fries. She'd ordered the thoroughly messy gravy fries, but the catsup smell mingled with salt and hot grease appealed to her at this moment.

Max shrugged. "No wounds suggesting human attacker."

Something about his response made Raleigh pause in the journey to her mouth with her stolen fry. He was withholding something.

Mrs. Marie shuffled over carrying glasses of water with lemon. Recently, Max had given up sugar and had attempted to drag Raleigh into the black hole of sugar free living. Water tested her will power. She hadn't adopted his "grown up" living as he'd called it when he'd proposed the idea to her and tried to convince her it was time. If she could sneak a sugar packet into that water without him seeing, she planned to do just that.

"Here y'all go," Mrs. Marie said, setting down the glasses and then putting one hand on her hefty hip. "Mr. Henri said to take care of you two special. I imagine you had a rough night Mr. Pyles. And you too, Raleigh."

Mrs. Marie's chest heaved upward and then her shoulders drooped.

Max nodded but remained silent. Mrs. Marie's expectant stare left Raleigh feeling as if she needed to say something.

"It wasn't one I want to repeat again." Raleigh shuddered as the image of Deon's body covered in bite marks resurfaced in her memory. Even as traiteur to the dead, she had her limits.

"Please tell me that what everyone is whispering isn't true," Mrs. Marie whispered, leaning forward and doing the sign of the cross as she spoke.

Max rested his elbows on the table and looked up at Mrs. Marie. His expression remained neutral. "What is everyone saying, Mrs. Marie?"

Mrs. Marie looked around the diner as if people were watching, as if she was about to divulge a secret. Raleigh leaned forward, feeling part of the conspiracy.

"The animal walked on two feet." Mrs. Marie's eyes widened. "Everyone's already talking about how it's the real rougarou, beb."

Raleigh gripped the booth seat with both hands to avoid the outburst of laughter threatening to overcome her. Cajun folktales about swamp monsters weren't proper leads in an investigation. If Max took these reports seriously, he'd be laughed at more than when he utilized Raleigh's ability to connect to the dead. Not that this didn't cause enough strain for his career. He faced much scrutiny at work over any case she was involved in.

"Mrs. Marie, we are in the middle of an investigation, and we don't have all the answers yet, but I'm sure it isn't the rougarou."

"I sure hope not. The idea of a monster running around is cagoo." Mrs.

Marie did the sign of the cross again before stepping away to a table on the other side the restaurant.

Crazy alright. Just the idea that people would believe that was *cagoo*.

Max swore as he pushed his fries away.

Raleigh looked up at him from her fry and her thoughts. "What?"

"There was a set of footprints near the body. Obviously, someone leaked it although it was supposed to remain on a need to know basis."

Raleigh put her own fry down. "Footprints? Like human footprints, not animal?"

Max nodded. "Yes, and since you and Madison were careful not to go within the five foot radius of the body, these footprints belong to someone else. We found where you two stood so we have those prints, too. We are probably going to take your shoe impressions today anyway, just to be thorough.

Raleigh sunk back into the booth, Paw's tales of the rougarou swimming in her mind. She remembered being terrified of the dark for months after he told her the story, since he'd concluded with how the monster attacked bad children. It was just a story to scare her into behaving or going to bed on time though. The rougarou was simply a myth. Footprints had to be a person, not a monster. But bite marks?

"So it was a *person* who did that to Deon?" Raleigh asked, unable to mask her skepticism.

Max huffed. "Of course not."

Raleigh couldn't tell where his thoughts were, and her forehead began to ache trying to figure it out. "But footprints?"

"Someone else was at the scene which creates questions. My first one, besides the obvious who, is when were they present."

Raleigh chewed on this bit of information as she delved into her sloppy gravy fries with her fingers. She'd asked Marie to add shredded lettuce and pickles in between the layers of fries and gravy, and it created a delectable mess. The fork had proved an inadequate tool.

While placing fingers full of mess into her mouth, she considered this new twist. If a person was there after Deon's attack, then why didn't they call the police? But if they were there during the attack, that could tell an entirely different story. One that Raleigh couldn't imagine a possible logical scenario for with some kind of wild animal involved.

"When will you know what kind of animal?"

"The guy says he will get it to us ASAP. It'll still be a few days after the teeth impressions are done and sorted though."

Finding a complete impression might be difficult with how mangled the body had looked, but the number of bites on Deon's body had to have given at least one good impression. Days with an unidentified wild animal running loose wasn't a pleasant thought either.

Max pulled out his wallet and fiddled through cash, counting it out. Even with their haphazard dating, Raleigh knew this sign as his readiness to get back to work. The leaking of that detail must have put his thoughts into overdrive, and he was ready to work the case before it got away from him.

"I have the dance lessons tonight, so I will be working late again."

Max nodded. "I'll probably put in extra hours this week with this case. Until I find the owner of that footprint, I'm not ruling it an animal attack. Too many unanswered questions."

He set money down on the table and then looked up. "Don't print that yet though. I don't know what the official statement is going to be, especially if people are whispering about the rougarou."

Raleigh nodded, biting down on her bottom lip. Finding someone else to put it on record would now be a priority for her afternoon. Her mind ticked through the list of police officers she had connections to, from the ones she graduated from high school with to the ones she'd babysat while in diapers. She'd need to work quickly before Max enforced his gag order over the precinct, and no matter how scared Nick was of her, he wouldn't talk. Max's boss didn't allow him to work cases with her unsupervised, but Sheriff Breaux had learned that Raleigh didn't cooperate well with anyone else. They'd reached a mutual understanding that Max would take care of his cases and someone would oversee from a distance, but Raleigh didn't want to ruin this new arrangement by dragging Max's name into the paper for something he wasn't supposed to be releasing.

Back in Max's Caprice, Raleigh texted Mike to get a statement about the footprint from Nick, thinking that time was of the essence. The Gazette was only a seven-minute drive from the diner, and then Max would only have about a ten-minute drive to the station.

Max dropped her off and absentmindedly kissed her on the side of her lips before rushing off through the parking lot.

"Mrs. Marjorie, relationships are hard with a workaholic." Raleigh announced going through the front entrance where Max had dropped her off. The side entrance required an ID card these days that Raleigh had forgotten on her desk yet again. Delacroix Senior had decided that security needed improving. The decision had come after a big blow up between Robbie Delacroix and Sam Delacroix at a family mixer, and many thought Sam's radio station would be finding a new home, but old man Delacroix had intervened and made Robbie stop encroaching on Sam's on-air talent for his television station. At least temporarily. Many believed the security was so Senior could keep an eye on his boys.

"Dear, relationships are just hard. Pick someone who's worth the hassle and hold on for the long haul." Mrs. Marjorie didn't look up from her typing. Her hunched over form seemed to diminish every day, but she arrived every morning with her glasses hanging off her nose and her purse clutched across her chest. Nearing 84, Mrs. Marjorie would probably work until she died. If she showed up five minutes late, they'd probably send the coroner to check on her.

"Wonderful advice, Mrs. Marjorie." Raleigh said, as she strolled through the swinging double doors.

In his cubby, Mike leaned back in his chair with the phone to his ear. Raleigh slid into her own cubbyhole chair, rolled into his area, and waited for him to finish the conversation, openly listening to Mike's sparse questions.

"Are you sure, Nick?" Mike asked, leaning over and jotting down small grip. A moment later he wrote rubber boot with a question mark behind it.

"Thanks, Nick," Mike said. "I'll be in touch again to see what else you've discovered."

He hung up the phone. "Nice call on that one. I'm guessing there will be a gag order in about ten minutes because he thought nothing of giving himself credit."

Raleigh nodded, squirming in her chair. Max wasn't stupid. He'd figure this out. But he had his job, and she had hers. "Max didn't want me to print anything he said today, but Nick always talks to us."

Mike chuckled. "You're going to be in hot water."

Raleigh scrunched up her nose at him. She didn't have the good guy charm he possessed in the flirting department, so she usually left the "hot water" to him. "So what did you learn?"

Mike glanced down at his note, a serious expression overtaking him. "They believe the footprint was a rubber boot from the grip. Lab should confirm in a day or two. It's not an overly large print at a size 10, possibly a woman or a man with a smaller build. That last part is conjecture on Nick's part."

"At least we have confirmation of a footprint though. I don't know how much we will get after Max lays into them this morning."

Mike shrugged. "Once we make it public knowledge, there's less of a reason to keep the answers from us. The footprint changes things a bit though, huh?"

Mike flicked his fingers through his hair and the sun-streaked blonde bounced up and fell back into place. His thoughts were reaching. Raleigh had noticed this movement quite a bit recently.

"Like, is the rougarou real?" Raleigh smiled.

"What?" Mike asked, his eyebrows furrowed.

"Just what someone said this morning." Raleigh could imagine the stories being passed along today. "It does create more questions, though, about a simple animal attack."

Mike nodded, settling back into his thoughts. "I think I'm going to try and observe those dance lessons tonight. No interviews, just watch."

Raleigh nodded. As Madison's assistant, Raleigh's observations would be drive-by at best as she ran around putting out the small fires that arose as the show's contestants squabbled over wardrobe or dance partners or camera time or whatever the issue of the night was. With this crew, issues always came up. Still, she could do her part.

"Theory?" She questioned, studying his out-of-focus green eyes.

Mike shrugged. "Just a hunch really. All the contestants were here that day for interviews. What if the animal didn't attack without command?"

Raleigh dwelled on that for the rest of the afternoon as she finished a special interest piece on the new farmer's market and made a few calls for a local Mardi Gras parade story. She'd settled into small town life again, writing small town stories. Although the people of Barbeaux kept life interesting, Raleigh couldn't say she was chasing anything big. Mike enjoyed the small town angle, but Raleigh preferred the hunting down of the investigation story. Maybe it had something to do with being traiteur to the dead. She could give them closure when she exposed what had happened. Is that what she wanted for Deon though? Did he deserve it? Maybe it was about Shawn though. That she could live with.

At 5:30, she and Mike jumped in his Jeep to head toward the Cajun Top Hat dance studio. Tucked away down a limestone drive, the dance studio was an old, weathered gray cypress barn that Brenda and Leonard DeWhite had converted into a dance studio nearly thirty years ago. Fully air conditioned, the barn's features also included a stage and a bar area. During the week, the DeWhite's offered dance lessons, but on Friday and Saturday nights you could rent the place for parties, and on Sundays they hosted regular Cajun bands and dancing. Raleigh's childhood had included a visit here a time or two with her grandparents.

The barn theme extended inside with a rough wooden stage, bar, and picnic style tables, as well as bleacher style seating on one side for observations. Potted trees softened the wood up a bit as well as the inside lighting strung across the ceiling in a crisscross pattern. Pleased to notice they'd freshened the place up a bit before the filming, Raleigh could cross the worry of the place looking like a dump on camera off her list.

"I'm going to be invisible," Mike said, brushing her arm with his hand before pointing toward the three-tier bleachers.

Raleigh nodded. That was Raleigh's goal for every filming.

Raleigh located Madison among the milling contestants, many of which had long, drawn faces. A smile replaced Madison's frown for a millisecond as she looked up into Raleigh's face, but then the sternness reappeared as she gripped her clipboard even tighter to her chest.

"A few days off would have been a fabulous idea." Madison rolled her eyes.

Raleigh assessed the room. A small, gloomy group had formed with Aryanna at the center. Benjamin, Deon's lone male buddy among the group, comforted Aryanna with a beefy bicep around her shoulders. Several of the other female contestants also had heads down and a few had tears trailing down cheeks. But, Winter stood to the side studying her nails, her tight blue jeans showing off the curves accentuated by her four-inch heels. Winter nodded at Raleigh in recognition, but her expression didn't change from boredom. Winter and Raleigh had come to a mutual understanding of acquaintance after Raleigh had solved her best friend's murder a few months ago, but Raleigh had nothing in common with the stripper turned party hostess and dating contestant, and that had made any conversation between the two awkward.

Leaning against the bar, Tiffany and Frank whispered to each other in hushed tones. The two had become fast friends on the set of the first challenge when they'd been paired up for a pirogue race, but nothing romantic had appeared in the footage as far as Raleigh could tell. The two had an air of guilt around them with their concerned expressions and furious whispering.

"What do you need?" Raleigh asked Madison, hoping to get closer to the two to see if she could catch a few snippets of their conversation.

Madison opened her mouth, but just then a powerhouse of a petite woman, wearing a flared blue jean shin length skirt and her long, auburn hair pulled into a ponytail, strolled onto the middle of the dance floor.

"Well, good evening ladies and gents. I trust we are ready for a good time." The big booming voice traveled from deep within the chest of the five-foot-one woman.

A few mumbles went through the crowd, but nothing near the level of excitement Brenda DeWhite expected. Deon's death had dampened the group's spirit, and even cheerful Mrs. DeWhite would struggle to get an enthusiastic response.

Raleigh moved out of the camera shot as the three-member camera production crew rose to life. Madison motioned to the outliers, and Raleigh moved in their direction to herd them onto the dance floor.

"Well, that just won't do, will it?" Brenda laughed, throwing her arms into the air. "The jig is going to require a little more pep, people. So, again, no matter how bad things seem, a little Cajun music will lift your spirits."

Raleigh motioned for Heather and Patrick to move toward the center. Patrick, as usual, looked uncertain and held back. Heather's shoulders heaved upward and then downward before she pulled Patrick toward the floor. Heather had changed her mind two episodes in about being on the show, but Madison wouldn't allow her out of the contract. To protest being forced to participate against her will, Heather did everything with as little enthusiasm as possible. But even with this lack luster protest, Heather's grandmother still refused to speak to her until the show finished filming. Patrick, on the other hand, had the clean-cut good looks that caused women to swoon. His amber eyes were deep and sensitive behind his glasses, and there had been a shirtless scene for a swimming challenge that had left him leading the popularity vote among the female demographics. The fact that he was hesitant around women had limited his connections during the matchups though.

Raleigh moved back toward the center and grabbed Madison's clipboard just as Frank handed her a microphone for her hosting duties. The rehearsal would only be about twelve minutes of the finished show, so Madison's package here would be brief and really free advertising for the DeWhites since they'd volunteered to be a sponsor this week.

While Madison recorded her piece, Raleigh moved around the crowd pairing up the contestants using Madison's notes. Madison had made some pretty interesting combinations. Frank and Kimberly together created a new pairing, since she typically gravitated towards Adam. The two had become the only repeat pairing over the course of the last several weeks. Benjamin and Aryanna seemed an obvious choice. The two were the showiest of the contestants if you didn't count Deon, and Raleigh supposed they weren't counting Deon anymore.

Winter's eyebrows rose when Raleigh called her name out for Patrick. A devilish grin appearing on her red lips.

"Yummy," Winter said, laughing.

Patrick smiled, but from the quick movement of his thumb over his fingers back and forth, Raleigh could tell he'd instantly grown nervous. Winter easily intimidated most of these men with her overt sexual tactics. She did make for good entertainment. Casting her on the show had been a good move by Madison. Nothing boring there.

Raleigh finished the pairings, leaving Clara, Lauren, and Adam as a rotating threesome. The show's formula had been pairs from the beginning. This odd person out deal would be difficult to work into their format, and Raleigh wondered how Madison planned to do it in the actual challenge Saturday. Adding a new contestant with only a few weeks to go would probably not work for the dynamics, but knowing Madison, it would be a way for her to add more drama.

Sidestepping the camera's view, Raleigh moved in front of a large potted tree as the attention returned to the contestants. The dancers shuffled around on their feet, anxiously awaiting instructions, all looking like they wished to be somewhere else.

Brenda DeWhite stepped into the center and clapped her hands together. "Well folks, when that Cajun beat is makin' your feet tap, it's the jig you'll want to be doing. We're going to get you swinging to the swamp pop in style."

"I need you and your partner to face each other... but no touching yet." Brenda laughed, a full and hearty sound from the hundred pound woman, as she weaved in and out the uncomfortable looking pairs. They needed to show more personality than this if they expected to earn votes for the show's airing.

Peering over the cameraman's shoulder, Madison motioned for Raleigh to move behind the bar. Avoiding the lights of the cameras, Raleigh made her way toward the corner. From this angle, she had a view of Clara, Adam, Lauren, Patrick, and Winter, but not for long, as Brenda had them moving around the dance floor performing some fancy footsteps with the jig and then the waltz.

Raleigh watched as they stumbled over each other in an attempt to find a rhythm with their partner. Most of them laughed, but Raleigh noticed a few other reactions besides humor. Patrick spent most of his time blushing as

Winter used his awkward missteps as a way to have her hands all over him. Of course, Raleigh caught the twinkle in Winter's eyes, and in a particularly bold derriere-squeezing incident, Winter even winked at Raleigh when she noticed her prying eyes. Raleigh was sure Winter was having fun with him to ease her boredom. Winter was an excellent dancer, so she picked the steps up the first time and had her fun while waiting for those with two left feet to catch up. On the other hand, Lauren's frustration grew with Adam until she allowed Clara to step in. Leonard DeWhite stepped in and Lauren became all smiles as he whirled her around the floor. Aryanna and Ben didn't understand the instructions, and Mrs. Brenda had to demonstrate again for them. Many of them just proved that the Cajun dancing hadn't been happening in their homes.

Two hours later, both of Raleigh's feet hurt from trying to stay out of the camera angles and trying to keep up with anything going on worth filming. Madison called a wrap to shooting, and Francois's guys began packing up the camera equipment.

Dark-haired Lauren approached Mike as he bounded down from the stadium seating in one big step. Her pink, plump lips curved into a sly smile as her hand reached out and touched his bicep, lingering there for a moment too long. Moving toward them, Raleigh became distracted by Tiffany and Frank's furious whispering by the bar. Something was happening with those two. Lauren laughed and tossed her long hair over her shoulders; Raleigh noticed Tiffany's hand flutter in the air to stress her point.

"Dammit." Raleigh muttered to herself before strolling casually toward the bar.

Tiffany stopped mid-word as Raleigh approached.

"So how did you feel the dance lessons went?" Raleigh asked, still clutching the clipboard to her chest.

Tiffany looked toward Frank, her eyes glaring at him. "Fine. I mean I'm not the best dancer, but the *fais do do* should be fun."

Frank grimaced. "I hope I don't leave my partner's feet bruised."

"I'm sure you will do just fine," Raleigh said, repeating the mantra she used to calm the nerves of the contestants, soothing and reassuring at the same time, if she delivered it just right. "Is something wrong? I noticed you two look worried about something. I want to assure you that we will do everything we can to make sure everyone is safe at the *fais do do*."

In interviewing, being direct worked great, but Raleigh had never done well with subtlety even when the situation called for it. It was a goal to work towards.

Frank's eyes widened. "Man, I didn't think of that. Shouldn't we move the location?"

Tiffany squeezed his arm. She appeared to have quite a grip as she left fingerprints in his shirt. "I'm sure we will be fine."

"Extra precautions will be taken of course," Raleigh said, making her voice soothing. "And we are attempting to be sensitive in handling Deon's death."

Frank's eyes shifted down to his leather loafers. "I won't miss the dude, so I'm more concerned about getting mauled by a wild animal."

Tiffany gently elbowed him in the side, widening her eyes at him. "What Frank means is that we weren't close to Deon, so we aren't as affected as some of the others."

Frank glanced down at her, staring at her as if he was lost for a moment, before nodding agreement.

Raleigh looked from one to other. One was obviously better at keeping a secret than the other. She'd need to get Frank alone to learn anything about what the two were hiding. She wondered if either of them owned a vicious animal. Neither of them looked the type though. But what did the type look like? That Raleigh wasn't sure she could answer.

"Let me know if I can help with anything though," Raleigh said, tapping the clipboard. "Madison aims to keep the show friendly."

They both smiled and nodded before Raleigh walked away.

Lauren still had Mike in her clutches as Raleigh approached.

"You need to help me out, Raleigh," Lauren said with exaggerated excitement.

"What am I helping with?" Raleigh asked, raising her eyebrows at Mike.

"He needs to be our other male contestant," Lauren said with a laugh. "He's perfect for the job. He's single, good looking, and he's here for the events anyway."

"That's my job," Mike grumbled.

"I'll help him think about it," Raleigh said, giving Mike a knowing smile. "But right now he and I need to get going. Stories to write."

"I bet Madison will like the idea," Lauren said, tossing her hair. "I'm going to go bring it up to her. You work on him, Raleigh."

She hurried off in search of Madison.

"Just so you know," Mike said as they walked toward the exit, "there's no way I'd date any of these women. I've been behind the scenes, remember?"

Raleigh laughed. "Don't worry. I didn't say I was going to help you think about saying yes."

Mike chuckled. "So what was going on with Patrick and Tiffany?"

Chapter Five

Even the deerskin hanging from the back wall sweltered in the temperature of the back porch where Halona Dardar worked. The shelves bowed under the weight of the mason jars, and the makeshift tables she fiddled around had cement blocks propping them up.

Raleigh felt sweat drip down her neck as she spread the leaves across the surface, careful not to overlap them as Halona had instructed. The porch gave off an overwhelming aroma of nature, sweat, and musk that Raleigh had come to know, but not quite comfortable enough to not be queasy.

"I take advantage of the gift of the camellia leaves. It is early in the season, but it makes a nice tea to ease anxiety and not bad for the headache." Halona laughed, a deep, course, throaty sound, and her long gray braid swished across her back.

Raleigh couldn't help but smile, although she never knew what was funny when Halona laughed. A cheery person, the woman always had a thin-lipped smile or a good-hearted chuckle with every tidbit of advice.

Through the screen door of the enclosed cypress back porch, a welcomed breeze tingled the back of Raleigh's neck. The old porch boards had worn through the last coat of sealant long ago, but Halona kept it spotless from dust and dirt to preserve her supplies and remedies. Even more so than Me'Maw, Halona used nature's gifts to treat her own people.

"So why you think you didn't connect?" Halona threw a sideways glance Raleigh's way as she continued washing the leaves in the ceramic basin sink.

The ceramic washboard already had a stack of cleaned leaves awaiting Raleigh's hands.

"I don't know." Truthfully, Raleigh didn't believe she wanted to connect to such a horrible death, and perhaps she'd pushed it away as she once had for most of her life. But if this was the case, it would be her fault they didn't discover what had happened to Deon. For over a decade, her connection to the dead had been broken, disconnected by her need to suppress the weirdness. She didn't know if she could give it up again. She'd proven its usefulness to herself as well as to everyone else who'd sought her out when they'd died. If she hid from it again, Me'Maw's disappointment would be crushing.

Halona's bosom rose with a deep inhale as she wrung her hands against a dingy, threadbare bath towel. "When was the last spirit visit?"

Raleigh twirled a leaf between her fingers, only feeling the stiff stem with the pads of her index finger and thumb. Not death. Of course, its end had happened when it had been plucked from the camellia bush, so its death had technically occurred before this moment. But if she were to have pulled the leaf herself from the tree branch, would she have felt its essence stop? That small popping in her fingertips to let her know that its life had ended.

"At least three weeks."

"And you're thinking?"

"What if by trying to control the connections, I've pushed them away?"

Raleigh stole a glance at Halona as she put the towel on top of an old rusted washing machine in the corner. The two had been working together for right over a month to help Raleigh maintain control even during a connection. Uncle Camille's friend Dardar was her son and had suggested it in passing, and Raleigh had thought that it would be good for her to accept this curse instead of fighting it. But maybe that's not how it was supposed to work.

"Or maybe the spirits have granted you a reprieve because no one has needed you." Halona's wrinkles on her forehead rose and disappeared as she waited for a response.

Raleigh shrugged. "Maybe." She couldn't help but feel that gifts like hers didn't get a reprieve.

Halona sighed heavily, rustling the turquoise feathers on the gown she wore. "My sister struggled with the spirit visits, too. She told me once that the visitors had claimed her mind, and her life would be sacrificed for this purpose. She gave up on any effort to control the intrusion, and her body gave out under the stress. She was only 54."

With a looming thirtieth birthday, the warning didn't escape Raleigh. She'd hoped Halona could help her ease the physical reactions to the connections, understanding that to continue being dragged to another's death could be detrimental to her own health— not to mention dangerous if she was in the middle of driving or anything similar. But was that the price she must pay? Was it some kind of package deal and to connect to the dead, she must walk in their shoes.

Me'Maw had always been selfless, putting others before herself and her family. Raleigh could remember many times where people would show up for treatment at dinner time, and Me'Maw would leave a hot meal to attend to them. Paw would always wait for her, meals getting cold, hours passing until it was late night. She'd miss family outings when others needed her without complaint. Maybe Raleigh shouldn't be complaining at the inconvenience, or maybe what Raleigh needed was to hear some of Me'Maw's good, homespun advice.

"We all need to find our own path. Maybe with time?" Halona smiled, tight lines creased at the corner of her deep golden brown eyes.

"A connection right now might be reassuring." Raleigh said, rolling her eyes as she continued spreading out the leaves to dry.

"Be careful what you wish for." Halona chuckled.

Raleigh laughed. So true. Not too long ago she'd wished the dying would take an extended vacation from her head. She supposed she'd grown accustomed to their comings and goings over the last several months, but had she become so comfortable with the dying that she wished they'd visit more often? Maybe not. If this was a reprieve, she may need to enjoy it.

"Same time next week?" Halona asked, leaning against her screen door as Raleigh stood in the dirt path leading to her car. A few black and white chickens pecked at the grass feet from her, and a black lab lay lazily under an oak tree.

Raleigh nodded. The old woman would not give up saving her from the dead taking her with them.

The long dirt road led past trailers and other shotgun homes. Halona had mentioned that several relatives lived on this family land, including Dardar, Uncle Camille's lone friend. This back stretch of land was out of the way and left it feeling like a separate community from Barbeaux Bayou, for better or worse.

As she approached civilization again, she phoned Madison about the show, but the girl didn't answer, as usual. If it didn't come in the form of a text message, Madison didn't respond. As far as Raleigh could tell, the girl didn't know that a phone did something else besides text.

As usual, Cheramie Lane lay sleepy even in early evening. Typical of Louisiana, winter had only come in short bursts and the leaves had turned as ugly as dirt before falling. The tree branches reached barren up to the last rays of sunshine. Even her wispy crepe myrtle in her front yard looked defeated, but the steep roof of the Acadian stood formidable above the car's windshield, and she admired the fish scale trim on the roof steeple and the deep pecan of the French doors leading onto the wide front porch of Aunt Clarice's old house. Having loved this house since she was a girl, Raleigh had never imagined she'd call it home. Her life had changed so quickly in the last six months, she wasn't sure if she was keeping up. If only Aunt Clarice's confidence could rub off on her along with the inheritance of the home.

Max's navy Caprice bordered the road, blocking her mailbox and the picket fence view from the street. Since it was his weeknight with his son, Raleigh had expected a quiet night with a Twix bar and a glass of wine, especially since she had interviews tomorrow and a long day of making peace between bratty contestants.

She should miss him. The thought occurred to her as she yearned for the silence she'd looked forward to all day. They hadn't spent any time with each other since before Deon's death, but there was the little matter of her slipping details into the story he'd asked her to keep quiet, which meant her quiet night had the potential for massive drama. He was bound to have read it in today's paper since he made a point of scanning the issue on his lunch hour.

His anger couldn't have reached a ten since she hadn't heard from him yet.

But he might be at her house to tell her what a horrible girlfriend she was in person. She didn't keep anything stronger than wine in the house, so she could have at least been phoned a warning to stop and pick something up.

Raleigh parked the car beneath the carport, the white seashells crunching beneath the trees. In the rearview mirror, she watched the braless young woman wandering around Ms. Margaret's yard gathering the white clover flowers into a bouquet. Nothing about these flowers spoke of beauty, so Raleigh could only imagine what she was doing. Ms. Margaret must be turning over in her grave with this flower child living in her house. Ms. Margaret preferred women prim and proper and behaving like good girls. She and Aunt Clarice had experienced a tiff or two in their younger days, as there had been nothing prim with Aunt Clarice's vices.

Aunt Clarice offered more to admire in ways of courage. Raleigh was completely unsure about flower child.

To avoid attracting the neighbor's attention, Raleigh avoided the creaky porch board and stepped lightly on the oak planks. Just another sign that she needed me time after her day. Through the rattling panes of the French doors, Raleigh could hear stomping feet and high-pitched laugher.

Mason's tenor voice emerged from the rumble.

An orange foam dart whizzed past her head as she opened the front door. The two boys' shoes scuffed the floors as they ran up the hallway into the living room clutching Nerf guns. Max's son Mark towered a head above Mason, but Raleigh's nephew giggled as Mark overtook him in a shower of darts.

"What's going on in here?" Raleigh asked, forcing excitement in her tone.

"War, Nannan!" Mason laughed as Mark flipped him over his side and they scuffled on the rug.

"Well, let's avoid total annihilation of the house." Raleigh continued down the hall towards the kitchen, her sinuses clearing from the delightful smell of cayenne pepper and crab boil lingering in every crevice of her home.

Max hovered over the stove, steam rising from an oversized boiling pot she'd stuffed in the cabinet a few months ago and forgotten about. Me'Maw had cleaned her cabinets when Raleigh had moved in and given her a box of kitchen supplies. Since Raleigh spent little time home to cook, the wine bottle opener and the glass got the most use. That Max even knew there was a pot buried somewhere in the cabinet was surprising.

"Hello, there," Max said, turning away from the stove to watch her come in. "I hoped you'd make it home soon."

Raleigh crossed to him, embraced him from the side, inhaling the buried earthiness beneath the spicy seasonings. He bent down and brushed a quick kiss on her lips before returning his attention to stirring the boiling water where orange shrimp tumbled in the foam.

"You thought you'd surprise me?" Raleigh inhaled the smell of lemon and cayenne, allowing it to fill her. The smell made her miss Me'Maw and all the cooking the woman had done for her, and she realized she hadn't stopped in to visit in over a week with her work schedule, a fact she needed to remedy.

"Mark wanted to play with Mason, so I figured we could make a night of it."

Raleigh ran her thumb over the scar on her wrist, a reminder these days of how far she'd come. Could he not have just said he'd wanted to see her? In only several months of dating, they'd moved to old married couple, the kind that grumpily bickered over who would pick up the milk. He'd grown comfortable that was what it was. Although she hadn't taken that significant step and given him a key—he knew where the hide-a-key was so what was the point — he felt comfortable enough to come into her house when she wasn't home, putting Aunt Clarice's valuables at risk. They'd skipped key steps – steps where Raleigh could have figured out her boundaries.

Raleigh sighed, and Max glanced back at her again, pausing in his stirring.

"I thought we might talk about my case too since the paper appears to have its own investigation going on as usual."

His tone was level without a hint of the anger Raleigh knew was there. He'd asked her before to stay away from his cases, to let him do his job without interference. After the article, he must know that she'd once again done her job, not concerned herself with his.

The air grew humid from the steam, causing Raleigh's throat to tighten against the spices clinging to the air.

She cleared her throat and walked to the fridge and pulled out a bottled water. "I'm going to go get some fresh air for five minutes on the front porch. It's been a rough day."

Max nodded as he clicked the burner off under the pot. "Just enough time for these babies to soak."

Raleigh turned and walked back through the shrieks and laughter of the boys and back through the original French doors, feeling the strain between her and Max grow with each step. It was the anticipation really. The mental preparation of another argument coming tonight about work.

Out in the setting sunset, Raleigh released a deep breath through her lips, knowing she needed to breathe in a new mindset before going back inside.

This house was her sanctuary, dammit. A place for her to escape all the chaos of work and family. He'd invaded her space, his argument already prepared. Should be some kind of relationship rule about that. No matter how many times they hashed out this argument, he couldn't seem to understand that this was her job, too. It didn't matter if she was right though; she always felt horribly guilty after he reamed her for jeopardizing his position due to the sheriff's dislike for her.

She sat down on the steps and wondered, not for the first time, if she was destined to end up living here alone forever with only her relative's inheritance of odds and ends to keep her company. Even Spencer, the family beagle, couldn't make it off Me'Maw's back porch anymore to visit her. She'd considered a puppy, but it would be cruel to promise an animal she'd take care of it when she couldn't take care of herself.

"Hello, neighbor." The blond braless wonder appeared in front of her as Raleigh's vision snapped into focus from her thoughts. A crown of white clover flowers framed her tangled mess of beach-combed hair. The flimsy white cotton shirt she wore revealed a boney frame beneath.

For a moment Raleigh couldn't think further than braless as her name, which is why she avoided assigning nicknames. Raleigh forced a smile. "Amber, right?"

Amber nodded, pursing her lips together, a slight hum vibrating through her lips. "I can sense a powerful spiritual energy here. It called me from across the street."

"It did?" Raleigh scanned the quiet neighborhood. Cheramie Lane didn't show any sign of life, nor any visible spiritual energy.

Amber nodded, wetting her lips with her tongue. "I would normally suggest a spiritual cleanse, but I believe it suits you."

"So are you some kind of psychic or new age practitioner?" Raleigh asked, avoiding the peep show of her chest and instead focusing on her light brown eyes and amber colored eyelashes.

"I dabble." Amber hummed again. "I was hoping to get a chance to speak to your charming friend from earlier."

"He doesn't live here." Her response was too quick, defensive.

"Oh," Amber said, regarding her with dreamy eyes. "I think I remember that now." She exhaled slowly. "Well, it wasn't a total waste. The energy says we will be great friends. It must be so."

Raleigh studied her, unsure of her thoughts on this woman. In her early twenties, Amber appeared the type to play with pot, eat health food, and spout out sage advice. A new age hippie, really. But she came off slightly… crazy.

But connecting to people in their last moments before death wasn't usually considered sane. Raleigh was sure people looked at her the way she was looking at Amber at this moment. Raleigh could pretend to be normal, obviously better than Amber managed, but she had a reputation. No matter how normal she wanted to be, people thought she was just as loony as Amber, so sitting on this porch and judging Amber's sanity churned her insides.

"Well, I must be getting back inside before my dinner gets cold. I'm sure we will see each other around again, neighbor."

"Of course we will." Amber smiled. "We are going to be the best of friends." She twirled on one foot and skipped back toward her house.

Raleigh wasn't sure about friends, but she would try to withhold judgment. Unlike what she was about to go back inside and face with Max.

Chapter Six

In the large mirror overlooking the hairdresser chair, Raleigh furrowed her eyebrows and squinched her nose and forehead together. The wrinkle on her forehead deepened, and she quickly relaxed her face so that it would return to its smooth exterior. Her birthday ticked steadily closer, and thirty felt uncomfortably near with relationship woes and wrinkle watch. She didn't need to deepen the creases.

"I mean," Sheri continued as her yellow gloved hands scrubbed containers in the sink, "am I supposed to keep waiting for him to decide if we are dating or if we are just friends? I can only chalk it up to taking it slow for so long."

Raleigh nodded and uh hummed at the right moment, attempting to remain neutral on the budding romance between Sheri and Jeff. Besides the fact that Raleigh failed at relationship advice, Jeff and Mike had remained chummy since high school. She had to hang out with him on several Saturday nights, shooting pool and cooking out under the patio when he and Mike would show up with a sack of crawfish or fileted fish ready to fry. Raleigh would remain Switzerland in this hookup because Jeff knew his way with a spatula.

"And then there is the drama over Deon's death," Sheri griped. "I don't blame him for wanting to stay away until everything clears up."

"Did he say that?" Raleigh spun the chair around, rethinking her neutrality. Sheri deserved better.

Sheri leaned against the sink as she turned the hair bowls upside down to dry. "Well, Deon's mother is causing trouble over the funeral arrangements. She wants Shawn there but not me, of course. But Shawn doesn't want to attend without me, and I don't blame him. That family has been pretty much strangers until recently. She called at least five times yesterday though, which didn't leave Jeff and my time together yesterday drama free. He probably thinks my life is a mess."

"No," Raleigh said, offering a smile of reassurance. "I'm sure he's just trying to give you space to deal with all of this. How is Shawn handling it all?"

A change of topic could do her friend some good.

Sheri shrugged. "He's confused, and everyone talking about the rougarou killing his dad is a nightmare. He doesn't know what to think."

"Barbeaux exists for its gossip." Raleigh couldn't understand the gullibility of the town. The only monsters around Barbeaux Bayou were of the human variety. "Something else will happen soon, and everyone will forget all of this."

"With that faux reality show, I'm sure something will happen soon. Ray at the bar said sparks were flying between Aryanna and Josh the other night. Something about some pictures."

"What pictures?" Madison asked as she breezed in through the front door, the bell jangling her arrival. "You are so difficult to track down, Raleigh Lynn. Can't you take a lunch like a normal person?"

Raleigh sighed. She tried as much as possible to escape work, even though lunch breaks were often spent working at her desk these days. "Sheri and I have a standing lunch date on Wednesdays. I try not to spend every waking moment working."

Raleigh didn't mention that she'd had to cancel the last three Wednesdays because of Madison's prep work for the show. Raleigh's life revolved around work these days to the point where her friendships, what little she had, were falling to the side. She still needed to work in a visit to Me'Maw and Paw, but she'd rarely made it home before their bedtime every night.

"I have some things to run through with you, and I figure with tonight's dance lesson, we won't have much time."

Madison slid into the chair next to Raleigh and pulled a stack of mismatched notes from her purse. "Setup starts tomorrow afternoon so the scenery can be ready for rehearsal Friday, which is scheduled to be filmed this week. But this episode is still missing a close interaction between the couples, and that's what makes the audience show interest. Any ideas?"

"Did we get any footage of the couples interacting during dance lessons?" Raleigh asked as she tapped on the armrest of her chair in frustration. She couldn't escape work; even in her dreams she thought about the complexities of this show. Now Madison invaded the one free hour she'd attempted to squeeze from her day. Raleigh couldn't wait until the show completed its filming.

"Nothing personal or explosive." Madison pursed her lips together as she clutched her notes in her hand. Madison must dream in catfights and scandal.

"Maybe you should spice things up and have them do confessionals after they dance for rehearsals. I bet they have something to say after they have their toes stepped all over." Sheri laughed a big-chested laugh as she sunk into the hair-washing chair.

"That's not a bad idea," Madison said, waving her notes in the air in a fanning motion. "We can film those Friday. Maybe we can make sure we do something to pair them in configurations that will cause sparks to fly?" At this, Madison looked to Raleigh for reassurance.

Raleigh stifled a groan. "We know who doesn't get along if that's what you're talking about." Madison and reality television made a perfect match. This truly was her calling. It would be a shame if her show never made it beyond the local market. Raleigh, on the other hand, couldn't help but imagine all their neighbors chasing them out of town with pitchforks for ruining the sleepy, laid-back reputation of their hometown.

Madison nodded as she rummaged for a pen in her purse to add to her notes. "Don't forget about Deon. Maybe we can bring that in as well." Their parents must have been tired by the time Madison was born. Aside from the six year age gap, it was the only explanation Raleigh had for what was wrong with Madison's sense of decency.

Jingling again, the door swung open and Max strolled in, looming over the hair studio. Reaching up to remove his sunglasses, his eyes traveled to each of them, sliding over Raleigh quickly. So the ashes of their argument still hadn't settled. He'd been steadfast in his stance, but so had she. She'd had her alone time last night after he'd left early. It hadn't been relaxing though.

"Sheri," Max said, looking at only the salon owner. "I needed to ask you some questions about the argument you and Deon had the day he died."

"Oh," Sheri muttered, her face whitening.

Max tilted his head, his lips neutral. Raleigh recognized it as his way to assure his interviewee. Too bad it didn't work in relationships. "We are simply trying to create a timeline of Deon's day to see who he came into contact with before his death, and Ms. Rachel said you two had an argument in the parking lot at the grocery store. Can you tell me what happened?"

Sheri's chest rose and fell heartily. "Shawn had asked his dad to go with him to a field day at school, but Deon had backed out the morning of the event. Then I hear from his mother that in the upcoming custody trial, he's going to say that I didn't allow him to participate in events with Shawn. I questioned him about it when I ran into him that morning, and he told me he couldn't talk about our upcoming litigation."

"And the argument was heated?"

"I was livid," Sheri said, her cheeks reddening. "As if our son's feelings are litigation. Do you know how upset Shawn was when his dad canceled? I had to deal with his foul mood for days, and of course Shawn blamed me, too. He always thinks that his dad doesn't show up because he and I don't get along."

"Did you two leave at the same time?"

"No," Sheri said, shaking her head. "I was going in the store, and he was leaving."

"Was he alone? Did you see anyone waiting for him in his vehicle?"

"That blonde from the show was crouching down in the passenger seat, trying not to let anyone see her."

Max looked to Raleigh and Madison, mostly Madison. He seemed to be going with Raleigh not being in the room as his dealing strategy.

Madison fiddled in her bag and pulled out a group shot from the promo shoot. "I'm sure you are talking about Aryanna. Apparently, the two were an item the last two weeks, but they couldn't show those sparks on camera for us."

Max took the picture and walked it to Sheri. Sheri studied it only a moment before pointing to a face on the picture, and Max returned to Madison.

Madison nodded as he pointed out the woman. "That's her."

"Okay, ladies," Max said, nodding and returning his sunglasses to his face. "I will be in touch to check out those surveillance videos of the studio sometime tomorrow after the judge signs the warrant."

Madison frowned, but Raleigh had expected it as a natural part of any investigation. The footage would be grainy at best. Even though Mr. Delecroix put money into the television studio occasionally, the surveillance cameras weren't top notch. Rumor was he only used the footage to spy on his children, and he didn't need clear faces to do that.

Madison let the door close behind him before she hissed. "Can he just leave it alone? I mean, obviously it was an animal attack, not a human mauling. He should be setting traps instead of wasting our time with video."

Sheri's chest heaved forward and she moaned. "Raleigh, I think I'm in trouble."

Raleigh zoned in on her and saw the tears brimming at the edges of Sheri's heavily charcoal outlined eyes. "What did you leave out?"

"I was there that day. At the station." Sheri gulped. "I swear I didn't do anything to him, but I went with his messages to Shawn printed out to wave them in his face. He grabbed my arms when he saw that I'd saved them, and I slapped him. I promise I left him there alive though. You know I'd never hurt anyone."

The tears spilled over and Raleigh could see the fear in her friend's eyes. They both knew that it would have been caught on camera. Max would know tomorrow that she'd left part of the story out, and that would make her look guilty of something. And what Raleigh did know was that if Sheri was to ever wish someone dead, it would be her ex-husband.

"You should have told Max," Madison said, twisting in her chair. "Now it's going to make you look guilty."

Raleigh glared at her sister. It must be nice to have made it to twenty-three and to not have had anyone slug you for not having a filter between your brain and mouth. With the crowd Madison dealt with, it was surprising.

"I know," Sheri whined. "I knew it would make me look guilty, but I forgot about the surveillance footage. Now he's going to see I was there."

Raleigh released a slow breath through her lips, her thoughts gathering as her lungs emptied. "When he sees the video, you need to tell him that he only asked you about the argument in the parking lot, so you didn't get to mention later on you saw him again. Tell him you went to drop off the text messages and then left right after and that you know nothing more."

Sheri picked her head up. "Do you think that will work?"

"Of course it will," Madison said, nodding. "Raleigh dates the pig. She can vouch for you."

Raleigh bit her lip for a moment and silently counted to five, but then Madison looked up from her phone. "No offense, Sis. I've just been rooting for Mike as a brother-in-law since I was nine. I may come around to Max someday when the jerk learns how to treat you better."

Considering that Max had completely avoided her and they could have very well been strangers just now, Raleigh didn't have much of an argument in his defense. Not to mention, coming from Madison, considering it was an unselfish thought, Raleigh should be impressed.

"Don't mention this conversation. You didn't tell me about it until after you talk to Max," Raleigh said, thinking that she'd need to keep this one to herself or risk starting another argument. Of course, this was more than printing a piece of evidence; this was hiding evidence in an ongoing investigation. But Sheri hadn't killed Deon. She knew her friend well enough to know that no matter how much she hated him, Sheri wasn't a murderer. She already knew Max wouldn't see it that way. Dating a detective wouldn't be so tricky if her friends didn't keep turning up as murder suspects.

Sheri nodded, mascara trailing down her face. She pulled a tissue from behind her, eyes unfocused. Raleigh imagined she was worrying about what Shawn would think if this got out and became gossip fodder.

This became more of a tangled mess by the day.

Chapter Seven

The mason jar bounced against the grass once again, the glass holding together. Raleigh climbed back down the ladder to retrieve it, feeling the ache in her calves from the many reps on this ladder. If she could stop dropping the jars, the string of lights around the grounds would be complete. After returning to the top rung of the ladder, Raleigh hung it from the metal loop and moved onto the last three without incident. Her luck might be changing.

Once down from the ladder, Raleigh looked around to admire their work on the staging area. The potted trees, picnic tables, and palmetto leaves established the Cajun theme of the fais do-do and the other elements were in the making as their small crew puttered around. Thankfully, Dan, amateur weather extraordinaire, assured them of clear skies until Monday. With the trickiness of outdoor events, especially two weeks in a row, Louisiana weather had been particularly nice to them instead of shooting their plans to hell.

Bumbling along the uneven ground, a navy extended cab truck and trailer strapped down with wooden rocking chairs flowed over the sides of the black metal railings of the trailer. Madison glanced over at the approaching delivery, but her attention returned to the two men attempting to set up a faux wood floor to her exact specifications. H&R rentals probably regretted agreeing to help her out at this moment in time.

Raleigh walked over as Patrick stepped out of the passenger side of the truck.

"Ms. Raleigh, Gramps has the rockers for this shindig. Any special place you want them?"

Cringing at being called Misses, she reassured herself that the fresh-faced, barely-looking-eighteen Patrick didn't intend to make her feel old. "We are going to set up clusters of them around the dance floor. I'll show you the exact spots, and we can divide the rockers among those areas."

Patrick nodded, as his older, more leathery-faced Gramps appeared from the other side of the truck. His plaid work shirt and hide work gloves in his hand indicated he'd come prepared for work, whereas Patrick's uncalloused, smooth hands didn't look as if he'd done any manual labor in his life.

Raleigh shielded her eyes against the glare off the windshield of the navy Caprice pulling in next to the truck. Max exited his Barbeaux Bayou Police unit, his collar and tie straight. Madison's head was going to explode. She'd waited all day for him to come, and he had to arrive at six in the evening when they were fighting approaching nightfall and mosquitos to complete set up.

Max strolled over gripping folded papers in his hand, sunglasses hiding his eyes against any reading of his expression. "Evening," he said, nodding to the group. He then gripped the out stretched hand of Patrick's grandfather. It was all so Southern. Max probably didn't even know the man, but it's what you did.

"We will start unloading them while you take care of this," Patrick said, staring at the paper clearly labeled search warrant at the top.

Raleigh nodded and turned and moved toward Madison, who had already spotted them moving in her direction. Those two etched lines across her forehead would become permanent if she weren't careful.

"You couldn't have worse timing," Madison uttered as they approached. The gentleman on his knees laying out the floor straightened up to look at her, probably thinking she was offering some new criticism.

Max handed over the warrant. "It's never convenient when someone dies. I'm sure Deon had plans today, too."

Madison glared at him a moment before she unfolded the papers and scanned through them. "Wait, you want the show's tapes too? Not just the surveillance footage?"

"Specifically, I'm looking for anything that links any of the other contestants to Deon. Those confessionals are probably the place I would like to start, after the surveillance video of that day, of course."

"Francois will pull it all up for you." Madison shook her head, those two lines firmly etched in her forehead to display her aggravation. "Raleigh, can you get him started while I give out some directions here and then join you?"

Raleigh nodded, her body tensing against what she knew was coming. Perhaps Sheri and Deon's argument had taken place in one of the many blind spots. She could only hope.

Max followed her through the metal door and into the dark hallway that led to the offices. Turning left, they entered the door that led to the studio, where the lights lit up the vacated space. The offices had emptied for the night except for the few stragglers working the party set up. Max reached for the door handle and held it open for her, but she was too nervous to acknowledge his peace offering. It could just be his good manners since he'd yet to acknowledge her, and she didn't want to give him undue credit.

Stooped over in his chair, Francois studied video on a screen in front of him as his hand hovered over the mouse. He glanced up as they entered.

"I want to be paid overtime if this is what I think it is," Francois uttered, his brow furrowed. "It's bad enough that tonight's *Talk with Ted* needed to be reedited because he didn't like his hair."

"Detective Pyles is here with a search warrant to see the surveillance footage from Sunday as well as the confessionals of the week."

Francois pointed to the screen farthest from him. "That computer is queued to the video of that day. The surveillance cameras aren't the best quality so the detail is grainy at best."

"I'll make do. I'm assuming there are no cameras in the back area?"

"No," Raleigh said, "Until *Barbeaux Hearts*, the back area was never used."

"As far as the confessionals," Francois said, refocusing on his screen. "Sunday's confessionals had about four and a half hours of green screen time. I suggest I burn you a copy and you spend your time listening to that dribble in small doses."

Max nodded and slid into the chair at the computer. Raleigh pointed out the time stamps and the toggle buttons between cameras. The T.F. Delacroix building had a total of eight outdated cameras that provided recordings of the front parking area, the front receptionist area, the three main hallways, and the two larger studios. Mr. Delacroix didn't feel the security camera update necessary anymore after he added the keypad entry system, which allowed only employees to enter doors that weren't the front lobby. As the receptionist, Mrs. Deloris had reached retirement age fourteen years ago and wouldn't be stopping anyone from coming past the front doors, but her shrill, commanding voice would be sure to alert anyone else to danger.

Max placed his notepad on the edge of the table and began forwarding through the front lobby footage of the day. Raleigh watched him jot down in his neat print the time each contestant entered through the lobby. Raleigh watched the screen as Deon, wearing the same fishing shirt she found him in hours later, held the door open for Aryanna. Minutes later at the lobby entrance Sheri entered and glanced around. Her skintight pants and animal print shirt clearly identifying her even in the grainy footage.

Max paused the video.

"Strange that Sheri didn't mention coming to the station when I questioned her yesterday."

His nonchalant tone didn't reveal his thoughts and put Raleigh further on edge.

"I'm sure it's nothing. Sheri would never hurt anyone."

"What I know," Max said, scribbling on his page in handwriting that Raleigh couldn't read from where she stood, "is that anyone can kill if they are pushed, especially if they are afraid to lose their son."

"You know Sheri personally," Raleigh said, infuriated. "All she wanted was to show him that she could prove he was lying."

"So you knew she was there that day and didn't tell me?" He glanced at her with narrowed, disgusted eyes, as if she were a criminal instead of his girlfriend.

Madison chose that moment to swing the door open in a huff. "Raleigh, can you go oversee the rocking chairs. Here's the diagram layout."

She tossed a sheet towards Raleigh, clearly frustrated by this entire situation.

"Gladly," Raleigh said, gripping the paper firmly. "You know Max, maybe if you wouldn't be such a horrible, stubborn boyfriend, we could have discussed it like a healthy couple, but clearly we don't have that relationship."

Raleigh turned and allowed the door to slam behind her. Guilt and relief charged through her instantly. She didn't want to agonize over the mixture, so she hurried outside to finish setup before a mosquito swarm drained them of their blood after all the sweat and tears that had gone into this show.

In the staging area, the wooden flooring had taken shape during the time she'd been gone and had only a few plants left to completion. Patrick and his father had unloaded the rocking chairs and awaited placement instructions. Someone had delivered the three pirogues during her visit to the video room, and the band would set up tomorrow night for rehearsal and again Saturday night for the recording. All that was missing was the guests and the catering service.

Hurrying over to Patrick, Raleigh began issuing instructions, explaining the diagram. Gramps and Patrick, gloves on hands, puzzled over the arrangement a moment before starting to move the rockers into the seating patterns. Deciding to pitch in to keep her mind off of Max, Raleigh picked up a rocker and half carried, half dragged it into its place.

"You know," Patrick said, patting his head with a bandanna that had stuck out his front pocket. "My gramps still makes each of these by hand. He used only driftwood when he began, but he received too many orders to keep up, so now he picks out his own lumber at the mill. Still finds driftwood for the swings though. He brought two of those lagniappe for the show, being he's getting free advertisement." Patrick blushed, realizing he'd rambled.

"That's wonderful," Raleigh said. "I know exactly where we can put the swing. Madison and I were talking about a hole in the staging now that the guy with the Cajun house scenery backed out. We thought about more reeds and trees, but this will look so much better."

Patrick grinned. "Coo-wee. Gramps will be thrilled to hear it. He's super proud y'all picked him."

"I really hope the show isn't causing you any trouble," Raleigh said, following him back to the rockers. "I realize some of the other contestants have had some issues; Madison can be intense sometimes even though she means well." *Most of the time she means well.* There were many times Raleigh hoped she wasn't lying to herself about that.

"What trouble might that be, Ms. Raleigh?" Patrick asked, gripping another chair to his chest as if it were a toy.

"Well, I know that some contestants have wanted out of their contracts and weren't allowed. There have been a fight or two between some of the girls that expensive makeup had to cover up. Recently, I've heard that there's some drama over pictures."

Patrick's jaw clutched tightly and he didn't speak until they lowered the rockers into place. Well, Raleigh dragged hers into place.

"No one knows who has the pictures, so of course that causes drama. Rumor was that it was Deon, but then he died and another one turned up so we know it isn't him unless he's sending them from the afterlife."

Raleigh took this in, turning it over in her brain as a bombardment of questions pummeled her.

"What kind of pictures?" Raleigh asked, and then rethought that question. "I mean obviously pictures that people don't want anyone to see because that's where the drama comes in, but are we talking criminal or just private affairs?"

"Private affairs, I suppose," Patrick said, thinking. "No one has really shared the pictures with anyone else. When I received the picture of me and...." Patrick's eyes flickered around the area and his pale cheeks reddened.

"It's okay, Patrick," Raleigh said, "I'm not going to tell anyone. I just want to figure out what's going on. Obviously, someone's targeting the contestants, and it's my job to take care of y'all."

He looked at her a moment, his face pained, but she saw the moment flicker in his acorn eyes where he decided to trust her. "It was a picture of me and Wayne in a... uhh, compromising position in my home. Please don't tell anyone, Ms. Raleigh. My grams and gramps don't know that I'm, you know, gay, and my grams so wanted me to do this show. They raised me right, but they ain't real big with the open-minded ideas of our times. They real good people though."

Raleigh nodded. Change didn't come easy in Barbeaux Bayou. It could weather a hurricane by buckling down and holding on, and that's pretty much how its residents held on to its traditions and ideas. Patrick had his work cut out for him. But then she thought of her Me'Maw and Paw, who weathered every storm and held on with fierce pride, but also rolled with the changes and allowed the storm to shape their path.

"So you were sent just a picture. What about a message?"

He shrugged his shoulders. "A simple typed slip saying, 'I know who you really are.' Apparently, everyone received the same message. When I got mine, I believed it was Deon since he and Wayne are friends. But he denied it when I confronted him. Everyone had their own suspicions and confronted one or another person, so it began to get around."

Raleigh considered this. "So if I find out who hasn't received a photo, I may be able to narrow down who might be sending them."

Patrick looked at her with an expression of surprise. "Why, I didn't think of that Ms. Raleigh."

"I'll figure this out Patrick." Raleigh nodded. "And you know, Patrick, I have some of those old fashioned grandparents, and I bet they would surprise you if you told them the truth. They really only want to see you happy. That's why your grams wanted you on this show. There may be a small amount of shock, but I bet those old people have a little more ability to adapt to change than you think, especially as Cajuns."

Patrick looked doubtful. "I don't know about that one. They haven't changed the way they do things since they met fifty years ago."

"You told me earlier that your gramps went from driftwood to lumber. The old people around here are better at adapting than we give them credit for." Raleigh smiled.

Patrick chuckled. "Maybe you're right."

Just then another truck hauling a trailer behind it pulled in, and Raleigh figured the food service tables had arrived. Thankfully, this was the last delivery today until the finishing touches arrived tomorrow. Fantastic, she might not go home tonight covered in mosquito welts. She'd be alone after her words to Max, but at least she wouldn't be tearing at her skin to end the itching.

Chapter Eight

A netting similar to a trawl net wrapped the entire chicken coop against any flying intruders, yet Mr. A.J. Thibodaux had found a total of thirteen egg-laying hens dead in the last two nights. This morning she and Mike had received a total of five complaints, all within a few mile radius that did not include the T.F. Delacroix station, so they couldn't immediately draw the conclusion that the same animal was attacking people and animals. David had sent them out to investigate since the major complaint by the five grumpy farmers was a lack of police interest.

Mr. A.J. scratched his balding head with black stained fingers and the ten hairs on top sticking up with the motion. "It's the darnedest thing. A trail of blood into the woods and feathers clear across tarnation, but nothing of the bird left."

"Did you happen to see animal tracks?" Mike asked, gripping the creosol pole and yanking to see if it gave under a pull. It leaned a half inch toward him, but held steady. On a walk-around inspection, no hole in the fencing or openings had revealed themselves. The gate appeared the only way into the chicken yard.

Shaking his head, A.J. pointed toward the dog cages thirty feet away with dirt covered floor. Several thin lips drooled as brown eyes studied them through a metal kennel. "Hard to tell. Leave the muts out at night to guard ma property, keep the coyotes away. They didn't even bark. Scared 'em, I guess." He glanced toward them and spit onto the ground in disgust.

Raleigh figured he was reassessing his security choice.

"I'm guessing no cameras, huh?" Raleigh asked, assessing the small farm. Under a few shade trees sat a small cypress shotgun house with an old white ceramic bathtub in the front yard. From her vantage point, Raleigh wasn't sure if it was a cast off or a water feature. Under an oak tree just beyond the house sat a rusted red and white tractor. Raleigh could appreciate the antiqueness of it. Her paw would be able to tell the exact year, its engine, and its model. Raleigh could say with certainty it was at least forty years old. If Mr. A.J. kept it running, then he had more talent than his run-down farm indicated.

"Nah," Mr. A.J. patted his hairs down on his head. "I'm old-fashioned. Don't want anything to do with those gadgets and computers. Old man Elmer may have cameras though. He's the paranoid type, and he lost a few rabbits and a chicken or two a few nights ago."

Mike looked back at her, and she jotted his name on her notepad. An Elmer had not been one of the phone calls in, but people in Barbeaux weren't too difficult to track down.

A.J. kicked his thick brown boot at the dirt. "Me and some others are thinking of going hunting, you know."

"What would you be hunting?" Mike asked, shielding his eyes in the morning sunlight as he looked at the tree line surrounding the carved out area for the house, the coop, and a small garden.

"Well." A.J. looked at his work boot, a black spot in the toe of his left boot capturing his attention. "Rumor is that we have ourselves the rougarou. We figure we can catch him. Might be worth some money."

"And what if it's a person?" Raleigh asked, thinking that a bunch of armed men going after a folklore might not turn out well.

A.J. shrugged. "Then we will have caught ourselves a thief."

"Well, thank you Mr. A.J.," Mike said, sticking his hand out to shake. "We will be in touch if we have any more questions as we talk to the others."

Mr. A.J. nodded. "Sure nice for y'all to come out."

Raleigh followed Mike back to his Jeep and climbed in, taking one last glance from the chicken yard to the woods again. From the location of the gate, a person or animal could have opened the coop's door without being heard at the house. If the dogs didn't react. If the chickens didn't cluck in fright. The fact that Mr. A.J. had heard nothing felt questionable.

She glanced over at Mike, his forehead creased in concentration. "What are you thinking?"

Mike cranked the engine and backed out of the dirt driveway back to the main road. "Well, I'm leaning more toward thief but maybe we need to look into the history of the rougarou."

"Why?" Raleigh asked startled. She hadn't expected him to believe in folklore.

"Well," Mike said, smiling, "maybe there was a real person behind the rougarou stories, and it might give us a clue as to what kind of person we are looking for now. Plus, it would help us debunk the rougarou gossip taking hold."

Raleigh laughed in relief. "I can get behind that, and Paw can probably help us with that. I thought for a moment you wanted to form our own hunting party."

"Isn't that what we do?" Mike asked. "Solve the murder ourselves? Like our own Scooby gang, albeit a much smaller one."

"Yeah," Raleigh grumbled. "Max wants me to stay out of the mystery solving business, breaking up our mystery solving gang completely."

"Trouble in paradise?" Mike asked, raising his eyebrows. "I'm guessing printing that tidbit of info didn't go over well."

"That, and the fact that Sheri hid a bit of information from him that I knew and didn't tell him."

Mike whistled. "You're in deep." He smiled. "He has to see that this is difficult for you, too. Our jobs require us to search for the truth."

Frustration throbbed at Raleigh's temple. "To him the law is black and white, and what he does is more important than the public knowing what is going on."

Mike glanced her way. "And you disagreed, right?"

"Of course I did," Raleigh said, and then released a deep breath through her lips. "I get that what he does is important, but our job is important as well."

"I can't give up my partner," Mike said, signaling on the highway toward Cheramie Lane. "I mean, how lucky are we to spend our day with our best friend doing what we love to do?"

Raleigh glanced at him and laughed. Aside from the television show right now, her job didn't feel like work most days. She liked her work. She wished more would happen some times, but she could live with the slow nature of the town. It's not like she had a large skill set. Even her previous job working as a detective's assistant had used the same talents. Besides, she did get to work with Mike every day; her beach blonde, six-pack-abs, sexy partner was like the icing on the cake.

Raleigh chided herself. Being googly-eyed over Mike would only make things with Max more complicated.

On the back lot of Cheramie Lane, her grandparents' white wooden house sat peacefully, and within thirty feet her parents double shotgun home rested under the canopy of oak trees. Within the old cypress barn between the two homes her Paw's old Ford pickup was parked inside its dark interior. No sign of life played out on the lawn.

Mike coasted his Jeep right up to the back of the pickup, and they made their way toward the back porch, where at midday they'd likely find her grandparents cooling off from the afternoon sun. From his dog bed next to the screen door, Spencer raised his head as Raleigh stepped onto the back step, but he didn't struggle to his feet, as he would have not too long ago. Paw said the old canine's arthritis had grown too painful, and in a show of sympathy Paw didn't usually extend to animals, the old Beagle had been given a heating pad. He didn't move much from his bed these days.

The screen door creaked as Raleigh yanked it open. "Me'Maw, are y'all home?"

Me'Maw chuckled from her rocker. "Why, look who's come to call finally."

Paw rose from his chair to shake hands with Mike, and then eased back into his usual cherry wood chair at the table. "You two must be real busy these days with all the foolishness going on in our town."

Raleigh nodded, noticing Me'Maw's hand over her worn set of playing cards she used to read for people. Me'Maw could read the cards and see glimpses of what was to come, but she typically only consulted them when she was worried. Catching Raleigh's eye on her, Me'Maw removed her soft wrinkled hand from her cards and folded them together in her lap.

Mike pulled up a chair at the table with Paw, like he'd done since his feet couldn't reach the floor. "Rumors spread like flood waters around here, we're chasing them all down. Plus, Raleigh here has Madison's show to work on and that's like dealing with a bunch of ornery alligators."

Raleigh sat in the chair next to Me'Maw. "Two more weeks, though, and we wrap up filming. Then maybe I can do something useful."

Me'Maw nodded, her shoulder-length white hair grazing her chin. Due to family traditions, Me'Maw remained quiet on Raleigh's training, especially since she'd gone outside the family. But, she wanted Raleigh to keep the family inheritance going, and who knew how seriously Madison would take her lessons? All of this went unsaid, but Me'Maw's eyes always spoke volumes.

Paw leaned back against the kitchen wall. "So what is fueling these rumors? Any real facts?"

Living here all his life, Paw felt as though it was his town and every matter was of his concern. He kept up with the news around Barbeaux Bayou with a passion. Because of this, he enjoyed questioning them about their articles, oftentimes shedding a new light on stories with his questions.

"A human footprint was found near Deon's body," Raleigh said. "Otherwise the evidence on the body is strictly from an animal attack unless something is discovered in the toxicology."

"And it's not possible it was put there when you and Madison found the body?"

"No," Raleigh said. "When I realized it wasn't Mike, we kept at least five feet from the body. I think the investigator said we were actually eight feet away. They picked up our shoes though to verify it wasn't us."

She glanced at Mike sheepishly, who offered her his goofy grin. When she'd confessed that she'd thought it might be him, he'd scuffed up her hair and joked that no animal wanted him. Raleigh couldn't help her paranoia though. With the rate that people around them turned up dead, it wasn't like the idea was far-fetched.

"Then there are other mysterious animal disappearances going on now. Chickens, rabbits, the like," Mike said.

"Only more fuel for the rumors," Paw said, bobbing his head up and down.

"We are looking into them," Raleigh said. "Strange inconsistencies though causing doubt that it's strictly animal attacks."

"What we came to ask though," Mike said, before Paw could jump on his supernatural lecture, "is has there ever been a time when someone used the rougarou lore to hide behind? I mean like a real killer pretending to be the rougarou?"

"Well now, that's a decent theory y'all have worked up," Paw said, resting his head against the wallpaper, his expression grim. "And I'm guessing that would explain some of the evidence?"

"Well, the bites speak of an animal, but opening gates seems more human, not to mention the footprint." Mike tapped the table, glancing at her for confirmation.

Paw cleared his throat. "The story of the rougarou isn't like the Loch Ness Monster or even Big Foot. It really did just begin as a story. The French told the story for a long time before they brought it here, and then the story traveled up and down the bayous of Louisiana and changed from town to town. The French told of a half wolf and half man. You know, the face of a wolf and the body of a man, but since we don't see too many wolves here, some tell of a rougarou that is pig or dog or I even heard one about a half bat. No consistency there, except that the swamp monster had glowing red eyes, sharp teeth, and rose to almost eight feet tall."

Mike leaned forward. "But no proof that it ever existed, right?"

"Oh, in the 1960s there were some pictures that a woman claimed to be of a rougarou, but many dismissed it as that of a decaying carcass of a dog. A Chihuahua, I think."

"But," Raleigh rubbed the scar on her wrist as she began to think, "the animal would have to not only be vicious but also trained by a person. How many animals in this area meet those requirements?"

"You'd have to check the exact laws," Paw said, "but it is illegal to own a wolf in our state. Now a hybrid is a different story, but you have to have papers if I'm not mistaken. A coyote wouldn't attack if it were trained except maybe if it were provoked. Even then, they tend to be too nervous unless they are starving. We didn't really have a bad winter around here to say that's the case. I don't see a panther being trained."

"What we need," Mike said, tilting his head. Behind those deep green eyes, now glazed over with thought, Raleigh recognized his wheels turning. "Is to know what kind of animal those bites belong to."

"I don't see Max turning that information over to us," Raleigh said, hoping whatever idea percolating in his head didn't involve her speaking to Max. She'd decided he would have to come to her first.

"He might." Mike shrugged. "Especially if he thinks it will help stop the town talking about the rougarou."

"I've always thought that the police needed to work better with the newspapers. People love to talk to a reporter and hate to talk to an officer. It could be the perfect relationship," Me'Maw said, rocking forward, her yellow tulip duster gently moving with the motion. In her eighties, Me'Maw looked in good shape, but every time Raleigh went weeks between visits, another wrinkle crossed the velvety cheek of her alabaster skin. Raleigh didn't know how much longer her grandmother would be around sitting in this old kitchen for Raleigh to just to drop in on, and the idea made her throat throb in pain.

"Okay," Mike said, clapping his hand on the table. "Let's see if we can track down this Elmer and see if we can get lucky with video. We may be able to end these rougarou rumors soon."

Raleigh rose, bent over, and squeezed Me'Maw tightly into a hug, inhaling her Dove soap and lingering hint of a fried ham lunch.

"Don't be a stranger," Me'Maw said. "I'll tell you what, in two weeks, I will cook dinner for you two and we can celebrate."

Raleigh smiled.

"Fantastic," Mike said. "Nothing like Me'Maw's stew."

"You should know." Paw chuckled. "You ate enough to grow up real tall."

Mike hugged Me'Maw and they allowed the screen door to snap behind them on the way out. Spencer didn't lift his head this time as they walked across the porch. Maybe Raleigh should get a dog instead of a boyfriend. Spencer had been a great companion until age had tired his body out. Of course, she didn't know if she'd trust herself to keep it alive. However, she had managed to keep a plant alive for the first time in her life. She supposed everyone had to grow up at some point.

"You have a way to get those footprint results?" Raleigh asked as she walked around to the passenger side of the Jeep.

"More of an idea." Mike grinned.

Raleigh groaned. "That sounds like trouble."

Mike laughed as he started the Jeep and backed out the drive. "What we do best, Ree."

Wasn't that the truth. And he wondered why it wasn't difficult to believe that he'd end up dead somewhere. And with no connection in weeks, Raleigh might be looking at a normal future after all. Considering she'd wanted that forever, she didn't know why it made her feel uneasy now.

Chapter Nine

The hanging mason jar candles lit the fais do-do staging, casting a romantic glow over the faces of the guests surrendering their ticket and moving along to find their seats. The last twenty-four hours had blurred into a massive list of finalizing details and refereeing the contestants into separate corners. Plastering a smile on her face, Raleigh accepted the ticket Richard Delacroix presented her as he strolled in with a young blonde on his arm. As usual, his salt and pepper hair didn't have a hair out of place and his forehead was flat as a television screen. Everyone whispered about his Botox treatments, not that these rumors were confirmed, but Mr. Delacroix had to be at least sixty-one. As the station manager and part owner of the entire company, tonight could be a catastrophe for Raleigh's career if the contestants couldn't play nice for the cameras.

Last night's rehearsal had crumbled as soon as it began with snide remarks, bickering, and some outright refusing to dance with their partners. Raleigh had no time to question anyone about the pictures because she and Madison had played mediators the entire night. Although plenty of tension had been in the air, no one would divulge what had sparked the newest issue.

Raleigh searched the area for Madison, but instead, she glimpsed Max speaking to a curly-haired woman at one of the sponsors' picnic tables. Raleigh knew for a fact that Max's name wasn't anywhere on tonight's guest list, and Madison would not have added him with all the trouble likely to happen with tempers at their peak. How he'd finagled an invitation would make an interesting conversation, if they were speaking.

"Sue, I'm going to check with Madison and see what needs to be done before filming begins."

Sue, the new secretary in the television studio, nodded as a younger couple dressed in denim and flannel approached the makeshift gate.

Adjusting the sunflower and cattail table arrangement as she walked past, Raleigh smiled at a few gentlemen already sipping canned beer from the iced pirogues located near the serving area. With their cowboy boots, jeans, and similar styled shirts, these must be some of the extras brought in for the dance scenes. Madison had recruited from her "other" party crowd to appeal to the camera, and Raleigh couldn't meet their eyes knowing that they'd once partaken in that lifestyle. Of course, the contestants could be former partiers as well. Raleigh had only seen a few pictures from the craziness of the illegal parties. In hair and makeup inside the studio, the contestants had about six minutes left before their appearance and the "matches" began. Raleigh felt panic hopping around her stomach. Like an animal feeling a storm coming, she felt the approaching disaster.

Madison clutched a clipboard as tightly to her chest as the pinned messy bun on the crown of her head. Her button-down shirt revealed just enough cleavage to be sexy, but the rest of her pencil skirt outfit spoke of her new professional role.

"Good," Madison said, "My mic is going to be turned on in a moment for testing, so you can take over now."

Raleigh took the clipboard as Madison handed it over. "Did you add Max to the guest list?"

Madison glanced in his direction, "Of course not. He came as Diane's guest, which as a sponsor I assumed she'd bring her husband."

Raleigh raised her eyebrows, ignoring the insinuation. Madison had made her dislike for Max known at every opportunity. "He needs to stay away from the contestants. We certainly don't need them any more riled up than they already are."

"That will be your job," Madison smiled. Her eyes revealed a slight fear though. She may be human yet. "Okay, audience selection first, then fan favorites followed by guys pick and then girls pick."

Raleigh glanced down at the clipboard, noticing all the labels typed neatly with the selections revealed. This is why she'd clutched it so tightly. "Will we announce the top couple of the week after, or will we let the dancing go on for a few rounds?"

Madison straightened her skirt and pursed her lips. "I think we need to get everything over with and just let the party go on after the announcement. I have a bad feeling that something is going to go wrong, and I don't mean in our favor."

Raleigh nodded. For Madison to be worried about drama, they'd reached explosive territory. "I'll get these to the sound man and get everyone in their places. You keep things rolling for the cameras, and I'll attempt to put out the fires before they get started."

Madison grimaced and then headed toward the stage area.

Raleigh turned and headed toward the sound table. Handing over the lists, she noticed a scantily clad, curvy woman leaning back against a table, fiery auburn hair brushing against the wooden surface. Scott took the lists and placed them under his headphones, catching her looking at the scowling young woman.

Scott glanced back as he twiddled with buttons on his equipment. "My niece wanted to be my assistant tonight. She's not so willing now that we are here."

The tickets to tonight's event were limited. Very limited. Sponsors who donated to the show received two tickets and each contestant received two tickets for family. The remaining tickets went to station bigwigs and the extras needed for filming. After the airing of the first show, many had called to beg and plead for tickets, but due to a limited budget, extra tickets weren't available. People like Scott's niece thought they'd be creative in getting an invite, but production were not allowed to socialize due to the possibility of being caught on camera.

Raleigh went over the order of the announcements as Madison had instructed and then turned to watch everyone gearing up for the contestants to enter. These fifteen people were the closest to celebrities Barbeaux Bayou had come close to claiming as their own, and they were enjoying every minute of it.

Mike strolled toward her from the back station door. "Are we giving an award tonight for the couple with the most tension between them?"

"Is that on or off the record, sir?" Raleigh asked, widening her eyes to express her concern. Mike would understand, after all he'd known her since they were four.

Mike chuckled. "You know we don't do anything off the record."

"Well, in that case," Raleigh said, "For the record, we are awarding the couple with the highest votes for best chemistry."

"Hmm," Mike said, "that can go all kinds of directions."

"Let's hope it all goes in a direction that doesn't involve another murder."

"Save me a dance once it gets started. I didn't sit in on all those dance lessons for nothing." Mike grinned, winking at her.

As the back door opened to release the contestants to the party, Mike squeezed her arm and returned to the sidelines where the press stood. As a courtesy, the Barbeaux Gazette covered the show each week, and since Raleigh worked the show that left Mike covering the local community piece the paper was known for, unlike the neighboring competitor.

To a standing ovation, the contestants strolled to the dance floor, and Raleigh motioned for them to take their places. Careful to stay out of Francois's camera frame, Raleigh managed to get the contestants into the two rows, even though they ignored her as they waved and called out to the audience. Obviously, Raleigh wasn't cut out to be a teacher when her charges pretended she didn't exist.

With a well-rehearsed Cajun call, Madison drew everyone's attention to the front where she introduced the fast-paced jig. After last night's disaster of a rehearsal, she and Madison had decided that a partner switch for some was in order, but the audience choice dance could potentially lead to strangling incidents, so Raleigh hoped a good night's sleep and an audience encouraged good behavior. Even she realized her naiveté sometimes.

Directing audience members out of the dancing shots, Raleigh stole quick glances at Max who conversed with his "date." His shoulders drooped slightly into that relaxed position, and he sipped from his bottled beer as if he weren't on the clock. But in typical Max fashion, his eyes scanned the area constantly, their eyes connecting several times with no indication of recognition. He and this Diane appeared to be having an animated conversation with her delicate features lit up with a smile.

Hard. He was tough. Stubborn and hard to reach emotionally. She squeezed her shoulders as the jig ended, preparing for the audience picks. Priorities. She could only handle one drama at a time.

Winter sauntered over to Raleigh, weaving unnoticeably through the crowd and the camera view. Raleigh waited as she slid in next to her as if she'd been standing there all along.

She leaned down, towering over Raleigh by at least six inches, and whispered, "Word is that Aryanna received a picture yesterday, which is why she's going around grilling everyone, causing a real ruckus."

"So if she received a photo, it wasn't Deon sending them."

Winter nodded. "I received one." Winter shrugged when Raleigh looked at her puzzled. "After the first ones came, I knew it was coming, especially with those pictures from Madison's parties floating around, so I didn't freak like these oversensitive people."

"Who does everyone suspect?"

Winter shook her head and smiled. "Each person suspects someone different, which is why this is going to be fun."

Raleigh couldn't help the eye roll, even though she'd attempted to stop after being annoyed so often by Madison's.

Fun? This waiting for a disaster wasn't fun.

"Are we ready for a great night?" Madison spoke dramatically into the microphone.

A cheer rose from the crowd with a round of polite clapping.

"It's time for your vote to become reality." Madison continued when it quieted. "Each of you cast a vote for your favorite couple when you collected your ticket. Your votes have been tallied, and it's now time for our audience favorite dance."

Madison nodded to the soundman and he began announcing couples. Frank was paired with Tiffany followed by Benjamin and Helena. Raleigh listened as each contestant was paired off until Aryanna and Joshua were paired. Joshua approached Aryanna, who glared at him with a contemptuous purse of her lips and a wrinkled forehead set in disdain.

Drawing in a deep breath, Raleigh prepared to intervene, but Aryanna allowed Joshua to take her into the waltz position. Deon and Joshua had argued briefly a few weeks ago, which had resulted in a shoving match between the two easily ended by the gentlemen teaching the contestants how to cast a fishing line. Raleigh wondered what that argument had been about and had it really ended that day as it had appeared on camera.

The waltz began, and the contestants began to sway around the dance floor. Clara moved off to the side, and then after glancing at Raleigh, she walked over. Terrible decision since it gave the camera an easy shot of her alone, showcasing her lack of pairing from the audience.

"I wish Deon was here," Clara said, frowning and tugging at her blue cotton dress.

"Were you two close friends?" Raleigh asked, noticing the animated conversation going on between Aryanna and Joshua. The woman's furrowed brow and forceful words spit at him as he clenched his jaw and looked around him continuously. At least their words weren't traveling further than the two of them, as far as Raleigh could tell from the other couples' lack of attention.

Clara shuffled her boot on the floor. "I've known him my entire life. He was good friends with my brother since grade school."

Raleigh remembered the video confession of her waiting for someone after the show finished filming. Had it been Deon? She didn't strike Raleigh as Deon's type, but maybe Clara liked that bad boy type. "Which guy are you going to choose for girl's pick? I'm sure there is someone you would like to be matched with."

"Does it really matter? I'm not really any of these guys' types. Don't really fit in with this group."

"Being different isn't necessarily bad."

Clara laughed a harsh sound. "I guess I at least don't have to worry about a picture showing up somewhere."

So Raleigh could add her to the "did not receive" list. Now she simply needed to discover who else. "Do you know who hasn't received a photo?"

Clara shrugged. "Maybe Heather, Edward, umm... Adam. I'm not sure about Lauren. I'm sure about some, but not everyone talks to me."

The waltz concluded with a hoop and holler from the audience, and Clara scooted back onto the dance floor for the guys' choice. When Madison announced the Cajun two-step as the guys' pick, Aryanna eased off the dance floor, blending into the table guests. Looking flustered, Aryanna leaned in and started whispering fiercely to a heavily made-up older woman.

The two-step went off without a hitch, well in terms of no unruly contestants dramatically stomping off the dance floor. Plenty missteps and toes were stepped on at some point, and an older gentleman in gray trousers stood up and announced loudly that they needed to watch how it was done. He grabbed his white-haired wife and swung her out onto the dance floor, and they seamlessly moved around the dance floor with such quick movements of their feet that Raleigh knew that she'd look like a clumsy toddler next to them. Madison motioned for the camera guy to get a shot of the couple, and Raleigh had to smile. Maybe Madison did remember that the people of Barbeaux Bayou were her audience and they didn't just want to see catfights and slugfests.

For the guys' pick number, Benjamin danced with Clara. Raleigh noticed he'd scanned the floor for Aryanna, but by the time he'd noticed she was gone, Clara was the only contestant without a partner. They were certainly an unlikely duo. Frank chose safe with Tiffany as well as Adam and Kimberly, who seemed to have become a couple in the last few weeks. Edward had surprisingly pulled Heather into his burly arms. As one of Winter's friends, he was not in the same solar system in terms of personality. His construction-built arms swallowed Heather's thin, bony frame, but Heather didn't appear awkward in his grip, as if she'd been there before. Maybe something was there Raleigh didn't know about.

The girls' pick number went much the same as the guys' pick to a point. Many of the contestants danced with the same partner. Aryanna floated back onto the floor and right into Benjamin's open arms. These two were like the prom king and queen of a high school dance. The blond, fit cheerleader and the handsome buff jock. All they were missing were the crowns and a personality that didn't bite.

Again, Clara was left without a partner, but after Madison's quick instruction, one of the hired dancers swooped in and had her two-stepping with the rest of the contestants.

Towards the end of the tune, other couples joined in and the older, gray-trousered gentleman two-stepped past the band and told them to play another. The fiddle player looked to Madison, who nodded her head and stuck up one finger, meaning one song before the announcement.

"So does that mean I can have this dance now?" Mike asked, stepping up behind Raleigh.

Raleigh felt his hand brush against the small of her back. "Only if you want me stepping on your feet."

"I can take it," Mike said, grabbing her hand and leading her onto the floor.

When they first stepped into the fray of dancers, Raleigh couldn't remove her eyes from her feet, trying to remember what to do with them. As a child, she remembered her uncles leading her around the dance floor, but back then she didn't care who witnessed her two left feet. After a couple of missteps and several bouts of laughter, she was able to look up at Mike and not just his canvas boat shoes.

"Not so bad after all," Mike said, with a half-grin that caused all the ladies to drool.

"Let me know how bruised your toes are in the morning and we'll see," Raleigh muttered, missing a step.

"Remember when your grandparents took us to the barn that one Sunday?"

Raleigh laughed. "Yes, we were what, nine? All the old ladies wanted to teach you how to dance. That's when you wore that cape everywhere, like Superman."

Mike shook his head. "They kept squeezing my cheeks. I thought my face was going to collapse, but I learned how to two-step."

"Oh," Raleigh said, visualizing the two of them running around the barn, "and remember you did the alligator on the floor with some of the other fools?"

Mike chuckled. "I'd forgotten that. If I recall it correctly, you were on the floor right behind me."

Raleigh laughed, hearing the slowing of the fiddle notes signaling the close of the song.

"I think that's what I need for a long-term relationship." Mike said, pulling away and looking down at her. "Someone to be a friend, you know?"

Raleigh's heartbeat quickened. "Where's that coming from?"

Mike shrugged, his lopsided grin reappearing. "I guess I've been feeling the pressure lately. My mom keeps on me about grandkids, and everyone wants to know why I'm still single. Makes you think, you know?"

Raleigh nodded. "We are past marrying age in this town, I suppose. Most people we graduated with are on spouse number two." Then she nudged him. "You can't replace me as the best friend though. I mean, I've known you since you didn't like the dark."

He chuckled again, but as she laughed along, she realized that one day she'd be replaced by a girlfriend, maybe even a wife. Sure, they'd always be friends, but a woman would want that intimacy to be with her. She'd be pushed aside, and the idea chilled her.

Madison's voice sounded over the speaker and the contestants began to move into their lines. Raleigh moved to the sidelines with Mike, out of the camera lens, and studied the contestants closely. Each week as the winners of the votes had been announced, the drama had grown. Considering Raleigh's feelings about tonight, she wanted to be ready to intervene at any sign, especially with all of her bosses in attendance. As Madison explained to the audience the voting process, Raleigh noticed Winter's disinterest, Tiffany's fidgeting, Frank's sweating, Aryanna's arrogant grin, and it went on. Each contestant offered something in the way of observation, but no one gave off a vibe of an upcoming tantrum.

The true winners of this week's couple vote had been Aryanna and Deon, but since Deon had become ineligible with his death, Aryanna was also not the winner. Tonight's couple had received the second highest votes, but Madison didn't mention this in her speech because this would draw attention to Deon's death. The executive decision had been made to include a two-minute memorial section of clips of him from previous tapings, but they were to refrain from mentioning him during live filming.

"The winners of this week's challenge and moving up in the ranks of Barbeaux Hearts is…" Madison paused for effect and the audience waited silently. "Joshua and Lauren."

As instructed by their servers, the audience members clapped as Joshua and Lauren stepped up to receive the crawfish statue that a local artist had molded for them as a favor, consequently putting the pottery business into a much sought-after position. The winners each week received these statues especially designed for the episodes, all fitting Madison's theme.

Expressions of surprise rose through the contestants as they looked around at each other. During filming Lauren and Joshua hadn't demonstrated any chemistry, and in fact their scenes together had been limited to slight interactions. Even now as Joshua walked toward Lauren, his face couldn't completely hide his own shock. Lauren glowed with the announcement, smiling big and waving and mouthing thanks to everyone. In front of the stage, she clutched Joshua's arm and kissed him brazenly on the cheek. Raleigh scanned the audience, wondering what had caused the viewers to say these two made a great couple.

Turning back to the contestants, Raleigh caught more than one of them rolling eyes or looking away from the couple at the front. Winter studied her nails, an expression of boredom clearly visible on her face. Aryanna's hands remained clenched at her sides even as everyone else clapped, albeit forced.

As Joshua and Lauren returned to the group to receive congratulations, Aryanna pushed her way to the front toward them. On instinct, Raleigh moved toward the group, ignoring the hissing coming from Francois as he waved wildly with his arm.

"You did this," Aryanna yelled. "You killed Deon because you wanted to beat him for once. You could never win otherwise with your pathetic way of following people around."

Adam stepped between Aryanna and Lauren. "Hold on there. No one killed Deon. You need to calm down Aryanna."

"Oh, get over yourself, Adam," Aryanna shouted again. "You didn't like

Deon either after he warned you to stay away from Clara, and you weren't man enough to stand up to him."

"A wild animal killed Deon," Joshua said, keeping his voice low as he looked around at all the eyes on them. "You are being dramatic as usual because you can't stand not being the center of attention."

Kimberly slipped next to Adam and reached for his hand. "Aryanna, you need to stop now, you are making a fool of yourself on camera."

Raleigh stepped in the middle of the fray. "We need to not handle this in front of the cameras. I want you to think about how you want yourself to be portrayed."

"Who cares?" Patrick said. "Since we are getting it all out in the open. Who's sending the pictures? That's what I want to know."

The voice decibel level compounded as everyone began speaking at once. Raleigh held her arms out to keep them apart as they began pressing in on each other, aggressively accusing one another of misdeeds. The cameras caught the entire deplorable scene.

"Please guys, let's keep this civil," she pleaded. "You have an audience."

The arguing continued with each accusing someone of sending or knowing who was sending the pictures. Recent date sabotage was also mentioned. Raleigh tried to signal out who said what, but too many voices speaking at once made that impossible. She thought it was Helena's voice that screeched about the sabotage though.

Madison appeared next to her as shoving began.

"Quiet!" Madison yelled. "This is not the place to hash out your arguments. We can do this tomorrow if you like. Right now people are watching."

"You didn't even mention Deon once this week," Aryanna cried. "Not once!"

"For Christ's sake, Aryanna," Joshua said frustration oozing from every syllable, "there will be a memorial at the end of the show. We discussed this in this week's planning meeting for the week. Leave it be."

Aryanna lunged forward. Raleigh grabbed her by the middle and was yanked forward by the momentum. A cry went through the group as Joshua moved sideways and Madison took the blow to the eye that Aryanna had directed at him.

Finally, Benjamin pulled Aryanna away from the dance floor by the arm. Madison clutched her eye with one hand and made a motion to the band with the other one, calling for them to start a tune. The fiddle strummed the opening notes immediately.

"Everyone smile and dance," Raleigh said, grabbing her sister by the arm. "Lauren and Joshua, make sure you two put on a good show for the cameras."

Raleigh led Madison off to the refreshment area where there would be ice and alcohol.

Reaching into the pirogue, Raleigh pulled out a bottled beer and held the bottle up to the redness and puffiness that was once Madison's perfectly made up eye. Madison clenched her teeth but kept silent as the cold did its work. An older, salt and pepper haired server brought Raleigh a plastic bag, and she filled it with ice from the pirogue. Madison switched with her, and Raleigh opened the beer before handing it back over. Taking a long swig from the bottle, Madison finally unclenched her jaw.

"I think they are trying to kill me or at least make me age ten years," Madison said, holding the ice to an already swelling eyelid.

"I think you are going to need something stronger than ice on this." Raleigh grimaced. "How did we find the craziest people of Barbeaux Bayou?"

"You should see the ones I turned down." Madison scowled. "At least I have the capital now for my business, but I'd prefer they don't ruin it with stunts like these."

"That's great," Raleigh said. She wondered who had invested in Madison's harebrained matchmaking party business idea, but she didn't want to ask when Madison was clearly in pain. Very temperamental, Madison was more prone to anger when she wasn't feeling well.

"I'm going to escape to the studio for a minute where I have something seriously stronger for this pain. Cover for me for the next five minutes, okay?"

Raleigh nodded, looking back towards the crowd. Many of the audience members had joined the contestants on the dance floor where an all-out party had commenced. Swiping her badge through the security pad, Madison went in through the metal door, and Raleigh wished she could go curl up in her own cubicle for a nap. These events exhausted her, especially when she had to referee. Hopefully, Madison realized that she would not be helping with her new business.

As she pulled herself out of her own thoughts, Max emerged from the crowd and sauntered her way.

"Hello," he said sheepishly. "I hope everything is all right with Madison."

"She'll recover. Madison always lands on her feet," Raleigh said, studying him for any sign to show her his intentions for this conversation.

"I think I owe you somewhat of an apology." He took a deep breath, his eyes meeting her forehead. "I don't think I'm wrong about there needing to be lines drawn for work, but I do think maybe I was too harsh and that we might need to figure these things out. Together."

Raleigh nodded. "We both have jobs to do, and we need to figure out how we can work around both our careers."

"I need you to promise not to keep information from me though," Max said, pleading with his voice and his eyes. "It's a trust issue for me, and I need to trust that you are being forthcoming with me."

She rubbed the scar on her wrist, considering what she needed to trust. To be trusted, maybe. "I'm sure you will be keeping things from me, so we may need to discuss some limitations where sources are concerned."

He nodded assent. "With us, I suppose it will be something we need to work on." He sighed, reaching out to her and pulling her close. "All I know is that when you were dancing with Mike, I realized that even with the obstacles, I don't want to not have you."

Raleigh felt his arms, not as comfortable as she'd like. Was it the tension and distance that had grown between them? Or something else? Something about his words nagged at her. Did he want her, or did he not want her with anyone else? Her ex-fiancée had taught her there was a difference. Maybe she was overthinking it, as she tended to do.

She allowed Max to lead her toward the dance floor. She spotted Mike chatting with a big bosomed brunette, vaguely familiar in that Raleigh had seen her around before at some point. Her stomach throbbed. Was this the same as Max? Did she not want to see Mike with anyone else, but not really want him herself?

Raleigh shook her thoughts loose. With tonight's event, she had more than enough to stress about. She could leave her own relationship questions until another day.

Chapter Ten

A low clatter rattling against wood tugged Raleigh from a deep sleep. Feeling disoriented, she sat up in bed, blew her hair out of her face, and tossed the quilt aside. She blinked against the blurriness of the darkness and the sleepiness tugging at her eyelids. At the same time, every night a noise downstairs would wake her up. She couldn't figure out what it was, but she also couldn't rest until she checked it out.

Glancing at the clock on the nightstand, the red lights glowed, revealing that it was an hour earlier than the usual 1 A.M. noise alarm. She should just go back to sleep. After the night's events, she needed more than an hour for her brain to function, unlike the blankness coming to it now. The old house, after all, creaked and moaned with the weather. But Raleigh had dealt with the dead long enough to know that the eerie feeling sitting on her flesh, causing the hair to rise didn't speak of normal.

Taking a step out of the side of the bed, a loud banging on the front door vibrated through the floorboards.

Now that certainly wasn't a figment of her imagination.

She hurried downstairs, the step creaking loudly as she stepped onto it with her bare foot. At the front door, she peered through the old French glass to see Madison standing on the other side and hugging her leather jacket tightly.

Unlocking the door, Raleigh let her in, her eyes drawn immediately to the purple swelling surrounding her eye. It looked worse than it had an hour ago when Raleigh had snuck out of the party after filming had wrapped. Staying for all night station parties weren't part of her contract, and Raleigh had been exhausted after her week of work.

Madison walked in as if the place was hers and plopped herself onto the sofa, huffing as she sat down.

"So Richard has decided that tomorrow you will do the on-camera interviews."

"What?" Raleigh asked alarmed. She didn't do on camera work, and she liked it that way.

"I don't like it either, but he doesn't want me on camera with the black eye." Madison rolled her eyes, which looked painful with the puffiness. She winced mid-roll. "The whole incident will be edited from the airing according to him, and he doesn't want it on camera."

"What about makeup?"

Madison shrugged. "It's an option when the swelling goes down."

"Can't we edit you in after? I'm sure there's some kind of fancy camera trick we can utilize."

"That's an idea," Madison said, standing again. "I'll work on that in the morning. Meanwhile, the group will do their commentary tomorrow as usual. You can do those as practice for the Q&A during the week. I'm going crash now because I promised Mason breakfast in the morning."

Raleigh walked her to the door and locked it behind her. Agonizing about having her image splashed across Barbeaux and the surrounding communities would have to wait until morning when she could hash it out over a Twix bar.

After crawling into bed again, she drifted to sleep within moments due to her exhaustion. A dream of treading dirty bayou water grew more detailed, but then a tapping sound jerked her from the panic of being unable to keep her head above the water.

She sat up, clutching the pillow tightly. Glancing at the clock, the 1 A.M. revealed that she'd been sleeping longer than only the five minutes it had felt like. She could bury her face in the pillow and attempt to return to sleep for the third time tonight, but her mind already raced over the possibilities of what the noise could be. Maybe if she could figure it out, she could put an end to it, even if it involved boarding something up or changing something out. She'd do anything at this point, even go out and buy a hammer because she was pretty sure she didn't own one of those.

Once again, she slipped out of bed and eased down the stairs. With the front porch luminary leaking through the front glass, shadows and light licked at the walls, creating an eerie glow through the hallway. The tapping sounded against a hard surface. From her living room.

Raleigh stopped mid-step on the second to last riser and listened, her heartbeat pounding in her ears. Clearly, she hadn't imagined it or dreamed it.

"Madison?" Raleigh hissed.

Had her sister used the hide-a-key again? Maybe Madison had gone home and realized she'd lost her own key. It wouldn't be the first time.

No answer returned from the living room.

And then the tapping sound again. Almost as if someone was placing something down on the furniture.

Carefully, Raleigh tiptoed to the wooden plank flooring and then slowly toward the living room, avoiding the play of reflected light. Easing into the doorway, Raleigh glanced in, her body ready to take flight at any moment.

Aunt Clarice's image sat in the aqua chair, flipping through a fashion magazine Raleigh had picked up on a whim the other day when she'd been standing in line and had recalled how her favorite aunt had always had them in stacks around the house. This house. A tall glass filled with ice and amber liquid rested on the coffee table.

The cross-legged, cloth curled pinned up hair woman before her was the one of Raleigh's childhood, circa ten years or so before her death. Of course, Raleigh only recalled this version from old family photographs. And that was the only place Raleigh should be seeing Aunt Clarice— snapshots.

Raleigh squeezed her eyes shut tightly and counted to ten, breathing evenly through her lips to slow the panic edging in. Rubbing the scar on her wrist once, she opened her eyes and the larger than life woman had disappeared.

The magazine rested on top of the stack near the sofa, the amber liquid glass had disappeared from the coffee table, but the elephant figurine sat on the table once again. If it weren't for that elephant, Raleigh would believe the whole incident was a dream, that she was still in bed and none of this had really happened.

The house creaked as the wind knocked at its windows, and her heartbeat counted out each second that she stood in the doorway, her body aching with exhaustion. Finally, she admitted that she would have to walk back upstairs to her bed; she was indeed awake. She couldn't will herself under her warm comforter.

Aunt Clarice had come home.

In the morning, she'd bombard Halona with questions to figure out what the heck had happened to give her a houseguest. Or was she the houseguest now? As traiteur to the dead, she didn't have visits from ghosts. She only connected to the dying, and that's how she liked it. "Liked" being the operative word because what she really liked was the predictability of her particular talents. Change equaled worry.

Returning to sleep proved difficult. Her body yearned for relief from her exhausting schedule, but her mind would not quiet for deep sleep to overtake her. After a long, sleepless night, she slammed her alarm against the nightstand and hurried through her morning routine. Interviews began at nine this morning, so that gave her a few minutes to stop off at Halona's house before going in and preparing the questions for today's confessionals.

She found Halona hanging sheets up to dry on an old clothesline behind a dilapidated wash shed. With pillowcases draped over her shoulder, she moved quickly among the lines with a cotton bag of clothespins draped over her strong, hefty arm.

Raleigh picked up the full laundry basket Halona had left at the edge of the shed and walked toward the colorfully adorned woman. This morning her calf-length gown bore the pattern of a peacock, with her signature gray braid hung down to her waist.

"Do you ever take a break?" Raleigh asked, shivering against the chilly wind. The warm morning sun had not touched the frosty air of February weather.

"Breaks are for the old." Halona chuckled, pulling a sheet from the basket and flapping it out in the air. "I'm guessing this morning's visit isn't to help me with the laundry?"

"Last night my Aunt Clarice appeared in my living room."

"And I'm guessing this is the same Aunt Clarice whose house you now live in."

Raleigh nodded as Halona whipped out another sheet. "She wasn't even the age that she died. Those curls and that dress were from when I was a child. I remember it distinctly because she wore it to my sixth birthday party; I have a picture somewhere in an album at my parents' house."

"Did she have a message for you?"

"Message?" Raleigh stared at her, confused. "She didn't even speak to me. She was drinking her club soda and gin on ice and looking through the fashion magazine I bought last week."

Halona sighed as she flipped the pins across the white, threadbare sheet. "Then she's probably settling in."

"Oh no, she can't, can she?" Raleigh gaped at her, her brain racing through the possibility of having a permanent ghost around, waking her up in the middle of the night and who knows what else. Aunt Clarice had been on the wild side in her day. Her living days that was. Her dead self seemed tame just sitting in her living room flipping through a magazine.

"Friend, your talents will grow. Surly a long passed relative whom you were close to can sense that and make use of it."

"Isn't it crazy enough that I connect to the dying to see their last moments? Do I need to see them after they are dead as well? I mean, aren't they supposed to move on to some spiritual place like Heaven or whatever hip place the soul is going to these days? I'm finally adjusting to being the receiver for the dying; I'm not ready for any growth yet. I still eat candy for breakfast, for goodness sakes! Does that sound like someone who is willing to grow?"

Raleigh felt her face burning as the anxiety gripped her. It had clenched and unwound in her stomach all night. Would ghosts come popping out of the woodwork now? Would that become her normal? She didn't expect ordinary, but she did have limits of comfortability. And this was definitely a breach.

Halona chuckled and her chest jiggled with the deep laugh. "You will need to get over that fear if you expect to grow at all. The dead won't hurt you. They may drop in unannounced, but they are usually confused and looking for a little guidance. Your fear will cause you to block them and miss the answers you seek."

"Aunt Clarice is going to have to answer for waking me up every night," Raleigh grumbled. She inhaled deeply and allowed the release to take some of the worry with it. "How do I communicate with a ghost?"

Halona shrugged. "Beats me. I can't even communicate with my own husband to clean his feet before he comes in the house, and he's very much alive." She laughed again. "Maybe try talking to her, but remember if you feel fear, your brain will immediately deny that it is happening. Some kind of defense mechanism. It's why children see ghosts more than adults. My grandson tells me ghost stories all the time, and he jumps off of bridges and climbs to the roof. The little daredevil is quite the handful."

Dismissing her fear would take work. She'd adapted to the connections, but it didn't mean that fear didn't prick at her flesh each time the blackness came and transported her into someone seconds from life ending. The unknown frightened her. A simple passing felt natural, but to cross into someone where violence awaited to share their experience terrified her.

After the sheets were hung, Raleigh thanked Halona and hurried off, wondering if she'd opened herself up to this with their control exercises. Maybe she could ask Aunt Clarice to leave. Didn't ghosts go somewhere after death? This mysterious light people talked about. She didn't want to be rude, but suddenly, the old house felt small with the addition of a roommate.

Chapter Eleven

The confessional room was really Studio 3 of the television studio, a mostly unused smaller studio. Madison had set up a camera facing a staged green screen where each contestant had a scheduled time to sit on a stool and reflect on the week's events. The concept behind these were to allow the audience to get to know the contestants better to increase votes, but most weeks the video had to be seriously edited due to ramblings. To keep them on target, scripted questions greeted them at the door. Raleigh had prepared these under pressure thirty minutes before Benjamin had strolled in with a latte in his hand from the new Hot Joe's coffee shop, which had opened in the old full-service gas station near the bridge.

He'd popped into the studio with only a curt nod in Raleigh's fretting direction and had exited without a word just as Adam slipped into the front doors. Sitting in Ms. Marjorie's comfy chair, Raleigh waited to buzz them in, noticing the condition they trampled in after last night's heavy partying.

While Adam was behind the closed door, Winter and Edward strolled in together. Winter's eyes were hidden behind movie star sunglasses, but her slicked back hair and makeup looked flawless as usual. Edward's sleeves covered most of his tattoos as he'd taken to doing during the taping, Madison wanted him to show his body art to add to his bad boy image, but the request seemed to make him more self-conscious. His goatee still hinted at the type, so the audience responded anyway.

"We really should push these back to long after the chickens have roosted,"

Winter said, covering her mouth in a pretend yawn. "Beauty sleep is good for the cameras, too."

As if. Raleigh restrained herself from groaning. Winter didn't need help in that department.

"Did the party go into the wee hours of the morning?" Raleigh asked as she fiddled with the clipboard that she marked off the contestants as they finished up. Madison wanted every box checked off just so. Her sister was only organized when it came to parties.

"Hmmm," Winter said, grinning. "Some juicy gossip was spilled as the beer flowed. You know I had to stick around to hear."

"Oh, really?" Raleigh asked, trying not to give away any enthusiasm. Rumors around this bunch usually ended in on-camera drama like last night. She couldn't seem to stay ahead of it.

"The juiciest bit seems to be that Aryanna has been keeping a little secret from everyone, and that's why she reacted the way she did last night."

Edward grunted before swigging a large gulp from his chrome thermos. Raleigh took him for someone who either drank his coffee straight up or spiked. She tried not to judge though.

"What secret is that?"

"Well," Winter said, licking her lips, her eyes lighting with the gossip. "It's not just her secret though. Apparently, she and Ryan were MARRIED right after high school. It lasted all of about thirty days before her parents had it annulled."

"So why did she go all crazy on Josh?"

Madison needed to seriously rethink her background check procedures. Even with a miniscule budget, living in a small town had to be good for something besides having to drive so far for a department store.

"Poor guy," Edward said, shaking his head before swallowing another round.

Winter leaned over the counter, smiling. "Josh served as the best man in the wedding and had one of the only pictures from the ceremony, which mysteriously got delivered in one of those manila envelopes."

"So does everyone believe he's behind the pictures now?"

Edward shook his head. "Nah, he swears that picture has been long lost since he's moved. Not to mention, my picture was of a situation… one I don't want to mention to protect myself from police involvement so to speak… and he would have known nothing about that. Winter here is the only person with that knowledge."

"And I have my own situations that I don't want mentioned, so Edward's secrets are safe with me." Winter studied him, her eyes searching. Raleigh wasn't sure if her look held absolute belief that Edward trusted her, but it did reveal her wanting him to.

Raleigh tapped on the clipboard, thinking of all the contestants. They didn't have much in common. Even age-wise they ranged from 18 to 29. Living in Barbeaux meant that their families probably knew at least one person in the other contestant's family, but it was possible for them to have come on the show without knowing much about each other. But maybe that's what Madison had counted on. Living in a small town, some of these contestants had to have some connection.

"So the question is how is the person getting the pictures has a connection to everyone?"

Adam strolled out the double doors. "What about the pictures? I'd like to know what's going on with that."

"Did you receive one?" Winter asked.

Adam shook his head. "But plenty of my friends have. It freaked Patrick out completely, and I thought the guy was going to lose it. I have to say I really did think it was Deon. The guy was such a jerk most of the time."

Edward bowed out at this time and disappeared through the double doors for his confessional.

Raleigh nodded. "Frank thought so, too."

"It's just that the guy acted like we were still in high school," Adam said, shrugging. "So what if Patrick wasn't cool back then? Dude, we've grown up since high school, you know? And then that creepy warning he gave everyone to keep away from Clara? I seriously thought he was the one."

"What warning about Clara?" Raleigh asked.

Winter perked up from her plastered counter position.

"If any of us showed any interest in getting to know Clara, he'd catch us on the side and tell us that he'd hunt us down if we touched her. Are we living in the civil war era, dude? But then he never showed any interest in her, so it was weird, you know."

Winter and Raleigh exchanged glances. Apparently, the girls hadn't heard anything about this either.

"What did Aryanna think of his little obsession?" Winter asked, chuckling. "I bet that jealous cat didn't like it."

Joshua and Ryan strolled up the front doors, and Raleigh buzzed them in, considering Winter's question.

Adam shook hands with the two as she and Winter watched. From the glazing over of her hazel eyes, Winter was getting bored. Living a fast life meant that the mundane wasn't palatable.

"So what about today's confessionals?" Ryan grinned, his one dimple showing. "Do we tell the truth, no holds barred?"

Joshua laughed. "If we all did that, we wouldn't have to worry about these pictures showing up."

"We were just talking about that," Adam said.

Winter stepped closer to the three men, immediately gaining their attention with her long legs and midriff-baring top. "So who do y'all fellas think is the guilty culprit?"

"I think it's Aryanna," Joshua said, his brown eyes sheepishly looking away from Winter.

"Josh," Ryan said, his tone indicating a warning.

"Sorry, bro," Josh said, shrugging, "but she had that photo too, and she's been acting strange. Sneaking around spying on people."

"Like who?" Raleigh asked from her spot as she stared at the clipboard, making notations on the side of each contestant.

"I know she scared the devil out of Clara a few days ago after she showed up at her house the night Deon died. The only reason Clara knew she was there was because the dogs barked. That girl's dad has like twenty hunting beagles. Stinky animals."

"Now that you mention it," Winter said, tilting her head, "she came into the bar where I work last week, and she was acting weird. She was alone and she didn't even order a drink."

Ryan held up his hand. "Hold up, I know Aryanna, and the fact is, if she had pictures, she'd have been more dramatic about the revealing. She wouldn't have kept them secret."

Edward flung the double doors open and looked around at the crowd. Winter grimaced and nodded her exit to the back.

"So you aren't denying that she could have the pictures?" Josh challenged him.

Ryan laughed. "I guess I'm not. She does like attention."

Edward leaned against the counter and picked up his thermos from where he'd left it. "Aryanna did corner Frank when we did the pirogue week. She showed up at his grandmother's house and made him real uncomfortable."

Raleigh jotted down a question mark next to Aryanna's name. All of these testimonies certainly made her look suspect. At least for the pictures. Raleigh had to hope that Deon's death was only an animal attack and not connected to any human.

Speaking of Aryanna, though, her interview time had come and gone. Typically, she and Benjamin or she and Deon would arrive together. Raleigh had watched ten weeks of interviews to know the order by now. Madison would be furious if Aryanna skipped after last night's outburst. With editing it out of tonight's program, the show couldn't not show her completely, especially since Madison had chosen her early on as the show's sweetheart. Of course, that decision was also up to the viewers, but creative editing had worked in Madison's favor so far.

In the back of Raleigh's skull, a familiar throbbing began. As if there was a door back there and someone was knocking, waiting to be let inside. Glancing up at the clock above the entrance doors, she knew Mike would not have shown up to put in last night's story as he had a roof repair to help Nate with early this morning.

Raleigh gripped the edges of the counter, wondering if she should ease off the chair or risk staying put. Black spots began to burst in front of Raleigh's eyes and her head weighed her neck down as if something had become strapped to it.

Fighting it only made the physical symptoms worse, so Raleigh closed her eyes and felt the rush as she tunneled toward whoever beckoned, as if propelled forward on a roller coaster.

Her eyes looked up into the sun and blinked against the harsh light burning her eyes after the darkness. Raleigh immediately took stock of her body lying on the ground, unable to move. Pain gripped her legs, her abdomen, and her arms. Fighting the nausea, she forced her neck to bend so she could look to the side and was greeted by pooling blood near her nose. The iron odor filled her nostrils and Raleigh or whoever's body she was inside closed her eyes to the sight.

Moments passed before Raleigh forced her eyes to open again, ignoring the blood, she searched for a landmark and found the distinct carving of an F on the back of a rocking chair.

She felt the faintness of the heartbeat—the one she shared for a moment— as it slowed. The woman's last recollection before blackness took Raleigh away was she'd heard a yell before the attack. Why hadn't the person gone to get help?

Raleigh felt the familiar pop as she snapped back into her own body, and then a sharp pain stabbed through her backside. She looked up from her position on the floor as Edward's concerned face hovered over hers. She shook her head, feeling as though she needed to disengage the last remaining remnants of the dying from her own conscious. She'd need a shower to dislodge the memories of the body as her own.

"Are you all right?" Edward asked.

"Umm," Raleigh said, feeling the bruise forming already on her hip. She must have tipped over sideways. She should have foreseen that one. "I think so."

Winter's head appeared from over the counter. "You had one of those freaky episodes, didn't you?"

Raleigh had connected to Winter's best friend Summer only months ago when she died, and Winter had only just grown warm to Raleigh. Her talent didn't always go over well when emotions ran high. Murder tended to do that.

Raleigh gritted her teeth together. "I need to make a call. Winter can you handle things up here while I get Max on the phone?"

Winter nodded but didn't ask any more questions, which wasn't typical of Winter. But even Winter had her limits sometimes when it came to gossip, it seemed. Edward helped her up, but he remained quiet as well, which was fine since Raleigh didn't want to answer any questions. With a body in the back of this building, she didn't need anyone creating any trouble.

Chapter Twelve

Max's temple scrunched tight in concentration as he looked around the empty *fais do-do* grounds. Aside from the missing band equipment, everything looked exactly as it had last night, the plan being to clean up today with the help of the building's Sunday custodial staff. As the last event outside in this area, Madison could tear down the entire staging and allow the grass to grow back up to its normal six feet high since the lawn service only showed up occasionally.

"Make sure no one comes through that door," Max said for the sixth time. Raleigh stood with arms crossed, standing in front the door where he'd instructed her to remain as he slowly made his way to the visibly crumpled form in the distance.

"Shouldn't you go see who she is first?" Raleigh asked.

From her position by the door, Raleigh could see a crumpled body in white and navy blue tattered clothing. A hint of blonde was visible but it was a shade of deep amber and swallowed by the shadows of a twisted body. Max's painstakingly slow progression to the body had Raleigh's feet arching forward to get a better view. If not for his reminders, she would have walked toward the area by this point. Raleigh could feel her in that empty pocket in her brain that the dead filled when they visited. When the body would be "found," the space would feel hollow again. Raleigh didn't know the science behind it all, but she did know what she felt like.

Max studied something a moment longer near a rocking chair Raleigh couldn't see from her position. "Nearly there."

Sirens shrilled through the morning air and birds scattered from the treetops, flying haphazardly before heading south. The Barbeaux Bayou police announced their arrival, and as usual Raleigh recognized the siren call.

"There's a dead chicken over here," Max yelled out, stopping a few feet from the body.

"Really?" Raleigh asked. "We've been doing a story on mysteriously slaughtered chickens at different farms around Barbeaux."

"Hmm," Max uttered stepping closer to the body. The blaring sounds pulled up to the side of the building just as they had only a week ago.

Two officers got out of the vehicle and sauntered over to Max. Max gave them orders that Raleigh couldn't hear, but the officers walked back to the squad car and busied themselves with marking off the crime scene with the all too familiar yellow tape. Another squad car pulled in followed by a navy blue truck marked Sheriff in fat white letters, which parked beside the squad cars. Raleigh groaned. After the incident in high school, dealing with the sheriff reminded both of them of their strong dislike for each other.

Getting out of his truck, Sheriff Breaux's portly belly folded over his pants, but his white button-down western shirt kept it all tucked in.

"Get that tape up now, Rogers," Sheriff Breaux rumbled, chewing on his usual Wrigley spearmint gum. "Rope off the back wall of this here building so no one comes out dat door. And would someone get Ms. Cheramie out of my crime scene."

Max glanced up at her from his study of the body, but he didn't speak in her defense. He glanced back down at the body instead, continuing to gather his evidence. Anger lit through her like a firecracker. She deserved to at least know who she'd shared the last moment of life with earlier. She had suspicions, but the fuzziness filling her head needed a name to leave.

The metal door smacked her hard in her back and threw her forward. She recovered her balance before she hit the ground and turned to see Antonio rushing over the threshold with one of those camera interns she could never remember the name of following on his heels. Antonio hurried over to Max, ignoring the shouts of the officers to stop. Working for the *Bayou Blend*, the only news programing for the station, Antonio's new-to-the-job enthusiasm worked hard to achieve his dream of moving to a bigger station quickly.

Antonio managed to make it to Max, although he had to swerve to the left to avoid the burly, bulbous-nosed officer tunneling at him from the right. Skidding to a stop feet from Max and the body, Antonio immediately stuck the microphone in his face and motioned for the camera guy to position the camera.

"I'm standing here with Detective Maxwell Pyles for the Barbeaux Bayou Police Department at the scene of where another body has been discovered. Detective Pyles, is it true that this is another vicious animal attack?"

"Uhh, as far as we can tell at this time," Max said, looking beyond the camera where the officers had frozen, unsure what they should do.

"So, the rumors are true that the rougarou is considered a suspect in these deaths?"

Raleigh groaned. Antonio would never be taken serious with this kind of story. The question had to be chalked up to youth and inexperience.

Max's forehead tightened and his shoulders pulled up. "The rougarou is simply a myth. These attacks are by a dangerous animal with the possibility of a human companion. Now if you'll excuse me, we have a crime scene to work."

"But don't you think you owe the people of Barbeaux a little more information on the type of animal that is running loose, killing people at the rate of one per week?"

Max stared at him. Raleigh waited, holding her breath. How would he respond to this question?

"Mr. Antonio Waters," Sheriff Breaux barked from his view from the sidelines. "If you don't leave my crime scene immediately, I am going to have you arrested for interfering with an investigation."

Mike came out the doors, quickly scanning the scene, and Raleigh wanted to hug him. She'd wanted to feel the warmth of another body against hers since connecting to the cold insides of the young woman resting 150 feet away, but Max had been complete business as soon as he'd arrived. She understood keeping it professional, but she needed a moment. A moment to ease the chill inside of her.

"Sheriff Breaux, what would you like to tell the residents of Barbeaux about protecting themselves from this creature?" Antonio asked, turning to face him.

Mike reached out and rubbed her shoulder. The warmth of his hand spread through her, easing some of the tenseness.

"Stay away from the suspects and you'll be okay," Sheriff Breaux said, smiling. "Now I've had quite enough of you today. Since your video…"

Mike hurried toward the group, his long, lean legs making quick strides. Everyone turned to look at him. "Antonio, you have enough footage for now. I'm certain the sheriff here will call a press conference to release relevant information as it becomes available."

"But I…" Antonio began.

"Inside," Mike said, adding force to his directive. Antonio nodded and followed him back toward where Raleigh had slowly crept closer to the fray.

Their group entered the building, Raleigh glancing one last time where Max was crouched down by the body, not giving her a second glance.

Inside, Antonio squared up against Mike, his chest puffing up. "Why did you do that? I had everything under control?"

"Because he was about to confiscate your video as evidence since you were in an active crime scene. It's just one of the things Sheriff Breaux does when you annoy him. Something you need to learn if you expect to keep your stories."

"Oh," Antonio muttered.

"Who was it?" Raleigh asked, her voice choking.

"That blonde. The one with the nice rack," Antonio said. Swallowing his ego was taking some work. His face held a sour expression.

"Aryanna," the camera guy said, glaring at Antonio with a steely look of disgust. "The one who always brought us lowly camera guys muffins."

The blood rushed through Raleigh's head, and she felt the wispy hint of a dying heartbeat in that hollow part. Her thoughts were alone once again; the dead trusting she'd figure out what had happened. She'd been so sure that Aryanna had been manipulating the contestants with the photos only moments ago that she felt guilty for thinking ill of the dead. Feeling drained from the connection, the guilt swirled and created a deep sadness. The contestants were dying, and all she had was gossip and pictures, her ability proving itself useless.

Mike put his arm around her and pulled her into the crook of his chest. "How about we go visit Paw for a bit? I think the fresh air might do us some good until we can do something useful around here."

Raleigh nodded, unable to speak. He always knew what she needed.

Chapter Thirteen

The rows of Paw's garden reached as far back as the eye could see. Raleigh held her hand over her eyes and squinted into the sun to glimpse what aisle her Paw worked today. Towards the back left quadrant, her Paw walked between the gray rows, tossing shucked peanut shells as he hobbled. Raleigh kicked off her shoes at the edge of the garden and stepped onto the February coolness of the dirt.

Walking barefoot through the garden had been her tradition since she was a child. She liked the feel of the dirt between her toes; the harsh lumps and the smooth water-beaten surfaces all mingled side by side so that each step created a different experience for the padding of her feet. Paw would tease her about this affinity she had to experience the garden with her toes, but he bragged to others that she was going to be a gardener one day. Raleigh didn't see how one had anything to do with the other.

Paw turned to see her approach and handed her a handful of peanuts. These would have been grown in his garden, dried on the back porch, and roasted in the oven. Me'Maw would have then stored them in bags and pouches and anything handy for Paw to grab and stuff his pockets with every day. The dry roughness of the peanuts in her palm offered familiarity and comfort.

"You and Mike off for the afternoon?"

Raleigh shook her head. "Another body turned up at the station, and I needed to clear my head a bit."

"Oh," Paw said, glancing her way before he began meandering down the aisles again, his right leg giving out just a little each time he stepped down so that it created a distinct swagger. Several years ago a tractor had fallen on his leg when he was working on it, and he said each year he felt the pain in his joints one step at a time.

Raleigh walked at his side on the row next to him. The rows had been recently tilled and must be awaiting new plantings.

"Another animal attack, I suppose?"

"It looked that way," Raleigh said, thinking of the footage that Antonio had managed. Even with Max blocking most of Aryanna's body, bite marks with rips and gashes could be seen up the arm that had been L-shaped on the ground. "When I connected with her though, it was long after an attack. She must have taken awhile to…"

Raleigh trailed off. The connection had come long after the attack. She hadn't died right away. In fact, she'd probably bled out like Deon, but hours had gone by with no help. Perhaps if it had been during, Raleigh could have saved her.

"Listen Raleigh Lynn, you can only do what God intends you to do. She wasn't meant to be saved." Paw looked at her and motioned to her peanuts, as if the magical salty goodness would make it all better.

On command, Raleigh cracked one open between her knuckles and popped it in her mouth, licking her fingers to get the full taste of the flavoring. Paw was liberal with the salting of the shells, and the flavor slid across her tongue, warming her, reminding of her childhood days of picking the nuts from the plants and stuffing them in these canvas bags to carry back to the back porch on her red wagon.

"What if I can't save them because it's some kind of animal?" Raleigh wondered aloud, walking in the direction of her grandparent's white Acadian farmhouse, a step behind her Paw's pace.

"Hmm." Paw uttered and then became quiet. Raleigh let him be, understanding he was thinking.

She didn't need to worry about something being off with the connections anymore at least, but after being inside the body of a dead person, her head felt wonky. Not quite like herself or grounded in her own shoes, so to speak.

Of course, she'd left her shoes at the edge of the rows, so it was more like she hadn't floated all the way back into the edge of her toes.

"Still no evidence of what kind of animal?" Paw asked quietly, tossing a peanut shell to the side.

"No," Raleigh said, squeezing the rough shells in her palm. "Max isn't giving too much away, if he even knows yet. Of course, the news station is now getting into the rougarou story."

"No such thing," Paw said, tossing his head side to side in disgust. "If this animal is being used to murder people, it's a human monster doing the using."

"Doesn't that make it worse though?" Raleigh said, crunching another shell between her knuckles as a way to ease some of her frustration.

Paw hobbled over a chunk of aisle that had fallen over. "Sure does, Raleigh Lynn. Sure does."

Mike stood between the rows and Me'Maw's back porch, waiting for them to return to the front. He'd been making a few calls when they'd pulled up, even though Raleigh was certain he'd used it as a clever ruse to give her time alone with Paw. Since she was young, Paw had been the strong force that had calmed her after connecting to death. Although Me'Maw was gentle, understanding, and warm, Paw's voice returned the strength to her and made her feel steady in her own skin again.

"Jeff called," Mike began, his lips twitching in agitation. "Sheri had to go in for questioning again at the station today."

"Why?" Raleigh asked. "They can't possibly think she has a connection to Aryanna, too. I don't think the two of them ever spoke to each other before."

"Apparently the last call that Aryanna made was to Sheri's cell phone. They found her cell phone near her body."

"Sounds like you got a witch hunt going on," Paw said, resting on his good left leg. "That girl would never hurt nobody."

Raleigh nodded. "Besides, it's an animal attack. What do they think she did? Borrow a dog to attack Deon and Aryanna? She doesn't have any pets."

Mike shook his head. "Sheri is terrified of dogs. Remember in junior high when the police dogs came? She had a panic attack and had to sit in the counselor's office the rest of the day."

"She has a scar from a dog bite on her eyebrow where she was attacked when she was really young. It barely shows anymore." Raleigh said, recalling Sheri's sitting on a bench outside the cafeteria at school, pointing to the scar, and telling her about how her dad had shot the dog to get it off of her. That was so long ago. Probably third grade.

"I wonder why Aryanna called Sheri though?" Mike asked, his eyes glazing over as his thoughts drifted.

"Maybe something to do with Deon?" Raleigh suggested. Deon's girlfriends typically avoided Sheri. After hearing stories about how horrible she was from Deon, many of the younger women felt intimidated by the boisterous, overprotective mother.

The back screen door slammed shut, drawing everyone's attention to the porch. Madison came out, noticed them, and walked in their direction.

"I'm wanted at the station." Madison muttered. "I thought I was going to have the morning off, but people on this show keep dropping like flies."

"They called you in?" Raleigh ignored the last part, even though Paw frowned deeply at the comment.

"Your detective needs me to walk him through the crime scene and tell him what has been disturbed since I was the last one to leave last night."

Madison didn't lower the overly large sunglasses on her face. With the sunglasses and a little more makeup to her nose, one couldn't tell that her eye was red and swollen. Too bad this week they were filming in an inside studio, and the glasses would be a noticeable distraction.

"When did Aryanna leave last night?" Mike asked.

"Early." Madison said. "The camera guys wanted to reshoot some of the dancing, but she was gone by 10:30."

"So I wonder why she came back then?" Raleigh asked.

"I will let you people handle that," Madison said, waving her hand in the air. "I'm going to go in and deal with these idiots, and then edit the footage, I suppose. My work is never done."

Raleigh's eyes strained as she forced herself not to roll them. Madison worked hard, when she wanted to. And that wasn't all the time, for certain.

Madison walked away, and Paw limped toward the porch at the same time.

It was time for his morning rest and then lunch with Me'Maw. Her grandparents had very predictable routines. After sixty years of marriage, they knew what they liked.

"Something else, Ree," Mike said.

When Mike called her by his nickname for her, she knew it was something that she wasn't going to want to hear. She steadied herself and looked up at him, waiting.

"Max has brought Sheri in for questioning three times this week. He's also been speaking to people involved in her custody battle with Deon."

"What?" Raleigh asked, heat rising in her ears. "Why didn't she say anything?"

"I don't think she wanted to worry us." Mike said, running his hand through his hair. A sure sign of his frustration. "Jeff says she's not handling it very well."

Raleigh should have checked in on her after that argument had been discovered, but she'd been so busy with the show and trying to find the chicken killer. Feeling like a horrible friend, she imagined how difficult this would have been for Shawn if he knew his mother was being questioned.

Max had done this though. He knew Sheri could not have killed Deon, and he'd pursued this like a vulture. It was an animal, for goodness sake! Yet, he kept digging in further. Was that why he'd kept his distance? So he wouldn't have to tell her?

Raleigh felt the fury building in her center.

Chapter Fourteen

"Are my eyes black?" Sheri asked, her voice quivering. "I think my makeup has completely smeared by this point."

Raleigh looked it over and squeezed her friend's hand. "It's good. You've almost completely rubbed your eye makeup away, so no smears."

Typically, Sheri had elaborate eye shadow and eyeliner drawn perfectly, but for Deon's funeral she'd decided on a more somber appearance. Waterproof mascara had probably slipped her mind with everything going on.

Sheri's shoulders shook. "I don't know why I'm so upset."

Raleigh glanced over at Shawn surrounded by Deon's family pulling him close into an awkward shoulder hug. It didn't relieve the deep frown on his face. Shawn's sadness had cut Sheri to the core, and the damaging rumors had left Shawn confused and angry. He'd lashed out at his mother and been driven into the arms of Deon's family. Sheri had been falling apart this week, and Raleigh felt awful that she'd neglected her friend.

"Shawn lost his father," Raleigh said. "You two will figure this out. He loves you."

"I know." Sheri glanced in his direction and another tear traveled down her cheek. "I hate that he's run to Deon's family after the hell they put me through. Does that make me a horrible person?"

Sheri looked to her, pleading with her for reassurance. "You are a fantastic person and a wonderful mother. This is just another obstacle to overcome."

Avoiding the open casket before her, Raleigh thought about how Deon had been a horrible person in life, spending much of his life on drugs, stealing from friends, picking a few bar room fights over a quick temper, and enabling parents who'd get him into a treatment program to avoid jail time. But after *Barbeaux Hearts*, the town would only remember him as the charming version he'd projected on screen, and Madison had memorialized him with last night's two-minute dedication. All of this proved that life wasn't fair in the least.

Sheri sighed, her chest heaving forward. "I'm so tired of all the obstacles."

Frank's eyes met Raleigh's for a moment before sliding to Sheri's hunched over frame. Frank and some of the contestants had gathered in a corner near the back chairs. Benjamin, Ryan, Helena, and Lauren's appearance didn't create any surprises, but Frank, Tiffany, and Patrick weren't Deon fans. Of course, southern manners could have intervened in their case.

And those good breeding manners continued as Frank walked their way. Raleigh squeezed Sheri's hand to let her know of his approach. Sheri pulled herself together, bracing her spine for the encounter. Each condolence drained her energy, and Raleigh didn't know if her friend would last the entire day.

"I'm so sorry for your loss," Frank said, forcing eye contact but then glancing away to look back at the others who'd hung back.

Sheri nodded. "Thank you."

"I didn't really know Deon that well," Frank said, fidgeting with the bottom of his untucked shirt. "He seemed... umm... nice."

"He was an asshole," Sheri muttered. She closed her eyes, and Raleigh squeezed her hand hard.

"Sheri is just emotional right now." Raleigh smiled, hoping no one else had overheard. No one appeared to be looking at them. Sheri didn't need to add anything to the rumors at this point.

"Well, I quite agree," Frank said with a grin. "So I'm happy you said it first."

Sheri looked up and a short laugh escaped her lips. She hid her mouth with her hand quickly. When she'd recovered, she said, "Thank you."

"I wanted to thank you, Ms. Raleigh, for your advice," Frank said. Raleigh cringed at the Misses. It always made her feel like her mother. "My grandmother said she'd known for awhile when I told her."

"What about your grandfather?"

He shook his head. "Not yet, but I'm working up to it. I guess our blackmailer will have one less victim now."

"Too bad the other pictures can't all be dealt with so easily," Raleigh replied.

Sheri looked at Frank. "What blackmailer? What pictures?"

"Oh, just someone trying to threaten the contestants with compromising photos. You know, the usual stuff." Raleigh shrugged.

"I love you, my friend," Sheri said with a smile, "but you attract trouble like feral cats on trash night."

The doors opened and Madison, sunglasses plastered firmly to her face, breezed in with her confident four-inch heel strut. With her black pantsuit, she looked the part of the television producer, all the way down to the no-nonsense expression she wore on the visible part of her face.

Madison did a quick scan of the wake attendants; Raleigh motioned for her to come toward them, but Madison ignored her and walked toward the contestants, signaling out Ryan. With one sleek motion, Madison put her hand on his forearm and whispered into his ear. He leaned in, listened, and then followed her outside.

Her Madison alarm bells jingled in her head. They usually signaled Madison was up to her former bad habits.

"That was weird, right?" Sheri asked.

Raleigh nodded, wondering what Madison had going on now. Besides being her typical insensible self, she had cleaned up her life recently.

"Oh, that," Frank said with a sheepish smile. "Many rumors about the two, you know, about their closeness. Only rumors, I suppose."

Raleigh looked at Sheri, and their eyes shared a knowing look. Usually, where Madison was concerned, the rumors held truth in them. Madison hadn't mentioned anything about dating though, especially one of the contestants. In fact, she'd been on her best behavior lately, and Raleigh would hate to not give her credit for her efforts.

"I could use a breath of fresh air," Sheri said, watching Shawn talking to one of Deon's relatives.

Raleigh watched Shawn avoid looking at his mother. Since he faced them, his eyes slid over his mother and he focused hard on the relatives standing around him.

"Let's step outside for a few minutes," Raleigh said. "Shawn will be alright."

Sheri nodded and stood shakily. Raleigh followed her out, Frank following behind Raleigh, but he stopped when he reached the congregated group of contestants at the back.

Outside the wide wooden oak doors, a few people had gathered on the portico, but they didn't pay any attention to the two as they strolled to an open column. Sheri leaned against the column and inhaled deeply and exhaled through her nude lips.

"I didn't kill him," she said, her fingers kneading her forehead. "I wanted to several times over the years, but I didn't. You know, I've only received child support from the man nine times. Nine times in nine years. And instead of making him pay the child support, the courts helped him because of his friends."

Raleigh had heard all of this before, but she could tell that Sheri needed to get something out, so she remained quiet, waiting for it to come.

"He dated many women. I never worried about any of them to be honest. Shawn just thought Dad had plenty friends. But the show made things rough these last few weeks."

Her chest heaved upwards. "I didn't know he was even dating Aryanna. In fact, I saw Helena leave his house early in the morning just two weeks ago, so I figured the two of them were dating."

Raleigh added this tidbit to her mental list of questions later on.

"Aryanna called me that night. She wanted me to meet her at the station, but I told her no. I didn't even know the woman, and something just felt wrong about the situation."

Sheri looked to Raleigh at this point for confirmation that her instincts had been right. Raleigh nodded. She agreed that something was weird about the request, but she also knew she would have gone. That whole curiosity instinct of a reporter, but that didn't mean it would have been the safe choice.

"When I refused to go, she asked me to at least tell her who had Deon been seeing before he died. I thought about Helena, but I didn't feel right about giving her that information. She was acting weird; well, at least what I thought was weird. I didn't know her, so it could have been normal for her."

"What was weird about it exactly?" Raleigh asked.

"She kept asking me about anyone stalking Deon. How would I know if someone was stalking him?" Sheri glanced at Raleigh again, keeping her eyes on the other bystander. "But she was insistent that someone he'd been dating when we were together was stalking him. She became irritated when I didn't know anyone. I mean, Deon and I dated for all of five months, maybe. I didn't know there was anyone else during that time."

Raleigh had been gone from Barbeaux Bayou by this time, so she hadn't really been in on any of the daily gossip. With her and Mike away at college, many of their friends that had stayed home had married, had children, got divorced, etc. Mike had come home after college, but he hadn't mentioned anything in their weekly phone calls. He wasn't big on gossip unless it led to a story.

"She didn't mention any other name?" Raleigh asked. "It seems like she knew something and was fishing."

Sheri nodded. "That's what it felt like to me. But I really didn't know, I swear." Sheri released a rugged breath. "But now, she's dead… I know it's an animal attack, but it just doesn't feel right that she was asking these questions and then ends up dead."

"Did you tell Max this when he questioned you?"

Sheri frowned and grunted. "He didn't seem real interested. Didn't seem to believe me."

Without making eye contact, Sheri revealed her dislike of Max. It was okay because Raleigh could completely understand. She'd been unable to answer his call last night, afraid that her anger would cause her to lash out.

"I'm sorry about Max," Raleigh said. "Mike and I are going to look into it. We will figure it out."

Tears pooled at the bottom of Sheri's eyelids, but she wiped them away. "Thanks, I knew I could count on you two."

"Always."

"I guess we better get back inside." Sheri smiled through watery eyes. "Don't want them thinking I abandoned my son in his time of need. Lord knows I would never hear the end of it."

Raleigh put her arm around her friend and walked with her back toward the doors. They'd almost reached the cherry wood doors when the one to the right swung open. Deon's mother in her flowing navy blue pantsuit strolled out, a deep crevice across her forehead leading the way.

"Well, there you are," she snapped. "This time is not about you but about your son. Maybe you should remember that as you socialize."

Sheri pulled her shoulders up. "I came outside for five minutes to catch my breath, and Shawn is fine with his relatives."

"Shawn would be great if you wouldn't have kept him from his father. Then he would have been able to know his father before he died, but you deprived him of that. For that, you should be ashamed, but that will be a guilt you have to live with the rest of your life."

"Okay," Raleigh said, feeling Sheri tense under her arm. "Everyone's emotions are running high right now. Let's keep these thoughts until a more appropriate time."

Deon's mother's frozen gray curls bobbed curtly, and she turned on her taupe pump and headed back through the door.

"After all of this is over," Raleigh whispered to Sheri, "you can deck her, and I'll cover you."

Sheri laughed and her shoulders slackened. Crisis avoided, at least for the moment.

Chapter Fifteen

Under Raleigh's feet in the Jeep, scattered quarters and dimes covered the gray floor mat, along with several, crumpled fast food wrappers and some dirty sneakers.

"Living out of the Jeep again?" Raleigh asked, moving an old parking pass from the dashboard.

Mike grunted. "I should give up my place and just sleep in here. It would be cheaper."

"Not very comfortable though," Raleigh said, glancing into the messiness of the back seat where wrinkled clothing mingled with rolled up newspapers and more errant odds and ends.

Mike only smiled. The tiny house he rented amounted to about five hundred square feet of sparse furnishings to allow for walk around room. As a perk, the house was only a few houses from his mother's, who needed help after his divorced sister had moved in with her four young children. The two women tended to make a mess of things on their own, but Mike remained quiet through overflowed toilets, busted pipes, and shattered light bulbs—all issues they couldn't handle without him, it seemed.

"So where are we on locating the man with the possible cameras?"

Mike's eyebrows furrowed, as he signaled to turn. "I've left messages, and he hasn't returned my calls. It's strange because I could swear the first time I called, he answered the phone, but it now keeps going to an old recording."

"Maybe we need to make a visit out there and see what's up?"

"Guerrilla style interviewing. Nice." Mike smiled as he pulled into a parking spot.

"Just trying to maintain our reputation," Raleigh said, taking in the old-fashioned window showcasing the bakery cakes. The white lettering on the window even resembled icing.

Mike laughed and then swung the door open. "Let's see if the tactic works with Helena first."

Inside the bakery, vanilla and confectionary sugar overpowered any thoughts of questions she'd come prepared to ask Helena. Raleigh always found a bakery intoxicating, especially with her love of sugar and chocolate. Maybe she could indulge a craving while they discovered Helena and Deon's relationship entanglements.

Curled tendrils escaped Helena's messy updo as she placed cupcakes into a large glass case. Her wide brown eyes met theirs as soon as the door jangled their arrival, and she froze with the chocolate swirled cupcake halfway to its shelf.

"Can… can I help y'all?" Helena asked, her lip trembling.

Mike moved toward the case, keeping a safe distance between them. "We had a few questions about you and Deon's relationship."

Helena's lip trembled, and then tears spilled down her face. She dropped the cupcake, and it landed on its side. Raleigh couldn't help but notice the icing smush against the tray, but she pulled her attention away from the deep brown glob and focused on Helena's waterworks display.

"What did you hear?" She gushed through tears. "I swear I believed him when he told me that we'd be together. He was always so sweet, but I didn't know he and Aryanna…" She trailed off and the sobs deepened, her shoulders trembling under the force.

"How long were you and Deon involved?" Raleigh asked, the awkwardness of the moment seeping into the thickness of the sweetness of the shop. She hated these moments and was much better at the arguing than the mushy tears.

"Oh." Helena sniffled. "Since the pirogue race. He invited me over after, and we hit it off, but we thought we'd keep things quiet to increase our chances on the show."

Raleigh counted backwards in her head with the shows. Five weeks. The pirogue race had been week two of the scheduled events, and the two had shown no chemistry on film. In fact, Deon had flirted endlessly with Winter on that show, and she'd played it up for the camera, even though later she'd complained of his breath smelling like onions.

Mike crossed his arms, his forehead wrinkling into his thinking expression. "Didn't you mind him dating other people for the show? I imagine it would be difficult circumstances to begin a relationship."

Helena shrugged as she reached behind a covered area for a tissue. "Deon wasn't really good at relationships. Getting him to settle down required waiting for him to get used to having you around long enough that he didn't want to be without you. I was willing to wait. Besides, I dated in the meantime, too."

That sounded so pathetic to Raleigh. Was this what today's relationships had been reduced to? Waiting around for someone to realize they wanted you. Sometimes she felt like she was waiting around to fit into Max's life, except she didn't bend very well to someone else's wishes. Therefore, their relationship wasn't experiencing much success.

"Did Aryanna know about you and Deon's relationship?" Raleigh asked, thinking she needed to create a flowchart to keep up with the relationships of this group.

Dabbing at the moisture under her eyes, she stared down at the glass cupcake cases. "Deon told me there was nothing between them, but then Aryanna visited me the Sunday he died, furious that I had called him. Apparently, the two were together the Saturday night when I called to see when he was coming over."

"Did she say what made her furious?" Mike asked, leaning forward, his voice gentle and sympathetic.

"He'd dropped her off at her house and spent the night at my house. She claimed I was sabotaging her chances by throwing myself at Deon and making him feel trapped. She accused me of stalking him. What she meant by that, I don't know. Deon and I had an arrangement, but um… she told me she loved him."

She crinkled her nose and a distant look glazed over her eyes. Had she become jealous of a budding romance between Deon and Aryanna and killed both of them? Raleigh still couldn't wrap her mind around an animal attack being controlled by a human. As far as she was concerned, more evidence was needed to prove that a human owner could direct a wild animal attack.

"Did you see Deon at all Sunday?"

Helena frowned. "He left my house in the morning. I didn't know he left to go pick up Aryanna." She gritted her teeth together.

"And you didn't see him at the station for interviews?"

Helena shook her head. "No, I went in later because I had to watch my sister's kid. I didn't know until Aryanna showed up at my house… she wasn't gentle with the news."

Raleigh could imagine the accusation. Aryanna hadn't left Deon's crime scene in the best of moods, but at least now, she knew where the woman had hurried off to when she'd left in such a weird manner.

"What are your ideas on who has been sending the pictures to you guys?" Mike asked, studying her closely.

Helena tilted her head as she gathered her thoughts, clearly taken aback by the change of topic. Raleigh looked from one to the other, waiting for her response.

"I haven't really given it much thought since I haven't received a picture," Helena began, her forehead wrinkling in thought. "I suppose the consensus is that Patrick is behind it. I mean he was all nerdy in high school with no friends and Deon bullying him nearly everyday and many others, truthfully."

"High school?" Raleigh asked.

"Well, most of the people who have received pictures have gone to high school together. I was two years behind them, but I remember the ones of that year."

Mike and Raleigh exchanged a knowing look with each other. That was something they hadn't put together yet. With everything going on, pulling the contestant's files had fallen at the bottom of their priorities, and no one had mentioned this commonality.

Mike nodded to conclude the interview. They made their exit with a few words of being in touch soon, and were soon back in Mike's Jeep within minutes and sadly without a cupcake.

"So, high school?" Mike said as he backed out of the parking slot.

"Does everyone's torment go back to high school?" Raleigh grinned, but she cringed as she remembered her own senior year of high school. Being responsible for the star football player's death—even if it had been self-defense—had made her tormentors many.

"It builds character," Mike said, chuckling. "But besides that, it makes sense that they went to high school together. Most of them are about the same age. Madison did know most of them when she chose them. Deon was older though."

"Yes, but he used to hang out with Winter, Summer, and Madison when they were in high school. You know, when they were dancing on the bars and getting everyone's attention? Winter told me he used them when he needed his drug fix."

Mike nodded. "That would make sense. Maybe we need to talk to Patrick then."

Raleigh looked around the console and spotted her cellphone under an old notepad. She pulled it out from the debris and dialed Madison's phone.

"What?" Madison's clipped voice rang over the line.

"When's Patrick's cooking lesson this week?"

"Ummm," Madison said, papers shuffling in the background. "Tuesday. He's with the first group."

"Can I host their lesson so I can do a little digging?"

"Fine," Madison snapped. "Everything is falling apart anyway."

"Madison," Raleigh started.

"Don't try to make me feel better," Madison snapped. "Two contestants have died and the station is considering canceling at the next sign of trouble. It's not even a disaster I can control to keep it together."

Raleigh sighed. "We're working on it. This week the contestants will be filming inside the entire time. Warn them there will be no outside activities allowed, and I'm sure they will listen with everything going on."

Silence greeted her response. Then the creaking of a chair in the background indicated she was still there.

"That may work." Madison spoke slowly. Raleigh could almost hear the thoughts processing like a turning wheel.

"I'll get with you tomorrow at work to discuss the segments. It's almost over Madison, just take a deep breath."

"Such bullshit advice, but I'll try." Madison's voice was lighter, so Raleigh knew it was her attempt at a joke. She really needed to work on her tone of voice. She always sounded like she was an angry hornet.

"So, you are going undercover?" Mike asked when she was off the phone.

"I don't know how undercover it will be, but we may learn something about Patrick and some of the other contestants at the same time if I go in and start asking some questions."

"I'll drop you off at home," Mike said, "I'll work on getting us the guy with the possible recording. Something seems odd about that situation though."

"Something is not right with this entire thing, Mike," Raleigh said, looking over at him. His blond hair fell perfectly into place as he drummed his fingers on the steering wheel. "Deon and Aryanna were attacked by animals, yet we are looking for a human? What is that?"

Mike's head bobbed up and down. "Maybe you need to see if you can get the results of the bite marks from Max. I mean, I'm with you. How does animal attack equal a person involved?"

"A person was there," Raleigh said, remembering her connection to Aryanna and shuddering. "But the bodies looked horrible."

Mike glanced toward her, and his hand reached out and patted her leg. Warmth spread across her cheeks, and she wanted to look away. "I know you don't like when it all doesn't make sense, but it will. We will figure it out."

Raleigh nodded, unable to get words over the lump in her throat.

As Mike pulled in front of her white picket fence, she noticed Max's navy blue Caprice in the driveway. She inwardly groaned. She'd looked forward to a little quiet to figure out what was going on with these deaths. Some idea or some inkling percolated just beneath the surface of her conscience, and Raleigh knew that if she could get just a few minutes of free time, she might be able to pull it out.

Mike glanced at the car in her driveway. "Looks like you can get started tonight working on those bite marks."

"Maybe I'm not girlfriend material," Raleigh blurted out. She inhaled sharply and back-pedaled. "I'm not that great at it."

"I don't think it's something you're born knowing, Ree." Mike grinned. "I'm sure you can't be that awful."

Raleigh admired the sweeping front porch of the house she'd grown up fantasizing about one day living in and wondered if Max had come alone or had the boys invaded her quietness as well. With working both jobs right now, she never had a moment to herself. But, she supposed she couldn't avoid Max forever. After a funeral and an interview, her anger had exhausted itself to barely a simmer.

"I suppose," Raleigh said, giving him a slight grin as she opened the door. "Tomorrow then."

He nodded as he looked toward the house without his usual sheepish grin. Something bothered him but Raleigh's instincts told her that it wasn't a conversation she wanted to have in this moment.

Raleigh closed the door and walked through her open gate and up the brick steps. Two days ago, she'd come home and Paw had mowed the lawn. With her recent hours, she'd let it slip, but Paw couldn't stand to see his sister's house get run down, even though Raleigh would prefer him to not overexert himself. She promised herself that in two weeks she'd take more time to take care of other responsibilities.

Letting herself in, she listened for familiar noises from within, but all she heard was a sizzling coming from the back kitchen. She set her key down on the entrance table and walked to the back. Max stood at the stove, sipping from a dark amber liquid glass and stirring in a skillet with steam rising out of it.

"This is a surprise," Raleigh said, sinking onto a barstool. "I figured I'd be eating a Twix tonight."

Max put the spoon down and reached for a glass in the cabinet near his head. As he poured wine into her glass, he studied her. "Maybe you can get your sugar from this tonight." He handed the glass over to her and smiled.

"My stir-fry is famous in some parts, and I'm sure a nice meal will do you some good."

Raleigh nodded as she sipped the sweet liquid. It glided down her throat and tingled as she felt it begin to work its magic.

He returned to the large skillet, picking up the spoon. "So, how was your day?"

"Chasing stories," Raleigh said, allowing more liquid to chase the uneasiness away. "The contestants on Barbeaux Hearts should be on an intervention show. Turns out almost all the ones receiving the pictures went to high school together."

"Hmm," Max said, glancing back at her. "Still no idea who is sending the pictures?"

Raleigh hesitated. She'd always liked Patrick. From the very beginning, he'd been good to everyone and had treated each of the women with such respect. Raleigh had a difficult time believing that he was behind the pictures, but maybe she didn't know much about him. She wouldn't have pictured the athletic gentleman as a geeky nerd bullied in high school.

"Everyone is pointing their fingers at each other, and each of them so far have a reason why it isn't them," Raleigh said. "We are still working on it."

Max's shoulders straightened out, but he remained quiet.

"What about those bite marks? Do we know what kind of animal is responsible yet?"

Max tapped the spoon on the side of the skillet and turned the burner off. "Tests weren't definitive. Canine for sure, but not pure dog. The expert says it is a mixture between dog and wolf."

"A wolf?" Raleigh set her glass down. "Do we even have those here? Coyote, sure, but I haven't heard of any wild wolves."

"Well, to have a pure wolf, you need to have it registered, but a hybrid would be possible to have, and of course, it's not like everyone follows the law."

Raleigh nodded. Her mind racing. Her paw had mentioned all of this before, but coming from Max, it became the facts of the case. A person would have had to have control of this animal in order to be involved. How much control could one possibly have over a wild animal? None of this seemed logical to her. Had it simply been a hungry wild animal drawn to the smell of the food from the parties? That theory seemed more probable to Raleigh. But when she'd connected with Aryanna, the woman had heard a person scream. Someone who hadn't helped her, but that expectation had been there for the help.

"Do you have any theories you are willing to share?" she asked, thinking that she didn't know enough about any of the contestants to know if they owned animals.

"Let's not talk about work tonight," Max said, placing a plate in front of her with shrimp and vegetables in brown sauce.

"Deon's funeral was this morning," Raleigh said, sipping from her glass again as she watched him move around her kitchen.

Max nodded. "I wanted to attend, but I had some interviews this morning."

"Sheri's having a rough time of it."

"Uh-hmm."

Raleigh watched him as he served his own plate and set it down next to the empty stool next to hers. He never looked at her though.

"When did you plan on telling me that Sheri was a suspect in an animal attack?"

"She's not a suspect," Max said, easing himself onto the stool next to hers. "I don't even technically have a case yet. There are just questions that need answers."

"But Sheri didn't do anything," Raleigh said, clutching her wine glass.

"And if that's the case, she'll be fine," Max said. He took a swig from his glass, and then looked to her. "Let's try a normal conversation. I know we can have one, so let's try."

He offered her a smile, a sign of peace.

She let it pass, as she tasted his famous rice dish.

Could they have a relationship if they avoided talking about anything that caused friction? Talking about work had become an issue. She left out details. Obviously, he left out information. Tossing ideas off of each other had become a non-option, but she didn't know when or why this had happened.

Maybe Mike could explain what went on in the head of a man to her. He certainly didn't think a subject was off limits with her.

Chapter Sixteen

The repetitive jingle wouldn't stop. Raleigh twisted in her sleep, her brain tingling as it began to awaken. The idea slipped into her conscious slowly, and she realized it was her phone. With her eyes closed, her hand felt around the nightstand until it landed on the smooth surface.

"Raleigh," Madison whispered.

Raleigh wondered what time it was. Should she be worried or terrified? The time of the call would give some indication. She'd recently installed room darkening blinds and curtains, so darkness surrounded her. But she couldn't feel Max in bed with her. Had he left for his five o'clock routine already?

Raleigh groaned. It was too early for thinking.

"Is something wrong?" Raleigh asked.

"I can't get Uncle Camille to wake up," she whispered again. "I'm not sure…" She drew air in sharply. "I'm not sure if he's breathing."

Raleigh bolted up in bed. "Did you check his pulse?"

"I…" Madison tapered off. "I can't do it Raleigh."

Throwing the comforter off, Raleigh jumped out of bed, stepping on her clothes from last night. "I'm on my way. Stay put."

Raleigh hung up and tugged on her jeans as she stumbled down the stairs. She tripped over her own hurried feet as she reached one of the last steps and caught herself with the railing. She stopped on the last riser and took a deep breath to steady the surge of anxiety coursing through her with the call. She'd be no use if she couldn't think. When the shaking in her limbs subsided, she rushed forward out the front door, leaving it unlocked behind her.

Uncle Camille's house lay only a few homes down the street on the opposite side of her own, and Raleigh made a quick walk of it. His shotgun home sat lost among the weeds and broken chairs and garden tools without even a car parked in the driveway. Madison must have walked here this morning as well. The fact that Madison had awoken when the sun had only begun to peek around the houses didn't speak of typical behavior, but Uncle Camille had to be Raleigh's first concern. His health hadn't been the best recently, but he insisted on self-treatment without really sharing much with the rest of the family, especially Raleigh who he didn't like much.

The front screen door squeaked open and the stale, musty air choked her. From the smell of the place, Uncle Camille was going without electricity again. Swelling with body odor and decaying food, the walls warped under the stench, which circulating air may have been able to mask. Madison leaned in the doorway, holding the sleeve of her jacket over her mouth.

"I'm sorry," she choked out from behind the fabric. "He's just lying there, and I couldn't bring myself to, you know, touch him."

Raleigh nodded and followed her to the back of the house to the only bedroom in the shotgun house. The stench through the kitchen and into the bedroom nauseated her, and she had to concentrate on putting one foot in front of the other instead of bolting back the way she'd come.

Once in the room, Uncle Camille's body crossed the bed diagonally with the old chenille bed comforter tossed about as if he'd thrashed in his sleep, but now he lay stiff with his arms stretched out across the mounds of puffy roses, probably a hand-me-down from Me'Maw.

Walking around the bed toward his head, a chill ran down Raleigh's neck, but she knew someone had to check. Strands of greasy hair poked out from the top of his head, and Raleigh could see long wiry nose hairs sticking out of his bulbous nostrils. Someone would owe her big time for this.

With trembling fingers, Raleigh reached toward his neck and made contact with his gray tinged flesh. She felt nothing but her own heart beating.

Suddenly, an arm jerked upward. "Come back tomorrow." He barked, and then snorted loudly.

Raleigh jumped back and knocked her hip against the wall. Madison screamed, but Uncle Camille only snored louder. Raleigh felt the wall behind her with her fingertips for balance as she steadied her breathing. A laugh of relief and of anxiety welled inside her.

Raleigh glanced at the nightstand to see a prescription bottle as well as an empty mason jar. She picked it up and after a whiff, crinkled her nose. Strong stuff. Certainly not from the doctor.

Madison motioned for them to leave the room, and Raleigh followed her out.

Back in the living area, a laugh escaped her lips, but a moment later she sobered up as she inhaled the stench from the overflowing trashcan and the sweltering walls.

"He's been like this all week, but at least he's been responsive when I come to get him up," Madison rambled, pacing the wooden floorboards of the living area. "He hasn't been very helpful with traiteur lessons this week, but he'll go over some of the home remedies he asks me to fetch at least. I mean I did learn how to make an arthritis concoction that smelled absolutely horrible."

"So you come in the morning for your training?"

Madison nodded, but didn't keep still. "Me'Maw insists I come every morning and wake him up. Some mornings he makes it to her back porch where she pushes biscuits and eggs on him. He hardly eats anything anymore, so she figures if I wake him up, he will come over for breakfast to get something inside him besides beer. Her plan has mostly worked, but this week he has been as ornery as an old mule."

"How has your training been going?" Raleigh asked, feeling a pang inside. She should be the one learning the family vocation, but Uncle Camille was a spiteful, dying old man.

Madison rubbed her palms against her bare cheeks. She looked so young without the layers of make up as a defense. "I don't think I'll be trained in time... you know."

She glanced at Raleigh and then looked away, returning to her frenzied pacing.

"Me'Maw will step in if anything happens to him."

Madison huffed. "She's old too, Raleigh. She won't live forever. All of this stuff is going to die with them. I can't even remember what goes in the arthritis cream, and I just mixed it two days ago. He gets so impatient with me, but I never thought I was going to have to learn all of this. I'm good with parties and people, not this mumbo jumbo stuff."

Raleigh didn't even want to acknowledge that Me'Maw might not be in her life at some point, and Madison just tossed it out there so blasé as if it didn't matter. Not to mention Raleigh longed to be the one training to be like Me'Maw, and Madison felt it was a burden. Raleigh took a deep breath, feeling the old aggravation welling inside. Recently, she and Madison had attempted a truce, but the age gap made liking her own sister difficult sometimes.

"I suggest," Raleigh said, then readjusted the harshness of her voice, "you get a notebook and write everything down. One day you will have it all memorized, but until then, you can't afford to lose the knowledge to time."

Madison paused in her pacing. "No one ever writes these things down, Raleigh. Damn tradition and all."

"I'm sure we can make an exception, and once you have it all in your head, you can burn the notebook."

"Yes, that could work." Madison nodded, deep in thought. "Of course, I can't tell Me'Maw or Uncle Camille about this. They'd have fits. So please don't mention it?" she pleaded.

"Of course not," Raleigh said. Since it was her suggestion, it would likely be her who Me'Maw chased with the broom. As if Raleigh would open herself up for that attack. "What was going on at the funeral with Ryan? You two dating?"

"As if I have time to date." Madison glared at her. "I had to ask him about the rumors surrounding his and Aryanna's marriage since her parents made some odd requests."

"What kind of odd requests?"

"They don't want any of the contestants at her funeral except for Ryan, and they wanted him to provide pictures for them."

"So, what were you thinking?" Raleigh asked, considering these details. "That the two of them were still together?"

"Sounds like something was going on there," Madison said. "He denies it. He claimed they hadn't spoken in three years before the show."

"I agree," Raleigh said. "If her parents had the marriage annulled, why do they want him there now?"

Madison shrugged. "I can't say I haven't thought about dating Ryan, but right now I don't know which contestant is lying, so I'm going to stick to finishing the show."

Raleigh nearly choked as she swallowed. Had her little sister taken a step towards growing up?

"I guess I'll go make excuses to Me'Maw," Madison said, frowning, oblivious to Raleigh's shock. "She doesn't take it very well. Sometimes I'd like to take one of those old iron pokers from Paw's barn to Uncle Camille's backside."

Finally, something they agreed on.

Raleigh escaped the stench of Uncle Camille's place and walked back in the direction of her house. Ms. Margaret's house had not changed since the new girl had moved in. The clapboard siding still hung broken on the side, and the old branch of the oak tree rotted where it had fallen in a storm. The swing though. The swing lay empty, rocking slightly in the wind. Ms. Margaret had occupied that swing almost as many hours as the sun warmed the ground, but she'd slid to the dirt and the darkness had welcomed her, but not before Raleigh had tried to save her.

But Raleigh couldn't save anyone. She could only find answers for the dead.

Boy, wasn't she a bundle of depressing thoughts this morning. Must be the early wake up call. Nothing a Twix couldn't fix.

"Well, you're up early this morning."

Raleigh stubbed her foot on the road and caught herself before falling as she glimpsed sight of the thin blonde spread out on a yoga mat beneath the tree. Damn, she hadn't spotted her among the overgrown shrubbery. If she had, Raleigh would have kept to the other side of the street to avoid the woman. Something about her made Raleigh cringe.

"A rare occurrence for me," Raleigh said, forcing a friendly smile.

Amber began walking toward Raleigh, her blond tresses flapping about her in the early morning breeze. "I like the quiet of the morning. Great for meditation. I've been wanting to speak to you about my dream though."

"Oh?" Raleigh asked, squinting at her as the sun blinded her, and Amber stepped out onto the narrow street behind her.

"Yes," she said, tilting her head with vacant eyes. "This dream has come every night since I met you, and I feel as though I'm supposed to tell you about it."

Raleigh kept quiet, wondering how much time did polite manners require her to keep her entertained.

"Do you own a green sequined dress? I keep seeing this dress over and over with a canine type animal clawing through it." Her green inquisitive eyes looked solemnly into Raleigh's.

Raleigh shook her head. "I'm not really the dress type."

"Odd," Amber said, chewing on her bottom lip. "I'm sure it means something."

"Maybe," Raleigh said, "I'll keep it in mind."

"Since we ran into each other," Amber said, smiling and reaching for a lock of blond hair to twist between her fingers, "what about that good looking yum, Mike? What can you tell me about him?"

"What do you mean?" Raleigh asked.

"Well," Amber drawled out slowly, "is he taken? I mean someone must have snapped up a hottie like that already."

"He's not dating anyone at the moment," Raleigh responded, feeling a heat rise through her.

"That's good news," Amber said, her eyes daydreamy. "I'm sure he has plenty of options. You two look very chummy. Are you sure you two don't have a thing going?"

"Quite sure," Raleigh said. "Mike's my best friend."

"That's a shame. You two would make a most attractive couple." Amber shrugged, stretching her arms above her head, her trim belly peeking out beneath her top. "But hopefully I will have a chance now."

Raleigh nodded, feeling awkward. "I need to get home, so I can get ready for work. It was nice talking to you."

"We need to get together soon," Amber said, smiling an ethereal glow on her face that should be outlawed so early in the morning. "Our psychic energy would be phenomenal."

"Uh-hmm," Raleigh said, taking a few steps away. "Maybe after the show ends. Real busy right now."

Raleigh continued walking away, wondering why was it so difficult for her to take the woman seriously. But she couldn't. She wanted to bolt every time she started talking about psychic energy. Considering her own talent, she knew she shouldn't feel this way. She also needed to consider her uneasiness about Mike dating.

Later. There would be time when the show ended to get her own thoughts straight. Right now she needed to get ready for her day hosting contestants learning to cook while trying to figure out the connection between blackmail and animal attacks.

Lucky her.

Chapter Seventeen

The exposed brick of the walls warmed the room, and Raleigh tugged at the collar of her button-down white shirt, feeling the heat from the bubbling pots steaming up the industrial kitchen. Lebasque's Restaurant had never fallen within Raleigh's radar before today due to its reputation and meals that would cost her a week's paycheck. She could see the draw though. Opening during her time away from Barbeaux Bayou, the restaurant had revitalized one of the old downtown two-story buildings, exposing the hundred-year-old bricks lit with chrome industrial lights. A wooden bar curved around one wall ending where a staircase led up to the top floor banquet room. This brick-columned open hall would film beautifully Saturday since Austin Lebasque had generously donated the space for this week's competition.

"What do you call this again?" Lauren asked, peering into the large stainless pot.

"Have you never made a roux before?" Patrick asked, a frown playing at his naturally easy blond looks.

Lauren shrugged. "I don't cook. Figured if I didn't learn, no one would ask me to do it."

Raleigh raised her eye brows in response to Frank's conspirator look in her direction. Perfectly logical if you thought about it, but not practical if you didn't want to starve or grew up with Me'Maw. Since Raleigh was old enough to stand on a step stool, she had been deemed old enough to learn to cook in Me'Maw's kitchen. She'd stirred a roux until her hand ached, and she hadn't dared let it burn to give her arm a rest.

"Stir more gently dear." A white-coated chef said, leaning over Lauren's shoulder. "You are not chopping onions."

Lauren giggled and glanced in the direction of the camera. Going into the final stretch of the show, the contestants appeared to be scrambling for airtime. By this time, they had figured out what Madison edited into the show, and these little silly conversations were right up in Madison's faves. Raleigh didn't know if this was good or bad for the show at this point. She was too far in to know which way was up.

"Oh, Lauren can't help it," Kimberly said, waving a mixing spoon in the air. "She's always been rough around the edges."

"You're one to talk," Lauren shot back, glaring over in her direction before she forced a smile on her face. "You weren't so polished in high school."

"I've heard recently that many of you went to high school together," Raleigh said, seeing a way in and hoping to de-escalate the upcoming argument. "How is it being on a show with the same people you may not have liked then?"

"We all got along great back then, didn't we, Patrick?" Lauren said, her face hovering right above the pot.

Patrick looked up from the sauce a sous chef was walking him through to glare at her a moment before he remembered the camera and looked back into his saucepan. "Best buddies."

Kimberly's lips puckered into a pout. "Well, I hated it. Couldn't wait to leave those people behind. Little did I know that I wasn't leaving anyone behind when I didn't have enough money to leave this small town."

A few pans clattered together, and Clara's voice gritted through the sizzling and hums of the kitchen. "Barbeaux Bayou may be as small town as it gets, but it is our home. Our families built this place, and we should be proud of it."

A moment of awkward silence followed where Lauren lifted a flaky lump of amber-colored roux above her pot and allowed it to plop back down into the mess. She probably would not be winning this contest; therefore, she would not get her pick of a sweetheart for the last episode. As the final episode going into the finale, the winner of this challenge earned the right to choose their match for the Mardi Gras ball. It was at this ball that the Barbeaux Hearts couple would be crowned sweethearts and serve as queen and king of the town's Mardi Gras parade.

Raleigh could finally see the end of this nightmarish work schedule. Now if she could just figure out all the other questions surrounding the show, she'd feel like it was actually coming to a close.

After everyone's entrees were simmering, Raleigh ushered them up the upholstered stairs to walk them through Saturday's cook off. With rich hues of burgundy and wrought iron, the décor was reminiscent of the French Quarter of New Orleans. On each table a black, candle-filled lantern rested on white table clothes with fancy place settings. Twenty-four round tables awaited the paid guests, as Austin Lebasque had insisted on selling tickets to the event. The contestants would be at the front of the banquet room, however. Each of them would have a small table to display their dish in whatever manner they wished.

Lauren giggled as she sat behind a table. "I feel like I'm presiding over court."

Patrick leaned against the doorframe, observing but not making a move to come into the room. Raleigh had yet to figure out how to get him alone to ask what she wanted to know. Not that "hey, have you been stalking your fellow contestants?" was going to be an easy conversation with or without an audience.

Kimberly walked along the judge's table. "So they really are going to eat all that food?"

Raleigh nodded. "Each of the three judges will taste test a sampling of your dish and score it on an evaluation sheet. Scores will be added up after the taste testing, and a winner will be announced. You should have your pick for the Mardi Gras ball ready for the announcement as you will be asked during the presentation. The viewers will then vote on other matches for the ball."

"Will the crowd be voting on something that night?" Frank asked, looking around the place cards at the tables.

"Actually," Raleigh said, "A fan favorite of the night will also get to pick their date. Waiters will serve a sampling to each table for judging as well."

"Good Lord," Lauren declared loudly, "No one said I needed to know how to cook to win this show. I may have paid more attention in the kitchen instead of my books."

Kimberly groaned. "That's just ignorant. You should have paid attention simply so you wouldn't starve to death. Even people with fancy law degrees need to eat."

Lauren frowned, but she shrugged when she noticed all eyes on her. In Lauren's short biography, she was serving as an intern at the largest law firm in town. Largest in Barbeaux Bayou meant four lawyers, so it wasn't that impressive. From overheard gossip, Raleigh gathered that she wished to leave Barbeaux Bayou after the internship ended for bigger opportunities elsewhere. Raleigh couldn't fathom why she hadn't stayed in New Orleans for an internship since her law school was located there, but that had not come up in any conversation.

Clara sat quietly at one of the guest tables, her almond-shaped eyes studying the linen napkins. "What about the rest of us? How will our dates be chosen?"

Raleigh hesitated a moment, realizing that Clara had already accepted defeat. She hadn't won a single challenge, but her simmering dish downstairs had smelled delicious, so she should feel some sort of hope.

"Will there be a lottery to lower the rest of our chances for winning this farce of a show?" Kimberly asked, standing and looking around the area.

"You will be paired by number of votes. Highest to lowest," Raleigh said, feeling the awkwardness seep through the room.

"Sounds fair," Patrick said, nodding his head.

"I hate to bring it up, but I'm trying to keep on top of it," Raleigh said, seeing no other opportunity like the present. "Any more unwanted pictures showing up?"

Silence followed as everyone looked at the floor or at a flower centerpiece.

"Is that a yes?"

"Well, I haven't received any, so I don't know anything much about what is going on," Clara responded.

"It's nonsense," Patrick said. "Someone getting her kicks off of weirding people out. I'm going back downstairs. I've seen all I need to see up here."

He strolled toward the exit. Raleigh tried to think of something to say to get him to say more, but the clench of his jaw said it wasn't a good idea.

Clara quietly followed him downstairs, looking back with her big doe eyes at the room one last time. Looking at her, Raleigh could tell she wasn't made for television. What Madison had seen during the auditions that had offered promise, Raleigh didn't know. Her insecurities crinkled at her eyes and twitched at her lips.

Kimberly placed her hand on her hip. "At least we can say it's almost over. The only reality of love is that it isn't found on television."

Lauren shook her head. "Negative Nancy may find it difficult to find someone."

Kimberly tsked loudly and then disappeared down the stairs.

"So did you find love on the show, Lauren?" Raleigh asked, trying to recall any matches Lauren had made. She couldn't recall any.

Lauren smiled. "It's irrelevant. I'm not really looking."

Raleigh studied her, waiting for the joke, the funny sarcastic comment to follow.

She smiled. "Believe it or not, most of the contestants are here for the attention. Take Patrick for instance, he's trying to get everyone to see how he's changed since high school. It's better than a high school reunion because he gets to show the entire town he's not this dweeby geek behind a computer who can't get a date anymore."

"So who do you think is behind the pictures then? Someone who is jealous of all the attention y'all are getting?"

Lauren shrugged. "Anyone can be guilty, I suppose. We all have secrets to hide, even in this small town. Some are saying that it's Patrick's way of paying some of them back for the way they treated him in high school." She smiled, her eyes twinkling in excitement.

"So what kind of attention are you trying to get?" Raleigh asked, filing the info away but more curious as to Laura's obvious interest.

She laughed, a harsh, jarring sound echoing off the walls. "That I can't say, but I'm going to get back to my cooking, so I can hopefully win this challenge and have the focus on me for a change."

She floated down the stairs, and Raleigh sighed. Maybe she should let this one go and not try to be the traiteur to the dead. Aryanna hadn't been all that nice to her alive, and Lord knows, Deon had never even shared a moment of kindness in his rise to the top.

Of course, Me'Maw would be chiding her for even having the thought. As traiteur—to the living or dead—her job was to help everyone who came to her. She couldn't refuse the dead, no matter how much a scoundrel they'd been during life.

Her cellphone rang in her pocket, and she was saved from imagining the chewing out she'd receive from Me'Maw for giving up.

"I'm outside," Mike mumbled, his voice far off. "We are going on a guerrilla interview."

"Gotcha." Raleigh giggled, heading down the stairs. "Heading your way. I've just finished up. No luck here though."

"Ever think that maybe we should just start a reality show where they kill each other off one by one instead? They seem hell-bent on doing it without wanting anyone to save them."

"Imagine the ratings," Raleigh said, reaching the bottom of the staircase and waving goodbye to the camera guy. "But then Madison may not have a chance for a season two if the death toll gets too high."

"I hate to break it to your sister," Mike said, "but I don't think she's getting a season two. Not enough love happening on this love show."

Raleigh exited the antique black French doors onto the red brick sidewalk and hung up the phone. Mike's Jeep waited at the edge of the sidewalk, and she climbed into the passenger seat.

"Do me a favor and let the boss break that news to Madison," Raleigh said, throwing a crumbled takeout bag onto the back seat.

Mike nodded. "So, our man Elmer will not answer my phone calls, so we are going out to see why. I figure you may soften the presence, and he may not perceive me as a threat this way."

"Weird that he wouldn't return our call. We only wanted to see if he had surveillance video."

Mike nodded as the tires spun on gravel. "May be something to it, but he does live in the back bayou, so it could be nothing."

Raleigh nodded, knowing that the back bayou had a reputation for being a bit strange. The long, winding road went through trees, swamp, and several junk piles that were mixed with the mobile homes and ancient shotgun shacks that families had owned for several generations.

After they crossed the bayou on the old drawbridge, Mike signaled their turn down a small road barely visible among the knotted vines and trees. The setting sun disappeared above the tree canopy and eeriness emanated from the underbrush. The Jeep bumped along the dirt road for a ways before they saw the first dilapidated mobile home set a ways from the road.

"That's where Deon grew up," Mike said, peering out the side window.

"Didn't he move out of there when he was a teenager?" Raleigh said, noticing the rotten porch had fallen off in some parts and there was a cracked window near the bent door. "Looks like no one has lived there since."

"He and his mom moved out of there when his dad died. As I heard it, she went back to her family, who didn't like the match to begin with. She remarried for money and never acknowledged that this belonged to her, not even to sell."

Raleigh wondered if Deon acknowledged his father's relatives, who must live back here somewhere. None of the people surrounding Shawn the day of the funeral dressed the part of a back bayou person, but she supposed some of the relatives could have been from this side of the family.

The trees opened up into an empty space and a newly mowed, small cemetery emerged in the stretch. Eight white tombs stood solemn against the dim rays of the sun, and a gray, baby lamb statue rested in the middle, eyes looking toward the road.

"Guess they don't leave back here even when they die," Raleigh muttered, feeling a chill start in her shoulders. A traiteur to the dead wouldn't be hanging out in a cemetery with all those sensations emanating from dead bodies.

Mike chuckled. "Might explain why Clara doesn't fit in so well. She probably hasn't left the back bayou too often."

"I forget she's from back here," Raleigh said scanning the surrounding structures, knowing that Clara lived close to where Deon had grown up. Isn't that what they had said when they'd spoken about him threatening the men to stay away from her? The big overprotective brother that Raleigh couldn't imagine him being.

Mike slowed to maneuver around a large pothole. "I think that's her to your right. I had to come here once with Ross pick up some crab cages for his dad. I couldn't tell the difference between the house and the sheds."

Raleigh raised her eyebrows at him, but then looked out the window to take it in. An uneven driveway led to several small buildings, each surrounded by automobiles in various stages of distress and two or three boats with cages stacked high. Painted on a piece of scrap plywood was a sign in the front of the house advertising crabs for sale, and another one with a little better quality of painted letters said dogs for sale. Dog cages peeked just around the side of an old barn with a rusted tin roof

"Maybe the house is the one with the screen door?" Raleigh asked, trying to study each structure as they passed.

"Well, I think someone lives in all of them. There's Clara's dad, her uncle, and a brother that moved into that small one in the corner. I think there's someone else as well that I'm not remembering."

"Wow." Raleigh gulped. "She turned out well, considering where she came from." She caught a glimpse of a hole in the roof, patched by a metal stop sign. She wondered if someone lived there, and if they'd thought not getting caught stealing the sign meant it was okay to showcase the stolen object.

Mike nodded.

"How far back is this guy?" Raleigh asked, noticing a few mailboxes along the road near the dirt driveways that disappeared into complete wooded areas.

"Should be one of the ones upcoming. That was 2227 just now, and we're looking for 2234."

Raleigh read the mailboxes as they passed and soon a clear driveway emerged among the tangled bushes to reveal a shell driveway leading to an old L shaped Acadian house. The cypress wood had once held a coat of paint, but it had flaked off in most places, leaving the gray, weathered wood exposed to the elements along with its rusted tin roof. A large chicken yard took up most of the left side of the front yard. It was neat though. The creosol posts evenly spaced with the fencing tightly pulled. A tractor rested under a tree in the right side of the yard. Otherwise, nothing stood out. There must be a garage or a place to park the car in the back because no vehicle indicated anyone was home, but someone watched from a glider rocker on the porch as they pulled into the driveway.

Raleigh slid out of the passenger seat and walked to the porch with Mike, as the man stood to greet them.

"Good evening," Raleigh said, smiling. "I'm Raleigh Cheramie, and this here is Mike Simmons. We work for the *Barbeaux Gazette,* and we heard that you had some rabbits and chickens turn up dead, and there was a chance you had it on video cameras. We were hoping you could help us out by telling us if this is true?"

"I reckon today people run their mouths too much," he said, rubbing his rough hand over the coarse stubble on his chin. "Chickens get killed all the time. Can't do anything about the coyotes and the cranes and the coons. All animals like to eat."

"What about the cameras?" Mike asked. "Would you have caught what kind of animal it is on tape?"

"No," he said, quietly staring at them.

Mike pointed to the corner of the house where a small camera was visible from the angle they stood. "What about that one? Did you maybe catch anything with that one?"

His jaw tightened. "It's not real. I just keep it around so my neighbors think I'm watching. Family is sometimes the worst thieves when they think it is borrowing."

"Do you have an opinion on what is attacking everyone's chickens at this time?" Raleigh asked as Mike crossed his arms and studied the man. They both seemed to be sizing each other up.

"I don't have any comments for the *Barbeaux Gazette.* If I did, I would have returned your calls."

Raleigh could see they were going to get nowhere. "Well, thank you for your time. If you hear of anything or think of anything in regards to the story, please give us a call at the *Barbeaux Gazette*."

Mike tossed a curt nod in his direction, and they walked back to the Jeep. Mike stood with his door open and looked at the chicken coop. He pointed to the corner of the coop where the chickens had clustered themselves, probably for the night. Raleigh looked in that direction and saw another video camera at the corner of the overhang.

"Why would you go to all that trouble to install fake cameras?" Raleigh asked, trying to see if something about the camera gave away that it wasn't real.

"I don't think they are fake," Mike said, glancing around the yard. The man stood on the porch glaring at them with one hand on his hip.

Raleigh hopped into the passenger seat. "Then the question becomes why would you not want to reveal the footage of the animal or person killing the chickens?"

"Exactly," Mike said. "You are either guilty or you know who is guilty."

Raleigh nodded, looking at the man one last time. His distrustful glare spoke volumes, but did he have something against the paper, or was he hiding something? Clearly, she'd need to find another way to find out.

"I guess I should turn this over to Max," Raleigh muttered.

"Trade it for information." Mike grinned. "You tell him something, he tells you something. Maybe you can negotiate."

Raleigh laughed. "Have you met Max?"

Mike shrugged. "Tall. Focused. Not very understanding. Yes, I vaguely recall meeting the man who takes away my best friend. He puts such a damper on our stories." Mike grinned after, but the description vibrated through her. She felt the truth of his words rattle her.

Chapter Eighteen

The outside of the Bayou Life Museum was nondescript, clinical even. A white brick structure, built in the 80s from the style of it, and nothing to speak of bayou life on its outside. Three vehicles parked in side parking spoke of visitors, but the dark film layered on the glass door didn't allow visible life from the outside.

"Are we sure this is the right place?" Raleigh asked, shutting the door of the Jeep behind her.

Mike looked around, his blond hair falling neatly back into place after he twitched his head. "David said this was the building. I would have thought it would look more…"

"Cajun?" Raleigh asked, noticing the small white letters on the door reading Bayou Life Museum.

Mike nodded in agreement.

"Maybe we should do a story on the irony of a Cajun museum being in the least Cajun building in the town. I'd feel much better about writing that article."

Mike glanced in her direction. "Think of it as fact gathering."

"You mean myth gathering?" Raleigh said following him toward the door.

David had ordered them to write a story on the rougarou for Sunday's edition. At least they'd missed today's paper with what Raleigh believed was an irresponsible piece of journalism. The town didn't need more superstitious fodder for the rumor mill. Enlightenment with actual facts might do it some good though.

"Hopefully we can give David what he wants today, but by Sunday we will have something to balance the madness."

"Hmmm," Raleigh uttered as they reached the door. "Maybe if I tell Max that everyone will be searching for the rougarou come Sunday if he doesn't give us something, he will help us out on proving it is a person behind this."

Mike held the door open for her. "Sounds like a plan. Maybe he can help us with our video camera issue."

Raleigh bit down on her lip. With their not talking about work, she hadn't mentioned it to Max. She knew she should have last night, but she hoped to keep it and trade it for information. Not a normal strategy for a healthy relationship. Perhaps if she offered it as an olive branch, they could salvage what was left of healthy.

"Welcome to our museum today." An older woman with a silvery bob asked from behind a heavily stacked desk. "What brings you in today?"

To the left of the lobby, a palmetto background with a pirogue dwarfed the small area.

"We were told we could find a Mr. Raymond Sydney here," Mike said, extending his hand to her with an easy dimpled grin to set her at ease.

"Why, of course," she said, smacking her orangey lips together. "Mr. Raymond is always here. This museum is his child."

"Yvette, did I hear visitors?" a voice called from an archway to the back. A stooped-over gentleman in a white cotton, button down shirt emerged from the back clutching wire frame glasses.

"Mr. Raymond Sydney?" Raleigh questioned, putting his age in the 80s from the wrinkles on his cheeks and wiry hair.

"Yes, ma'am," he said, extending his hand out for her to shake. "And I believe you are the granddaughter of Alcee Cheramie. She loves to brag on you."

"Yes, sir," Raleigh answered, caught off-guard.

He chuckled, raising his hand with his glasses. "She and I go back to Delilah's dance hall days. She'd always save a dance for me on her dance card, even though your Paw had her eye from the beginning. I couldn't compete."

Mike laughed, winking at her. Me'Maw, also known as Alcee Cheramie, was quite a looker back then. Paw had been proud when she chose him. They'd once seen a picture of Me'Maw dressed for a night out with her painted lips and long wool skirt. She'd said it was her Saturday dancing and Sunday church going outfit. Mike had teased her, and she'd retorted that she didn't do anything in that outfit on Saturday night that God would be ashamed of on Sunday morning.

"I will be sure to tell her that I've seen you," Raleigh said, wondering if she should ask for more detail. She loved stories about her grandparents, but this gentleman didn't know that. "I'm sure she will love to hear about it."

"We're actually here because David from the *Barbeaux Gazette* sent us," Mike said.

"Ah, yes." He nodded, rubbing his hand holding his glasses against his forehead. "The infallible rougarou. How about we go into this back area and have our discussion? It's much more comfortable."

They followed him through a corridor into a large area with displays of sugarcane farming and Cajun musical instruments and many other hidden displays behind chicken wire walls. Anything but fancy, stepping into the museum was like walking into a home of Acadians three hundred years ago.

He led them to two canary yellow sofas facing each other in the center of the room.

"The museum is lovely," Raleigh said, wondering about the choice of buildings. Had they been unable to find a different location?

"It makes do." He tilted his head as he sank onto the sofa. "The new museum should have been completed two months ago, but the holdups with the permits and the contractors have been awful."

"Oh?" Mike said. Raleigh could see his brain working, even if it was only in her imagination. No word of this had made it to their office desk, so he was wondering if there was a story here.

"Paperwork and funding falling through." He waved it off. "We haven't been real high on the totem pole of the parish. Preserving our culture isn't as important as stopping the area from flooding, and this I can understand.

Mostly." He offered a lopsided smile, saying that he understood, but he didn't like it.

Mike nodded, but from the set of his jaw, Raleigh knew he wasn't done with it. *The Barbeaux Gazette* would soon feature a story on the slow allocation of funding to this project.

"But you've come here for different reasons, haven't you?" he continued.

Raleigh nodded. "We've been asked to do a story on the rougarou, and we've been told you are our local authority."

"Ah, my qualifications may not withstand the scrutiny." He chuckled.

Raleigh and Mike waited for him to continue. Raleigh wondered what his qualifications were, but David insisted he was the authority.

"When I was six, my mom let me play outside all day long, but I had to be in when the streetlights came on. Now, I'm sure she could have just told me that I'd get my derriere paddled if I didn't make it inside by first light, but instead she told me that there was this monster that lurked in the swampy muck behind our street that roamed the streets after dark looking for kids just like me who weren't doing what they were supposed to do. For years, I was warned that the rougarou would get me after dark."

He smiled at them, letting them in on a secret.

"Then I got older and started to doubt the story, started arriving at the doorstep seconds or minutes later than the lights, but then Bobby Jean saw him in his backyard. He swore over his daddy's nudie magazines that he'd seen a creature with glowing red eyes, a human body, and a wolf's head lurking behind his barn when he'd gone outside after dark to retrieve his dump truck."

"Did he really see him?" Raleigh asked, drawn in by his voice. A true storyteller, his tone and manner drew her in, captivating her as well as anyone else he'd told a story to before.

"Who knows?" He chuckled. "But we believed him. And that's the power of the story. Everyone knows someone who has seen the rougarou, but it's never the person who is telling the story."

"So the rougarou has never been responsible for any deaths around here?"

"All stories and hearsay, never real evidence." He shook his head. "The story comes from very old French stories of the loup-garu, but I'm sure you know that the wolf isn't indigenous to our area. Consequently, many of the sightings have reported a dog or a pig. Local legend says that the rougarou is a man who has been cursed who must shed the blood of another man in order to break the curse. Some tell the tale with the curse lasting a year and a day. The story varies according to the storyteller."

Mike glanced at the recorder on the seat near him. "Have you ever heard stories of a real wolf in the area?"

He fiddled with his glasses, his coarse white eyebrows meeting in the middle. "I once knew of a man who kept one as a pet. He sent it further north after a few years though. He had to keep it registered with the state. Can't have them in Louisiana without that bit of red tape, legally of course. Around here, it's mostly coyotes and wild dogs."

"Would a coyote have attacked a person though?" Mike thought aloud.

"Well, I'm not an animal expert," Mr. Raymond said, "but usually they are afraid of humans unless they are starving."

"We've heard this," Raleigh said. "What I don't understand is why would an animal attack but not treat the body as food?"

"From the legend of the rougarou standpoint, the animal would bite to turn the person into the monster. The whole once you are bitten, you will be turned into a wolf at the next full moon legend." Mr. Raymond smiled. "As I said, I'm not an animal expert, but most animals will bite for defensive purposes. Maybe the animal felt threatened?"

"Well, that's a new angle to work," Mike said, leaning back into the sofa.

Raleigh had learned more from Mr. Raymond in ten minutes than she had from Max since the case began. Max had offered no specification on the footprint, except to say that it was a hybrid. How long did it take to analyze a footprint? Only so many animals resided in south Louisiana. Mr. Raymond probably could have identified the footprint on sight, and he felt no conflict oversharing information with her.

He reminded her of her grandparents, for more than simply the generation. They simply *knew* the area and its people and all of its stories. But they would not be around forever, and as she watched him rub his glasses against his blue cotton shirt with a distant gaze, she knew that forever was limited at his eighty plus years. All of that history and folklore would be buried with him and others like them.

Mike kept him talking about the history of the rougarou while Raleigh's mind wandered. Her Me'Maw's traiteur secrets would also pass with her. Entrusting those old traditions to Madison couldn't be the Cheramies' most intelligent idea. Halona, her trainer, must have thought about passing her ideas down to someone who would keep the traditions alive. Raleigh would need to ask.

An hour later after they'd visited the museum display on the rougarou, Mike stood against the Jeep, pondering something about the plain building.

"Care to share?" Raleigh asked, opening her door, seeing nothing of interest.

"Just an idea really." He flicked his hair to the side as he slid into his seat. "Maybe we are looking for someone with a pet that they shouldn't have, and it acted to defend them. If we knew what kind of animal prints we were dealing with, we could perhaps find the owner."

"Who else do we know down at the station who wouldn't mind slipping us that little detail?"

"Nick still works down there, but I've heard he's on desk duty after his last slip."

"Hmm," Raleigh mumbled, worrying about her old babysitting charge. She didn't like people to get in trouble over revealing information for a story. "Maybe I need to see if Cousin Joey may not mind being a spy. We can find another way to verify the information after we actually have it so we don't use his name. You know what I mean?"

He nodded, starting up the engine. "I need to meet Jeff for that planning commission story."

"Drop me off at my car," Raleigh said, rummaging around the center console for her phone. "I'm going to track him down and see if I can get him working on it."

Fifteen minutes later, Raleigh couldn't stop thinking about Mr. Raymond's story. It wasn't the story of the rougarou that bothered her, for she'd been frightened with stories of the creature when she was a child more than once. It was the fact that none of this would be remembered. The younger generation couldn't even make a roux, much less remember the culture.

On a whim, Raleigh turned down Ash Street, which led to the back woods where Halona lived. She found her sitting out on the front porch cleaning animal fur. Several flies buzzed around and an overripe stench emanated through the air.

"Didn't expect you today." She smiled, pressing a green plastic scrub brush over the deer hide. "You come to help make Ray a coat? He says he wants one like his grandfather used to have. Pity he couldn't have just found the original." She chuckled.

"I don't think I want to make any of those," Raleigh said, before thinking, and then figured she'd go in a different direction. "But how do you know how to do it? Did his grandfather write it down for you?"

She laughed. "His grandfather couldn't even spell his name. No schooling for him. I suppose I learned the same way I learn everything else. I listen."

"What will happen to this knowledge though? Will you have passed it on to someone else?"

"Ah, I hope my kids are listening," she said, pausing in her work as her thoughts deepened. "But I don't know most of the time if they really are. They would rather buy something in a store than make it. They don't really put much stock in the traditions anymore."

"Have you thought about writing everything down in case someone is interested?"

Halona shook her head. "Nah, that's not how things are done. Tradition calls for us to show and learn from the world around us. To experience our world through observation."

"But what happens if all of this dies out?"

"What has you bothered, Ms. Spirit Walker?"

"I guess I've been thinking about everything we are losing. No one seems interested in carrying on our culture. The contestants couldn't make a roux. One didn't even know what a bay leaf was. All of our shows have been Cajun themed, but none of our contestants have actually known anything without lessons."

"A changing world for certain." She sighed. "The best we can hope for is preservation. That's where you come in and hopefully there are others like you. But unfortunately, we can't stop the world from changing."

"I suppose," Raleigh said. "But I would still feel better if it was all written down."

"Then you write it down. An old woman doesn't have time for that." She grinned. "More than likely it became a tradition because our ancestors couldn't read and write. So be done with tradition and make new ones."

Raleigh laughed. "Maybe I can convince Me'Maw of this as well."

"Even the old learn new tricks," Halona said. "Have you had any more visits recently that you could write about?"

Raleigh shook her head. "I think I'm just exhausted with everything going on at work. Aryanna did show me her death, so at least I know I didn't break something inside me." Raleigh stopped, wondering if Halona understood this description. She'd broken the connection before when she'd seen death face to face, and recently she'd had enough dead bodies in her sights.

"I think you must get back to your calling. It's a good thing this television show is almost over." Her eyes were reproachful, almost as if she were channeling Me'Maw.

Calling? Curse? Who could say which?

"I'll be here Sunday for our session," Raleigh said, getting up to go. "I must get to Cousin Joey's now. I have a favor to ask of him."

"I sense trouble." She grinned as she continued to brush fur. "I'll see you on Sunday."

Raleigh left contemplating the permission she'd been granted to write the teachings down. Me'Maw may never give outright permission, but it may be time to get a record of family traditions before the family was no more.

Chapter Nineteen

After stopping at Cousin Joey's house only to learn from his wife that he was at Paw's house helping him work on a tractor, Raleigh pulled her car behind Joey's old maroon pickup truck. She shielded her eyes against the orange and pink of the setting sun behind the barn to watch the two men covered in grease spots tinkering beneath an old red and chrome tractor. Having no idea who this latest project belonged to, Raleigh could only guess that Paw was doing someone a favor.

"Me'Maw went down to the church if ya looking for her," Paw said as she approached.

"Not today," Raleigh said, stopping near the tire that came to her chin. "I was looking for Joey, and Leanne said you were here."

Paw wiped his forehead on a greasy mauve towel. "There was a time I remember when a little girl used to hang out under my tractors handing me bolts and screws."

Raleigh smiled. When she was young, Paw used to say she had an eye for things. She could find his screws in the grass where he'd lose them more often than not. She couldn't remember when she'd stopped working with him, but it was long before her exodus from the bayou. At some point she'd traded following Paw around with riding around with Mike and Katherine in the Jeep with the top off.

"What were you needing, Raleigh?" Joey asked, sitting up in the grass, wiping his hands on a dirty burgundy towel.

"A favor. Probably a bigger favor than I've ever asked before." She softened the news with a grin. The kind of look she'd give him before they'd go on some superhero adventure when they were children.

"Well, that sounds like trouble right there," Paw said, wiping down some engine part. Carburetor, maybe. Raleigh hadn't picked up much from following him around all those years. She'd been content knowing the difference between a bolt and a screw and a Phillips or a flat-headscrew driver. She'd mostly sit in the grass and wait for roly-polies to crawl by.

Joey grinned. "Doesn't Raleigh usually come with trouble?"

Raleigh pouted her lips together in pretend anger. "I can't help it if it follows me. It's not like I ask for it."

Joey laughed. "What kind of favor are we talking about?"

"I need to know the name of the animal expert or the kind of animal that left the footprints at the scene of the crime."

"Hmm," Joey said, rubbing his chin with a black stained hand. "I'm guessing Max isn't giving that information to reporter Raleigh or girlfriend Raleigh."

Paw glanced in her direction but remained quiet.

"Information hasn't been forthcoming," Raleigh grumbled, but then she felt guilty for feeling resentment towards him. She'd agreed with her silence to not talk about work, but she struggled with the resentment. "We can't seem to find the right working balance in our careers. I'm sure we will figure it out though. But I'm not asking you to sacrifice your career or anything either."

Joey nodded. "There is a gag order on the release of information."

"I know," Raleigh said. "David has us doing a story implicating the rougarou though, so we are trying to head this myth off with some actual facts. What I was thinking is that you can get the animal for us and then we can get the animal expert to confirm it. It leaves your part out of it."

"There ain't no rougarou running around here killing people," Paw said, his tone angry. "That newspaper shouldn't be getting people riled up over something like that."

"I know Paw," Raleigh said, hiding a grin by biting down on her bottom lip. "David says he's giving the people what they want. Mr. Raymond did a good job of giving us the facts though, so I don't see how anyone will believe we have a monster loose."

"I'm sure you and Mike will do the right thing," Paw said, leaning against the front tire.

Joey glanced from Paw to Raleigh and then back again. "I can tell you that the rumor around the office is that the results weren't exactly conclusive. Coyote – wolf hybrid is the best we can get him to commit to. I'm not on the case, so I didn't see the report myself, but if you talk to him, maybe he can shed some light on the matter."

"Oh, I'm sure we can get something from him if we ask the right questions." Raleigh smiled.

"That would explain your dead chickens," Paw said, bobbing his head. "They hungry at this time of year. Coyotes don't usually come near humans though."

"Maybe the wolf part?" Raleigh said, and then shrugged. "Mike and I will find out. Our theory right now is that this animal is someone's pet. A rather dangerous and untrained one, but it belongs to someone and in some way thought it was defending its owner."

Joey bobbed his head, looking much like Paw. "I like that. I may go with that theory myself and work it."

"Now that's how law enforcement and reporters should work together," Paw said, before disappearing back under the tractor.

Joey grinned and Raleigh rolled her eyes at him. Just like that, they were ten and eleven again.

"I owe you one though," Raleigh said before turning to go.

"I may collect one day," Joey called out after her.

She'd be in major trouble when her bill came due. Joey always came through for her when it mattered. Besides that, he was the only one who checked in on Paw and Me'Maw as much as she did. They'd spent many nights banging around this old house, chasing each other down the hall when they were too young to know where life would lead. Well, it had led them to chasing down bad guys like the superheroes they'd pretended to be, just not as partners in crime.

Raleigh fiddled around her house a bit, amazed at the laundry that had piled up and the dirty glasses in the sink. Having one night a week off meant many things went undone. Typically, she filled her Wednesdays with a board meeting, but lucky for her, none of them were in session tonight. Probably the Mardi Gras season kicking in and no one wanting to miss a parade or ball.

She was in the middle of scrubbing down a spill on the kitchen floor when a knock came at the front door. She leaned back on her heels and waited. Usually, anyone who knew her just walked on in, but seconds later another knock followed.

Throwing the dirty towels in the sink, she walked toward the door just as another knock sounded against the wood.

Clara stood fidgeting behind the glass, twisting a long string of hair in her fingers. "I hope you aren't busy. I was hoping to talk a moment."

"Sure," Raleigh responded, alert. It was odd for the girl to show up at her home, but Raleigh was sure it was just past experiences speaking.

Clara followed her inside, and Raleigh motioned her towards the living room. Glancing at the coffee table, Raleigh noticed the elephant statue. She'd returned it to the shelf after Aunt Clarice's visit, attempting to keep it safe from running children, but its movement acted like an announcement that she wasn't alone.

Sitting on the sofa, Clara scooted forward in her seat, grimacing uncomfortably. "I know it seems odd for me to be here. I told myself I was going to stay out of it, but then after yesterday, well, I guess I just want to be honest."

Raleigh surveyed her memories of yesterday. Nothing tragic stood out for her, so it had to be something she'd missed. "Is there something you want me to know?"

"Lauren slept with Deon," Clara blurted out, her hand reaching out to cover her mouth, her eyes widening.

"Really?" Raleigh asked, wondering if Deon had made it through all the female contestants. "How do you know?"

"It was so long ago," Clara said, casting her eyes downward. "In high school, Deon wasn't always nice to the girls. He used to tell me that he thought most of them were stupid. I guess he wasn't really a nice guy, but to me, he was still that big brother type who looked out for me." She glanced up at Raleigh and then back down at her folded hands in her lap.

"So this happened in high school?"

Clara nodded. "Lauren graduated with me, so she was several years behind Deon. She chased him for a few months before they had a thing for a few weeks in the summer. Lauren thought that he was going to be her boyfriend senior year."

"I'm guessing Deon didn't see it that way." Raleigh could imagine how this went. Deon and Sheri would have been over by this time, if Raleigh had figured the timing right in her head.

"Deon didn't really do relationships at that time, but Lauren's heart broke, like many others. It wasn't a great time for him."

"So why do you think this is important?"

"Well," Clara said, biting down on her bottom lip. "I saw Deon's picture. He asked me about it." She closed her eyes, and Raleigh had a feeling he'd asked because he'd thought she'd sent it.

"What was Deon's picture of?"

"A party from that time. A party where he'd stripped naked with a few others." She blushed. "Lauren had taken that picture that night. I remembered and I told Deon, but he was killed right after."

"Why haven't you told the police?"

"It's just a picture. I'm sure she didn't do anything to Deon," Clara rushed out, "but you were asking about the pictures, and I thought about that. And Patrick thinks Kimberly sent his. Something about she took the picture in high school. It's all so confusing. It's like it's not one person."

Raleigh nodded. Clara had stated the big issue with the pictures. One person having all these secret pictures felt impossible. A better explanation would be multiple culprits. But how was that logical when the contestants didn't get along? The pictures might not even have anything to do with Deon and Aryanna's death. If Raleigh could identify the animal, however, she could connect that animal to an owner, and that owner may be responsible for the pictures. She had to make this all make sense some kind of way.

"I will look into it, Clara," Raleigh said, giving the insecure girl a smile. "I'm sure Mike and I will figure out what is going on."

Clara stood, unsure of her next move. "I'm so sorry for coming over like this, but I just couldn't stop thinking about it after yesterday."

"Now you can put your mind on the season finale of the show. It's almost here. Any ideas for a final match?"

"Oh, I don't think anyone on this show wants me," Clara said, smiling wistfully. "Just between you and me, I always thought that Deon was going to grow up and figure out he wanted his childhood best friend. It's not the same without him."

Tears filled her eyes, but they did not spill over.

Raleigh reached out and squeezed her hand. "I'm sure we will figure out what happened to him, but I know he would want you to be happy."

Clara smiled. "You would think so, but you never know with him."

Raleigh walked the girl to the door, as she seemed unsure of how to do it on her own. Unfortunately, this television show may have destroyed the small amount of confidence the girl had.

After she'd gone, Raleigh couldn't get her mind to settle. Drawing a flow chart on a notepad, she mapped out the clues she had so far about these pictures and tried to find connections. She didn't know these contestants well enough to make assumptions. But at least she had a direction to go in. Lauren and Patrick remained the top people of interest, evidence-wise that is. Raleigh figured the truth would not be easy as it being the person who had taken the pictures.

Later that night, she sat up in bed, unsure what had awoken her. Disconcerted, she didn't know if she'd been dreaming or she'd heard something downstairs, but her heart raced as if something had happened. She racked her thoughts, trying to recall if she'd had an encounter with the dying while she slept, but all she could remember was a dress. A sequined number that she'd never own because she'd never have an occasion that required something that fancy.

Feeling the need to clear her head, she threw off the comforter and made her way downstairs for something cold. Perhaps that Twix bar she'd hidden in the fridge last week when she thought she'd attempt limiting the candy. Nothing like chocolate to burst all those residual negative vibes into smithereens. And that was why she'd never give up Twix, no matter how grown up she may get.

Coming off the landing of the staircase, she heard the laugh as clear as if she'd left the television on. She froze, recognition sinking through her.

Gritting her teeth together, she forced herself to walk toward the living room. Within its alabaster walls, an eclectic mixture of filmy spirits hovered in her living room. In the middle of it all, Aunt Clarice stood with a thin Virginia Slim dangling from her ruby red lips, flashing long, painted fingernails.

Catching the eye of the twentyish Aunt Clarice, the woman tipped her short bob in Raleigh's direction.

Raleigh swallowed against the dryness in her throat, willing her pulse to slow. Halona had advised her not to be afraid, but fear hammered through her with every throbbing heartbeat in her ear.

Raleigh opened her mouth, hoping words would come. Nothing.

The others, Aunt Clarice's guests Raleigh imagined, turned in her direction. One man with slicked back hair and a thin mustache even waved.

Raleigh's heart lurched forward, and she felt the overwhelming need to take a deep breath. Rushing toward the door, she unbolted it and stepped onto the front porch. The cool air hit her like a solid wall and jabbed at her flesh.

Coward. Raleigh muttered to herself bitterly. She was traiteur to the dead, dammit. Why couldn't she handle a few ghosts shimmering in her living room?

The dying were supposed to go, that's why. They showed her their last moments and let her be. Ghosts equaled a game changer. They meant death didn't leave her. She'd rather stick to the connections, thank you very much. Not that anyone in charge of this ability ever listened.

Headlights from the street blinded her, so she eased back into the doorframe so no one would see her standing in her own doorway in the middle of the night. The vehicle pulled up into Ms. Margaret's old house,

Amber's house now, she supposed. Raleigh pushed herself further into the door as she recognized Mike's Jeep.

Amber slid out of the Jeep, a long skirt fluttering in the breeze. Mike bounded out after her and walked her to the door. A strong, many armed oak tree blocked her view in seeing if there was a good night kiss, but as soon as Raleigh noticed Mike walking back to the Jeep, she ducked back inside so that he wouldn't see her if he glanced in her direction.

Questions raced through Raleigh's mind. When had that happened? Was that a first date or further down the list? Why hadn't he mentioned it to her?

Disappointment overwhelmed her. She wasn't sure if that disappointment was for her best friend dating someone without confiding in her or that he'd moved on while she stood still trying to figure out her own love life.

Too much change at one time for her. A person should have some adjustment period.

As she walked past the living room on her way to the kitchen, she noticed the party had ended. Maybe the chocolate would hold more than comfort tonight. Some answers instead of more questions would be great right about now.

Chapter Twenty

The bustle in the kitchen drowned out any chance at thought. Much planning had gone into what would happen upstairs during tonight's contest, but not enough consideration into the size of this kitchen versus the number of contestants roaming about trying to get their trays ready for the competition.

"Someone stole my last few bowls," Tiffany called out.

"There's extra on this rack over here," Adam called out, adding garnishes to his eggplant concoction.

With only minutes to go, Raleigh couldn't keep track of what dish belonged to whom, but the heat rising in this kitchen and the anxiety crawling through her made her wish she'd worn something a little thinner in the fabric department. As show host, Madison had scored posh upstairs duties while she had to contend with lost spoons, broken dishes, and overdone sauces. At least she felt gratitude at not being on dishwashing duty.

Madison counted Joshua and Benjamin's dishes in their trays as they filed past her. Each tray contained enough dishes for the judges as well as the sponsors' table. The contestants were to line up and make a grand entrance, introducing their dishes and receiving comments from the sponsors. Several servers would place samplings on the tables of the guests as the cameras filmed the judging. In some cases, Raleigh thought they should have insisted on a sympathy card for the questionable edibility of the dishes.

Rather unsteadily, Helena approached with small bowls rattling against each other. Raleigh smiled reassuringly, hoping for the best walking up the stairs. Frank followed, his small salad-size plates overlapping the sides of the serving tray.

Raleigh counted all thirteen servings in their trays and allowed them out the door. Winter glanced her way and swung her tray upwards like a pro. As the last of the appetizer dishes, her homemade drop biscuits smelled divine as she sauntered pass. Full of surprises, Winter had even whipped up a special butter from her great grandmother's recipe collection.

"Entrées line up in two minutes," Raleigh called out, watching Lauren stare into her pot, eyebrows furrowed.

The volume peaked as movement increased. Raleigh stepped away from her door guarding duty and approached Lauren's area.

"Something wrong?" Raleigh asked, noticing the bowls already lined with rice.

"Maybe," Lauren said, biting down on her bottom lip. "It doesn't really look like my mama's gumbo."

"I'm sure it will be fine," Raleigh said, hoping that no one received food poisoning tonight with all these inexperienced people serving food. "Every mama has a different way to cook a gumbo down here. No two are alike."

"I guess you're right," Lauren said, pulling the ladle through the mixture.

"So I wanted to ask you about something someone told me," Raleigh began, noticing the thickness of the mixture she spooned into the cup. "I've heard there was something between you and Deon in high school."

Lauren glanced her way. "Not at all."

"This person seemed real certain," Raleigh commented, noticing the twitching of her eyes as she ladled more gumbo into the bowl.

"Look," Lauren said, pausing above the bowl. "Whatever you heard, I'm sure it is none of your business."

"Well," Raleigh said, swallowing, "it's just that the blackmail picture of Deon was from that time and reportedly taken by you."

Lauren waved the ladle in her direction. "And so what does that mean? That I killed him? As if. I've studied the law, remember? I'm going to refrain from answering these questions."

"I'll let it go for now," Raleigh said, noticing the kitchen had quieted to hear their conversation. "But I'm real interested in who's sending those pictures, and I'm not going to stop looking for that person."

"Good luck," Lauren snapped. "I'd like to know myself."

"Showtime," Raleigh called out to the kitchen. "Dish count at the door for entrées. Desserts up in five."

Raleigh walked back to her position at the door, watching the contestants hurry to grab trays. Patrick lingered over Lauren a moment before grabbing his tray. A frown twisted at his lips and a faraway glaze overtook his eyes, almost as if he were remembering something.

Interesting. Raleigh may need to ask him about this later. She needed to ask him about his involvement anyway, being he was suspect number two.

By miracle, Raleigh managed to get everyone up the stairs, and when she reported upstairs to her coordinating duties, only seven contestants had completed the judging round. Raleigh walked to the back to check on the cameras.

Madison stood at the front with the other cameraman. She'd done a bang-up job with her makeup, leaving not a trace of a black eye for the viewing public. Her bright pink blouse complimented her perfectly layered raven hair, and her poise left nothing to question who was in charge.

At the judge's table between a chef and the owner of Lebasque's restaurant, Austin Lebasque, Jeffery Zedeaux sat with his hands triangled beneath his chin. If Raleigh wouldn't know Madison so well, she wouldn't have noticed the slide of her eyes over him every time she surveyed the audience.

Jeffery Zedeaux remained an off-limit topic. Raleigh suspected that Jeffery was Mason's father, a fact that Jeffery had not been informed of in any of the six years Mason had existed. Recently, Jeffery had shown a reinterest in Madison. Even though Madison had been close-mouthed, rumor spread that she'd turned him down and his pride had suffered. Knowing Jeffery the way that Raleigh did from similar experiences, he was probably looking for a way to get back at Madison for the slight. No matter how stoic Madison stood against gossip of her personal life, she had to feel threatened where Mason was concerned.

Raleigh moved around a table, walking around the servers who stood at carts, waiting to deliver the next taste-testing dish. Then, Patrick approached the judges with his tray.

Madison did her introduction of his contestant bio while he placed a saucer in front of each judge. After he emptied his tray between the judges' table and the sponsors' table, he approached Madison, where she asked him questions to the delight of the audience.

"So, are you looking for a woman who cooks, or will you be the cook of the relationship?" Madison asked, smiling with perfect gleaming white teeth.

Patrick grinned, his right dimple showing. "I'd like us to work together in the kitchen. Hotter that way."

An *ooh* went through the audience along with several chuckles. Patrick's grin deepened. The other contestants sitting at their long table clapped, but Winter rolled her eyes after a limp clap. Obviously, she wasn't a Patrick fan. She'd had her fun dancing with him, but pretty boys only held so much appeal.

Madison nodded to Patrick, and he returned to the contestant table. Kimberly smiled and pointed to several dishes on the table, and Patrick nodded as she scanned the audience, looking bored. Other contestants followed with taste-testing, each giving the judges a moment to fill out the scorecard and answering Madison's light-hearted questions. Raleigh walked around the tables, overhearing the comments of the guests, pointing Devin, tonight's college intern camera guy, to perfect shots. Frank's eggplant with seafood sauce managed to hold the most audience approval, but Patrick's ettouffee garnered some praise as well. Lauren's gumbo went untouched by most tables, while Winter's biscuits were a big hit and Kimberly's bread pudding received rave reviews.

Once each contestant took a turn and the judges were conferring amongst themselves, Raleigh sent Devin to video the judges since Francois had chosen this moment to have a conversation with a few people at table four. Helping Madison inform the tables to deposit their voting ballots in the large crystal bowl centerpieces placed in the middle of the table especially for the occasion, Raleigh kept her eyes on the contestants as they conversed and became restless.

When Austin Lebasque motioned for Madison, Raleigh nodded to the servers, who began collecting the audience's ballots from the vases.

"Ladies and Gentleman," Madison spoke from the front of the room. "We will begin to announce the winners of this week's challenge on *Barbeaux Hearts*. The winners will be able to choose their partners for the Mardi Gras ball, and you will have the honor of hearing their choice."

Raleigh watched as the servers handed David the ballots. David's job was to feed them through a machine that the town hall had lent them for the night. It would tally the votes, so the audience's choice could be announced right after the judge's choice."

Making her way to the front of the room, Raleigh motioned for Devin to move back. Francois would get the close up shots of the announcement, but Devin would need to get the reaction of the crowd, and he'd been distracted by someone in the front of the room.

As Madison waited for everyone to take their places and quiet, Max entered the room and walked to the back of the room to stand near the wall. His blue dress shirt managed only one crease, but he'd added a tie to make up for it. Raleigh smiled at him as his eyes met hers, but she continued moving Devin into the best vantage point.

Madison commanded the room. "Tonight's female contestant winner is Winter with her grandmother's mouth-watering drop biscuits," Madison said, turning towards a shocked Winter.

Winter stood up to face the judge's table, her expression not under control yet.

Austin Lebasque smiled at her. "You and I must talk, Ms. Winter. I would really like that recipe."

Winter smiled, regaining her composure. "Well, my grandmother said I was to keep it in the family, so we can see what kind of deal you want to work out."

The crowd laughed.

Madison looked into the camera. "Mr. Lebasque isn't a contestant, Winter. At least not yet." Madison laughed, and Mr. Lebasque joined in.

Raleigh caught Winter's wink in Lebasque's direction, and he nodded in answer. One had to admire her confidence.

Madison continued. "Tonight's male contestant winner is Frank with his divine eggplant in a white seafood sauce."

Frank stood, his cheeks reddening as the audience clapped for him.

"Near perfection, Frank," Jeffery Zedeaux said, leaning back in his chair.

"Thank you, sir," Frank said, nodding. "I've always enjoyed cooking."

"Our winners will now designate their chosen partners for our ball," Madison said, waving to the table of contestants.

"Well, hell," Winter said, tilting her head for the camera. "I was planning on going with Frank here."

Madison hesitated for a moment, her eyes flickering over the room as faces waited expectantly. "Well, if Frank accepts, he can choose to ask you as well."

Frank looked at Winter, and Raleigh could see something pass between them, although she had no idea what it was. If Raleigh had to guess, Winter knew that Frank was gay. Anything sexual in nature was Winter's business. Just whom Winter did this favor for—herself or Frank—remained questionable.

"Who would tell that gorgeous woman no?" Frank asked grinning.

"Well, that settles it," Madison said, her smile returning. "Our winners of the competition are our first match for the ball. Now we will have the audience's choice winners."

David crossed up to the front and handed her a slip of paper and then ducked out the camera angle.

"Our male audience's choice winner is Patrick with his crawfish étouffée."

A clap went through the audience as Patrick stood up. He waved to everyone in thanks.

"And our female audience's choice winner is Kimberly with her white chocolate bread pudding."

Kimberly stood and acted incredibly surprised with an overdramatized 'who me?' to the audience.

Madison turned to the camera. "It is time to announce your choices for a partner to the ball."

Kimberly glanced across the table, her eyes falling on Adam and Helena sitting side by side. "I choose Adam."

Helena's face scowled at her from Adam's side. As far as Raleigh could tell, Adam and Helena had been a couple for the last few shows. The fact that Helena had been involved with Deon hadn't been obvious with these two connecting during taping. From Helena's glare now, she'd moved on from those tears over Deon already. Kimberly smiled at Helena and tipped her head. This felt like retaliation to Raleigh.

"I choose Clara." Patrick announced.

All of the contestants went from staring at Helena and Kimberly to gawking at Patrick. Clara's mouth fell open and she remained seated until Tiffany nudged her arm to stand.

"There you have it folks," Madison said, her smile not quite as full. Patrick's announcement had shaken her as well. Clara skirted past attention on the sidelines; she was never anyone's choice. "These are our top three couples for the ball. The remaining contestants…"

"This is bullshit," Lauren shouted, standing up.

The audience gasped.

Lauren continued. "Patrick, we discussed this. And Frank, what the hell was that?"

Patrick and Frank looked at each other. Both of them looked guilty and surprised at the same time, if that was possible.

"Lauren, you need to sit down." Madison said, something bordering on rage edging in her voice. Raleigh recognized it from the many sister arguments.

"I am supposed to be in the top three couples. I made deals… I didn't come on this show to whine and complain like all of these losers. Ugh."

Swinging her arm in front of her, she collided with the various bowls and saucers on a serving tray and sent them flying in both directions towards the other contestants. Then she pulled herself up right, straightened her skirt, and walked around the table and strolled out the archway leading downstairs.

"Sorry, folks," Madison said, her eyes cold. "Finding love brings out many emotions. Let's try this again."

Raleigh ran out after Lauren. She'd already reached the bottom of the staircase.

"Lauren, what is wrong with you? Have you lost your mind?"

"Stay away from me," Lauren cried out. "I'm a freaking lawyer. I can take care of whatever you come after me with. I haven't done anything illegal."

She quickened her pace and disappeared into the first floor, probably out the front door, which was only ten feet from the staircase.

Raleigh stood on the third riser. She wasn't in the best shape to be chasing after someone in high-heeled boots. Frank and Patrick would need to answer for what Lauren had said, and she wasn't going to take an "I don't know" as an answer.

"You couldn't stop her?" Max asked, standing at the foot of the stairs.

Raleigh glanced up at him and then back down where Lauren had disappeared. "No, she's usually more level-headed than this."

Max gave her a long look. Raleigh imagined he was thinking that no one remained level-headed on this show.

A scratching panic smacked Raleigh in her forehead, and she gripped her temple against the strange feeling. She recognized the jarring pain in the hollow space the dead usually reached, but unlike the smooth awareness of how the dying typically arrived, this clawing anxiety raced through not just her head, but down her arm and chest as well.

With one hand, she braced herself against the wall, but then she remembered she was standing on stairs, and she eased herself to a sitting position on the riser. Rolling down the stairs would not be the way she wanted to go.

"Are you okay?" Max asked from afar.

Raleigh allowed herself to go to the dying, scared but needing to get this feeling gone quickly.

When the blackness dissolved, something scratched against her face. That something filled her face and part of her mouth. She spit it out, just as a jarring pain shot through her leg, ripping into every nerve. On instinct she yanked at her leg, but something tugged back, growling.

With every instinct alert, she tried to move her head to see, but whoever's body she was in was sluggish, his thoughts incoherent. Alcohol. She smelled it now on the collar, on her own breath, in the hair.

She needed a marker. A place. It was her, the body's, only hope.

Straining against the fire shooting through her leg, she lifted her head, but darkness and grass and shadows in the distance blurred before her. She blinked a few times and then squinted, feeling the time ticking each second that she could save this person.

An old beat up, dilapidated outhouse type building came into blurred focus. She recalled seeing it before. Where?

She needed to hurry.

Another jolting pain shot through her big as sharp teeth sink down into her calf. A scream escaped the lips, a deep animalistic sound.

Her last thought before the darkness enveloped her again was that the animal was massive.

Nauseousness swirled through her as the stairway of Lebasque's focused before her. Max's squatted down beside her, cellphone in hand.

"What's going on?"

The old house building, all those trees, no lights.

"Back Bayou," Raleigh swallowed against the taste of grass in her mouth. "We need to get there now. An attack."

Raleigh gulped as her heart lurched at the idea that it would be too late.

Max pressed something on his phone and it answered quickly. "Suzy, this is Max Pyles. What deputy do we have in the Back Bayou area?"

A brief silence greeted him before a high-pitched voice could be head through the phone even to where Raleigh sat. "Joshua is patrolling along that stretch tonight. Is something going on?"

"Tell him to get to Back Bayou ASAP." Max looked to Raleigh.

"The old out house in the front."

He repeated it into the phone, and they could hear the echo of the orders going on the wire.

"I will be there shortly," Max said before hanging up.

Raleigh stood shakily but quickly regained her strength. "How long do you think it will take us to get there?"

"We?" Max said, taking a few steps down. "There's no we. You are going to stay here and finish up the event. I will check it out."

"I need to go," Raleigh said.

Max interrupted. "No, you did your part. Now I'm going to do mine. I will call you with news."

He bounded down the stairs two at a time.

Raleigh needed to say something. Anything to cover the disappointment and anger she felt.

"This isn't how we work together," she called out, feeling the lameness of the statement.

Max looked back. "This is exactly how we can work together, Raleigh."

He continued out the door, leaving her on the staircase still feeling a panic filling the hollowness in her head.

Chapter Twenty-One

The doctors and nurses laughed good-naturedly over some blind date that had gone horribly wrong for the pretty redhead behind the desk. Aside from a beeping machine, the emergency room was having a quiet morning in terms of patients.

Raleigh peeked at Mike who at the moment flirted with a petite brunette who appeared to be right out of high school. The two stood near Luther Foret's closed door, and Mike's intentions were to get her to open it for them.

A moment later, Mike motioned to her to join him. The nurse entered his room and Mike followed. Raleigh slid in right after, attracting no attention from the doctors gossiping around the desk.

Luther Foret's head was elevated against a pillow and his eyes were closed. His bandaged legs stuck out from the white blanket.

"Mr. Foret," the brunette spoke loudly, "these people are from the *Barbeaux Gazette*. They are here to make you a celebrity."

He coughed, his eyes fluttering half way open. "Celebrity? I'm gonna be as famous as dos duck people on T.V. I'm gonna choot me a monster."

The brunette laughed as she checked his chest. "Are you feeling any pain? Would you like to up your pain meds?"

Mr. Foret waved his arm wildly. "I told you I don't want that garbage. Makes you cagou."

Mike stepped near the railing of the hospital bed. "Mr. Foret, we hoped you could tell us about what happened last night?"

His head inched over until his eyes could see them. "I uh… walk that stretch every night. You know, a few beers at Doug's, then I sleep it off. No harm done. It sho is dark though. Didn't see it coming until it clear done knock me over."

"Were you able to see what kind of animal it was?" Raleigh asked, noticing a smaller bandage on his left forearm. It must have happened after she'd left him.

"Big," he said, his eyes widening. "Hair like rough wires. But it was those red eyes, man. Those eyes gonna haunt me forever."

"So you couldn't tell if it were a coyote or a wolf or just a wild dog?" Mike asked.

"Nah, man." Mr. Foret closed his eyes. "I was face down. They say I passed out."

"Did you see a person anywhere near the animal?" Raleigh asked.

"You'd be cagou to try and get near this thing. I thought I was a goner until ol' man Richard's son showed up."

The door swung open, and Raleigh turned to see Max stroll through.

"Mr. Luther, you have guests this morning?" Max asked, looking them all over as he looped his thumbs through his belt loops.

"Gonna be a celebrity, Mr. Detective Man. Gonna get my fifteen minutes of fame."

"Is that right?" Max asked, walking around to the foot of the bed.

"He certainly is tough, refusing his pain meds." The nurse laughed nervously.

"I need to go over your statement this morning, if you are done with your red carpet appearance."

"I think we are done here," Mike said, brushing Raleigh's arm.

Raleigh studied Max who stood coolly wearing a tournament-winning poker face. He wasn't going to give her anything, so she followed Mike out the door.

When they'd made it safely through the large swinging doors leading to the waiting room of the emergency room, Mike whistled.

"So what exactly did Max tell you this morning?"

Raleigh rubbed the scar on her wrist. In some ways, cutting duct tape with broken glass had been less painful than the roller coaster of a relationship.

"He told me that Mr. Foret had been brought into the emergency room for his bite wounds, and he'd speak to him this morning and let me know how he was doing."

Mike chuckled as they exited the sliding doors. "So you didn't tell him we were coming speak to him?"

"Of course not," Raleigh said. "Last night he told me my job was done."

Mike remained quiet as they walked to the Jeep, and then left the parking lot, heading back toward the station.

"I didn't see you there last night." Raleigh said finally.

Mike stared ahead. "I took the night off. David covered instead."

"Did you have another date with Amber?" Raleigh said, attempting to sound casual.

Mike glanced over quickly and then back at the road. "Did she mention our date to you?"

Raleigh shook her head. "Let's just say I needed a break from my house the other night when Aunt Clarice decided to have a party in my living room. I saw you bring her home. I wasn't spying, I promise. My house felt a little claustrophobic."

"Aunt Clarice?" Mike asked. "As in former owner of your house Clarice?"

"Oh yeah," Raleigh said. "As if life isn't crazy enough, I now have a ghost showing up in the middle of the night."

"But a ghost, Ree," Mike said, running his hand through his hair before returning it to the steering wheel.

"Halona says my abilities are growing." Raleigh grimaced. "We both know how I like change."

Mike chuckled. "I'm going to think twice before I sleep on that couch again."

"I haven't decided if I'm willing to have a roommate yet," Raleigh grumbled, noticing he'd avoided the Amber question. The implications of that bothered her. Why wasn't he sharing? They didn't usually keep things from each other.

Pulling into the station, Raleigh noticed the few vehicles in the parking area. Madison had to finish the episode's editing before it aired at seven tonight, but some of the contestants had been enlisted to do a "chat" instead of interviews this week. Even though Raleigh wasn't on host duty today, she wanted to speak to Frank and Patrick about Lauren's outburst.

"What's on the agenda today?" Mike asked, shutting off the engine.

Raleigh grabbed her backpack and opened the door. "Editorial meeting with Madison, and then I have to get the announcements together for the editor."

Mike glanced as his watch. "Think I'm going to work on that bridge story. If I get that done, I can begin chasing a story on funding the museum."

Raleigh grinned. She'd predicted that one.

Inside the studio, the offices lay empty on Sunday as usual. Raleigh flipped the light switch, unwilling with recent events to walk through the darkened hallways blinded to anyone—or anything—hidden in the darkness. Not that an animal could get into the building – at least that she knew about—but two people had died here the last two weekends, and she didn't want to be next.

Mike headed toward their cubicle in the *Barbeaux Gazette* area, and Raleigh veered toward Studio C where the "chat" should be finishing up.

Inside, Madison stood behind the camera, clipboard firmly gripped in one arm against her chest. She looked back at Raleigh as she entered and then waved her free hand in the air.

Winter looked into the camera. "Who will find love and dance the night away at the ball? Stay tuned for the crowning of Barbeaux's Sweethearts."

"Cut," Madison called out. "Great work, guys."

Patrick stood and stretched, stepping away from the semicircle of chairs. Six of the contestants had gathered to discuss their ideas for perfect matches. After the last three weeks of interviews had been particularly nasty, Madison's solution offered an alternative and a better way to fill that five-minute segment.

Frank walked over to Raleigh, smiling.

"Well, hello, Ms. Raleigh," Frank said. "Is that man doing alright? Madison said you went to check on him this morning, and she was sure you didn't mean to leave her hanging." He gave her a wink.

Raleigh nodded, glancing over at Madison. Typical. "He's all bandaged and ready to go hunting."

Frank laughed. "Oh, I'd be staying myself in a building somewhere safe if I were him."

Raleigh noticed Helena had replaced Lauren on the panel. After last night's tantrum, Raleigh wondered whose decision that had been.

"Me too, Frank," Raleigh said, knowing that wasn't true. She seemed to let herself go straight into the middle of trouble. "So, I wondered what Lauren was talking about last night."

Patrick stopped as he was walking past. He glanced at Frank. "Oh, Lauren just thought I'd choose her. She wants to be in the top, you know? So she offered to help me win if I'd help her. She was just angry."

"And that's all it was?" Raleigh asked, looking to Frank.

Frank shrugged. "She told me I would only win if I picked her, since, you know, I'm gay. She said she'd help me. I never agreed though."

Patrick looked back at Helena. "I can't wait until this is all over." He offered Raleigh a small grin, and then walked away.

Frank leaned in. "Don't mind him. Gossip is there's a triangle between him, Helena, and Kimberly, and it's not going to end well."

Raleigh nodded. Madison should have called the show *Broken Hearts*. It may have been a more accurate title.

Madison approached. "We have editorial in five, and Nolan wants to see the cut in two hours. He's getting nervous."

"That's unusual," Raleigh responded, watching Madison bite down on her bottom lip. The owner of the station never watched the taping before it aired.

"I know. Something's up."

"Let's get it done, and it will all work out."

Madison nodded as she followed Raleigh into the editing room.

Chapter Twenty-Two

The building was a maze of white clinical walls and burnt orange doors. Besides an occasional water fountain, each hall appeared identical. Mike disappeared into the next corner hallway, looking at the room numbers on the doors.

"It's room 157, right?" Raleigh said, searching the small black plaques next to the doors.

"It's this one," Mike called from the corner of the university science building.

They'd driven the thirty-five minutes to search for the animal expert, but neither of them had attended school at the local parish university, both preferring to get away from Barbeaux after the disastrous events of senior year. The search for Frederick Byce's office had taken several minutes of wandering without direction in an unfamiliar place, but if either of them wished to return to school to study science, they could now find any classroom in the building.

Mike rapped on the door, and a muffled "come in" came from behind the door.

They entered a small messy office space with a young man, no older than twenty, sitting behind a computer. Several framed certificates hung on two of the walls indicating that perhaps he had expertise in something.

"Frederick Byce?" Mike asked, skeptically.

"Hold on a minute," the scruffy-haired gentleman said, pressing a few keys and picking up an old, beige desk phone at the same time.

While he mumbled a few inaudible words into the phone, Raleigh checked out the various animal prints hanging on the walls as well as the bulging bookcases along the far wall. Books overflowed into stacks on the floor, and they all looked to be about biology, zoology, countless species of animals, and anything science related. So this is what it meant to be an expert. As a journalist, she'd call herself an acquirer of small amounts of knowledge with little depth. Certainly no expert on anything, not even her traiteur to the dead abilities yet, for every time she felt she came to grips with it, something changed. Aunt Clarice had proven that with her unwelcome visits.

"Professor Byce will see you now," the young man said, returning the phone to its base, not glancing up from the computer screen. "He has about twenty-five minutes before his next class begins."

Mike and Raleigh shared a look as the other door within the room opened. It was a relief that he wasn't the expert; at least she wasn't falling that far behind. Raleigh followed Mike inside, smiling briefly at the young man behind the computer screen. His gaze slid over her back to the screen. He certainly belonged to her sister's generation, society expectations be damned.

A salt and pepper gentleman with thick, heavy black glasses was returning to his overly burdened desk. Stacks of paper protruded from every inch of space where they'd exceeded the area and moved to stacks on the floor near the corner of the desk as well as against the back wall. In this room as well, books weighed down bookshelves.

"So from your call, I assume you are looking for information about our furry foe?" His words were slow, gravelly. Raleigh could imagine the trouble of not falling asleep in his class.

Mike slid into an empty blue vinyl chair. "Yes, we are hoping for confirmation on the type of animal prints at the scene."

"Ah, see," he said, leaning back in his chair, "that information isn't to be released just yet."

"What we have been told," Raleigh said, jumping in. "is that the animal is some kind of hybrid between a coyote and perhaps a wolf. We aren't real sure how that shows up in a footprint though?"

"This is why I hate to try and explain science to the layperson," he said, shaking his head and clenching his thin lips together. "Science is not here to give you the answer you wish to hear. One can't dismiss the answer as a whole and only use the 2 percent that backs your hypothesis."

His rant came with spittle and banging on the arms of his rollout chair. He appeared to be working his way into an even larger diatribe on an obviously sore subject. Maybe falling asleep in his class didn't happen if the students had learned to work him up with questions.

"So," Mike said, heading it off, "this is not correct? It is not a hybrid?"

He refocused on them. "One can't prove that based on a single canine print. I mean, a trail of them, maybe, but one footprint is not enough to go on."

"So it is canine?" Raleigh asked. "Like a dog?"

"Not likely, but possibly," he said, his forehead wrinkling together. "Here, I'll show you."

He rummaged in the clutter of a pile to his left, and after a few moments of fiddling with a stack that Raleigh thought would topple over, he pulled a manila folder out and splayed it open on top of the other documents on his desk.

"This here," he said, pointing to three sets of prints, "are the general prints of a coyote, dog, and wolf." Raleigh glanced over them, not seeing much distinction between the three. "This here is our predator's footprint."

Mike leaned in closer, and Raleigh leaned over his head to get a better view of the print. She went back and forth between the two pictures, and Raleigh couldn't decide which one it looked more like, but it clearly wasn't a perfect match for any of the three animals.

"Well, the coyote's print is pretty small here, and the crime scene print is about the size of this dog's," Mike said, pointing to the picture of all three.

"Yes," Professor Byce said, "but this canine print right here is a fairly large dog. A small dog would have a similar size footprint to this coyote. And as you can see, they are very close in the shape of the pads and placement. The pads of a wolf will point directly forward, while a dog will splay outward."

"I can't tell if these are splaying outward," Raleigh said, turning her head to see it at a different angle and see if she noticed a difference.

"Yes, well that doesn't mean that it isn't a wolf." the professor sighed. "A wolf does not reach maturity until three years, so the age of the animal would also matter in footprint identification. Also, if we had more than one print, placement could be determined. Wolves and coyotes use direct registration when they walk, but a chaotic wandering pattern would indicate a dog."

"So I'm taking that your conclusion was that there wasn't enough evidence to make a conclusion?" Mike asked, studying the crime scene photo intently.

He nodded. "I believe the animal is a hybrid, but between what animals? I can't say until I have more data."

"Why do you say hybrid?" Raleigh asked, wondering what he saw that she didn't see in the impression in the dirt.

"Size, the deep claw marks, the size of the pads," he rambled on.

"If the police were to find the animal, would you be able to match the footprint?" Mike asked.

"Certainly," he said, smiling smugly. "This is a very distinct print. You know, many people decide they want to have wolf hybrids as pets, but as a wolf approaches three years old, maturity sets in as well as their instincts. They will no longer take orders from a master. They essentially become their own master and this creates issues for the people around them. A canine will typically take orders forever because they never reach the same maturity as a wolf."

"So you believe it is a wolf hybrid?" Raleigh asked.

"Likely," he said, "but I don't want to be quoted on that because I want more evidence before I speak with any certainty."

"Would the human owner be in danger?" Raleigh asked, her mind tugging at the beginning of an idea.

"Hmm?" the professor asked, staring at her.

"You said the owner of a wolf hybrid would lose ability to control the animal at about three years. Would that person be in danger, or would it just be others that are unfamiliar to the animal?" Raleigh asked.

"Well," the professor said drawing in a breath. "I'd say yes. An animal like that is unpredictable, but not for certain, you know? It would depend on the bond the animal had with the owner."

In her final moments, Aryanna had felt someone else present. Had that person been in danger too?

Mike stood up and stretched out his hand. "We won't take any more of your time. Thank you for speaking to us. If we have anymore questions, we will be in touch."

He leaned forward and shook his hand and then delved back into sorting through files on his desk, which appeared to Raleigh to be futile. At least Mike's mess consisted only of sticky notes. She may stop giving him a difficult time after seeing this.

After they found their way out of the maze of a building, Raleigh and Mike settled in for the drive home.

"So what was your line of thinking back there?" Mike asked.

"Maybe we are looking for someone who had a pet, but it's gone missing. I mean, how much control does this person really have over this animal?"

Mike nodded, focusing on the road. "Meaning is the person telling the animal what to do, or is the animal doing it on its own?"

Raleigh nodded. "But we still don't have anything concrete to offer in a story that the animal is not the rougarou. Of course that's because the rougarou hasn't offered its footprints for the record."

Mike tapped a beat on the steering wheel. "What other evidence was at the scene? Something had to be available there. Fingerprints. Fibers. Something like all those crime show people always find that cracks the case. I mean even Barbeaux Bayou's finest must have some of that technology."

"If we only had someone on the inside to give us that information," Raleigh grumbled, feeling resentful about Max putting her off. Every time she thought back to last night, a sharp stab went through her. She should expect it by now, but the realization that it was he that wanted her out of his work, not the sheriff, had come like a punch to the abdomen.

"Well," Mike grinned, "I can start dating a detective and we can get some information that way."

Raleigh glared at him. "Funny."

"Just teasing. Detectives have to follow too many rules."

Raleigh recalled the visual of him dropping Amber off, wondering if she should casually mention it again. Knowing Mike though, it would be a once and done. He typically dated women only once or twice, nothing serious. If she mentioned it, he'd wonder why. And she didn't know why it bothered her herself.

"Every time I think we've figured it out," Raleigh sighed, "we haven't. First, it's the sheriff, but now it's Max himself."

Mike glanced toward her and she caught the sympathy in his eyes. "Maybe you should call him."

"Maybe," Raleigh said. "Maybe we're at an impasse though. Neither of us willing to give in."

"So where do you two go now?"

Raleigh shrugged. "I'm figuring that out."

"This is why," Mike said, grinning, "I keep things easy."

"I've heard relationships are worth it," Raleigh said. Confusion again. She had to draw that line between her and Mike. Too risky for her heart otherwise.

"Maybe," Mike said, glancing toward her and then back toward the highway. "I want a partner in crime though, not all those divisions."

A piano tune strummed from Raleigh's phone. "Hold that thought."

Raleigh rummaged in the pocket of her bag and then saw Cousin Joey's name flashing on the screen when her hand finally came up with it. He didn't usually call during the day or even at all unless it was an emergency, which caused an uneasy feeling of panic for a moment until she pulled herself together.

"Raleigh," he said, his voice far away. A click resounded in the line and then she could tell she was off of speaker. "You said you would owe me, and I have a way for you to pay me back."

"Oh, really?" Raleigh asked, imagining him sitting at his desk, a stack of paperwork in front of him.

"Well, see," he said, a creaking noise resounding in the background, "I've been given a chance to prove my chops as a detective instead of just an officer, and I've been assigned to cold cases."

"Congratulations," Raleigh said. "I know you've been wanting this promotion."

"Right, right, not too excited until it sticks though," Cousin Joey said, "but that's where the favor comes in."

"Hmm," Raleigh said, wondering how his promotion involved a favor from her. Hopefully not something that involved Max because she wouldn't be able to help Joey.

"I was thinking that maybe with your skills, I may be able to get answers that weren't available in the past, and we can get closure for these people. What do you think?"

"What does your boss think about this?"

"I haven't run it by him," Cousin Joey said and then chuckled. "I was thinking maybe we would try it out and then demonstrate the success rate to him first."

Only a few months ago, she'd done the exact same thing by forcing a connection to someone who had been dead awhile to give answers to his distraught family. Not the far distant past though. She didn't know if something like this would even work. She'd briefly considered the idea of offering her services out, but she'd been unsure if it would work so had dismissed it.

"Raleigh?" Cousin Joey disturbed her thoughts, and Raleigh realized she'd been silent for longer than normal.

"Sorry," Raleigh said, glancing toward Mike. "I don't know if that would work. I mean, I've never tried to do something like that."

"Oh, I know it's a long shot that might not work out," Cousin Joey said, computer keys clicking in the background. "I just thought it would be something we could try. Kind of like fighting the bad guys together when we were kids."

"Give me a day or so to think about it," Raleigh said, "Mike and I are trying to track down a story right now."

"Sure thing," Cousin Joey said. "Just give it a real thought. I think this could be a good thing."

Raleigh hung up and glanced at Mike.

"A problem?" Mike asked.

"No," Raleigh said. "Joey wants me to help him with some cold cases, you know, with my connection thingy."

"Wow," Mike said, grinning. "Then we'd really have a way into a case. We'd be right in the middle of the investigation."

Raleigh couldn't deny the warm feeling of the "we," as if they were a packaged deal. "What if my ability doesn't work that way?" Raleigh asked, nibbling on her bottom lip.

"But what if it does?" Mike said, glancing at her. "Think of all the people you'd be helping."

That almost made her forget her fear of actually using her ability. Even though she enjoyed the after effects of helping settle the dead and providing answers for their death, connecting to them caused fear and pain and emotional exhaustion. It was a trade-off. Not an easy choice.

Chapter Twenty-Three

"So, I was checking out background on the contestants, and Madison really knows how to pick them, huh?" Max asked, sipping from his wine glass.

Raleigh laughed and picked at the Chinese food in the carton. "Yes, I've thought that a time or two. She claims they were the best of the auditions, but I'd hate to see the worst."

Max leaned back against the sofa. They were sitting around the coffee table, dining on Chinese food after he'd shown up with bags in hand from the local restaurant along with their favorite bottle of wine. No words about last night or this morning's interview at the hospital were spoken, and Raleigh tried her best to bury the words that struggled for air under the soy sauce and fried rice. Avoiding the trouble flitting at the edges made her feel as though they were on their first date— awkward.

"I know work has consumed all of my time lately," Max said, smiling at her as he tapped his fingers on the sofa. "We haven't been able to spend much time together, and that's put a strain on... us. But this case will end like the others, and things will go back to normal."

"Normal, huh?" Raleigh asked, setting the Styrofoam container down on the coffee table.

"Well," he said offering her a sheepish grin. "As normal as things ever are between us."

"Should we be worried about that?" Raleigh asked, leaning forward, studying his face for any twitches or tells.

"I can't say I haven't thought about it," Max responded, sighing deeply as he set his glass down. "The hurdles do make it tough, but we just need to figure out how to make it work."

"How?" Raleigh asked.

He shrugged. "Compromise?"

"I know we both have jobs to do," Raleigh said, searching for nice words, words that didn't come back and bite her in the ass later. "I wish we could figure out how to work together instead of against each other."

"It's not always easy with my cases. I can't share information on an open case, especially information that will be broadcasted to everyone," Max said, "but if we love each other, I'm sure we can respect the limitations and get past them."

Raleigh gaped at him. Love? Who'd said anything about love? Just yesterday she'd been trying to figure out if she liked him enough to deal with the hassles that came along with this relationship. She hadn't considered love at any point in time. Should she view that as a sign?

He studied her, waiting for a response. "You don't feel the same?" He asked after a growing silence passed between them.

Raleigh swallowed against the sudden golf ball in her throat. "I feel..." She cleared her throat and attempted to gather her thoughts. "I don't know how I feel. Everything has been so complicated. It's like our careers are in the way of our relationship, and I need to know how that's going to work out."

"Is that all you think about? Work?" Max asked, his voice tightening.

"My career is pretty important to me, about as much as yours is to you," Raleigh said, hearing the defensiveness slipping into her voice, knowing that an argument would be the result. "And lately I've felt as if you expect me not to do my job so you can do yours. It's not something that makes thinking about a future with you easy."

"What I do matters." He held up his hand as she opened her mouth to protest, feeling infuriation growing. "And you help. Your ability helps catch murderers, not to mention you help families of the deceased.

"Traiteur to the dead doesn't pay my bills," Raleigh exclaimed, frustrated. "And my career is at the *Barbeaux Gazette*."

"Can't you see that putting details of cases out there hinders actually helping people?" Max asked, moving from the floor to the sofa. "People are out there hunting the rougarou because of a detail you put out there that I asked you not to. No one needed to know that yet."

"If you'd release information, those same people would be reassured that a monster isn't out there hunting them. People have the right to know what is happening in our community. Would you prefer they not be careful and continue to be attacked?" Raleigh felt the heat of her anger in her forehead and her hands. She thought they'd moved past this.

"You are going to keep printing details unless you open your eyes to the reality of this situation."

Anger shot through her and her face tensed up.

"I shouldn't have said that," he said, pulling back, his face slipping into his poker face. "I think I'm going to go so both of us can cool down and think this through."

Raleigh let him rise without a comment or an attempt to stop him.

"I will see you tomorrow night, and hopefully we will have time to think about this."

Raleigh stood and walked toward the kitchen, away from him and toward her chocolate. It would taste stale and heavy in her mouth, but an overdose of chocolate would send her to sleep. And she would need help or her anger would fester and keep her awake.

The glass in the front door rattled as it closed behind him.

Later, after fitfully turning and twisting herself in her comforter, a distinct rustling sound below lulled her from the semi-consciousness she'd managed. Her frustration over Max propelled her downstairs without fear, for she knew that her only visitor must be Aunt Clarice. The rather predictable spirit would perhaps be entertaining or lounging around. Neither mattered because Raleigh wasn't in the mood tonight.

In the living room, Aunt Clarice draped herself across her favorite settee in the pink and maroon kimono that Raleigh had seen on her so many times growing up. In fact, aside from the shimmery glow, the woman appeared to be the larger-than-life figure of her childhood. Short gray streaked bob. Two wrinkles across the forehead, which she called her good time lines. Thin hands, long legs. The only thing missing was that thin Virginia Slim dangling from her fingers. As far as Raleigh remembered, it had spent more time burning in her fingers than it ever had in her mouth, although it hadn't stopped the cancer from spreading like a wisp of smoke through her insides.

"Well, hello, darlin'," the woman chimed. "Thought you and I could chat a bit."

Raleigh swallowed, her courage evaporating by the millisecond. "We shouldn't be able to chat at all. You do realize you died about fifteen years ago, right?"

"Well, that doesn't mean I have to act it, dear." She chuckled in her deep rich voice. "Death isn't quite as boring as all that."

Raleigh moved into the room toward the wing-back chair, noticing the elephant on the coffee table again.

"Why would I expect boring from you?"

"There's the favorite grandniece I remember." She chuckled. "I figured if we are going to share my home, we may need to work out a few matters."

"Your home?" Raleigh questioned. "Where's your half of the rent then?"

She chuckled. "Unfortunately, I had to say goodbye to such matters. Otherwise, I'd keep a better collection of reading material around here." Her thin arched eyebrows rose even higher.

"Reading materials, rent, it all requires money, and I require sleep to make it," Raleigh said, dropping onto the chair, getting the idea that negotiations could take awhile.

"Such a dreadful topic, but you know what isn't? Parties." She leaned her head back. "Ahh, it is so lovely to throw a party. You should try it sometime. Nothing like Madison, of course. Some decorum is necessary, but a little fun never hurt anyone. Liven up the place a bit."

"I'll consider it, if you limit yours to once a week," Raleigh said.

"Hmm," Aunt Clarice pursed her lips, thinking. "Agreed. If you keep a better selection of glossies. I do so miss the gossip and the fashion and, oh, the travel! Apparently, I can't just go anywhere I please, at least not far from that retched mausoleum."

"Done," Raleigh said, and then an idea popped into her head. "And no spying on me when I'm with private company."

"But what fun would that be?" Aunt Clarice said, and then chuckled. "I'll try, but I can only promise to stay out the bedroom, dear."

A knock came at the front door, and Raleigh immediately glanced at the clock above the small corner fireplace. 12:30. Who dropped in this late? Madison would just use the hide-a-key. Usually, late night visitors meant bad news.

At the door, legs all the way to the neck greeted her. In yoga tights, a messy bun, and no bra on, Amber appeared to have just rolled out of bed herself.

"Oh, good," she said, smiling lollipop sweet. "I was hoping I'd catch you still awake."

"I heard a noise," Raleigh said, looking back to see Aunt Clarice's head around the corner of the living room archway.

"Just my luck then," she said. "I was hoping to borrow a candle. I was working, and the electricity went out. It was so weird."

"Did you check your breaker box?" Raleigh asked, moving towards a large cupboard against the side of the staircase.

"I didn't think of that," she said, surprise edging her voice. "You're so good at this house thing. I couldn't figure out how the thermostat worked yesterday. Didn't realize how much my dad had to do before now."

Raleigh handed her a candle from the bottom shelf of a cupboard, even though after that comment, she hesitated giving the girl fire. She didn't want Mrs. Margaret's ghost haunting her because she was responsible for her house burning down.

"I was thinking about what you said about Mike," she said, clutching the candle to her chest. "I don't think he's as available as you think. He seems distracted."

"That's just Mike," Raleigh said. "He's difficult to pin down."

"Or maybe he's holding out for someone," she said, smiling. "Well, goodnight."

Raleigh closed the door behind her and felt exhaustion hit her. Amber's remarks warranted consideration, but the gears weren't working properly. Too little sleep.

"I like her," Aunt Clarice commented. "She has spunk."

"She makes me feel old," Raleigh said, locking the door and turning toward the stairs.

"Then you aren't doing it right."

"Doing what right?" Raleigh asked, feeling too tired for this conversation.

"Life."

Now she was being judged by a ghost. Time to go to bed.

Chapter Twenty-Four

Raleigh placed a platter of drumettes on the coffee table and scanned the living room for anything out of place to distract from the food and fluffed pillows. Only last night, Aunt Clarice had told her that she needed to liven the place up with a party. How ironic that Max had planned tonight's gathering without her knowledge. Of course, Raleigh knew an information collaboration wasn't the kind of party Aunt Clarice was talking about, but it did mean people in the house and an atmosphere of entertainment.

"Taco dip," Sheri said, placing a large casserole bowl next to her platter. "My specialty."

"It wasn't too much trouble leaving Shawn?" Raleigh asked, waiting for her to sink into the sofa cushions before sitting down next to her.

"He wanted to spend time with his *grandmother*." She shuttered at the word grandmother, but she visibly shrugged it off. "He's coming around to me though."

"I brought the important stuff," Mike said, setting two wine bottles down on the coffee table. "I'll get some glasses and the opener."

Raleigh studied him, wondering about the tense set of his jaw and his cursory glance over her. She could tell something was off about him tonight. Maybe there was something about what Amber said last night. Something she'd missed. Did Mike know how to be in a relationship? Was that the real problem? Not that she was an expert, and maybe that's why she hadn't recognized anything wrong with him before. Her men expertise proved nonexistent these days. For some reason she couldn't stop fantasizing about her childhood friend who could possibly ruin their friendship after one date. Not to mention, she couldn't decipher Max's complete 180-degree turn.

He'd arrived at 5:30 with groceries and party plans already made. While he'd prepared food in the kitchen, he'd notified her that he'd considered their issues and figured that they needed to work together. Getting along might help the case as well as salvage their relationship. He vowed to disregard his boss's repeated warnings to keep the details from her if they could work out how these details were relayed. She suspected concealment of identity may be part of that, but she simply listened while he rambled. The sheriff was due for reelection this coming year, and maybe she needed to volunteer to run the opposition's campaign, whomever that may be.

"Is Madison coming?" Sheri asked, picking up a cucumber from a veggie platter she'd chopped under Max's strict instructions. Apparently, rubbing the ends together wasn't part of his upbringing. Me'Maw would be ashamed.

Raleigh glanced at Max as he walked in with a large, table-size notepad. As he set it up on an easel he'd hauled in earlier, he scrutinized the space, fooling with it to get it to sit straight. "She said she'd try to drop in," Max said, moving a small wooden trinket that had belonged to Aunt Clarice from the top of the fireplace mantle so as the notepad didn't knock it over. "Something about editing."

"Huh?" Raleigh said. "There's no editing this week. The Mardi Gras ball preparations and ball all occur this weekend."

"No telling with Madison." Sheri said. "She's always up to something."

"Someone say my name?" Madison breezed in, removing dark shades from her face.

"Max said you were editing?" Raleigh asked, peering at her inquisitively. Madison avoided her eyes, but that telltale crease of guilt didn't indent her forehead.

"Just something I'm working on." Madison said, throwing herself across the rose-wing back chair. "You know the show ends this week."

Max pulled a marker out of his leather satchel. "Let's see if we can ensure everyone makes it to the end of filming."

"How's the last victim?" Mike questioned, returning with his arms loaded with wine glasses.

Max shrugged. "The animal got a few bites in, but he'll recover. He didn't see anything, of course."

"I don't see how," Madison said, reaching for a glass as Mike set them down. "I mean, if something is attacking me, I'm going to open my eyes to see what it is."

Max jotted down "Luther Foret" on the large notepad. "He was drunk and walking home from Doug's bar. He reports seeing mean red eyes and then being knocked to the ground."

"But if it is the same animal, then that means the contestants aren't a target." Raleigh asked.

Max wrote connection to *Barbeaux Hearts* with a question mark as a branch for his name.

"Well, Luther Foret used to work at Dangger Welding until he was fired for going to work drunk one too many times," Madison said, squinting at the board. "But he never had any association with the show. I checked into all the contestants to see if he was family or a friend, but only Lauren knew of him. His mama lives not too far from where her family used to live."

Max added these details to the paper.

"The professor said that a wolf would not acknowledge a master when he reached three years old," Mike said, handing Raleigh and Sheri a glass of wine. "Perhaps we have an animal going against its master, so it isn't a targeted attack at all?"

Max nodded. "I've considered that possibility, and it would explain the presence of a footprint near Deon's body." Max wrote these notes in the upper left corner.

Raleigh said, "It doesn't feel like a coincidence that the two contestants that were in the lead for the show ended up dead though."

Madison humphed. "Yes, and destroyed my show in the process. They had the most chemistry on camera, and everyone on and off the show knew it. Now it's just blah."

"Most are just trying too hard," Sheri said, sipping from her glass. "Deon and Aryanna were better con artists. More polished, I suppose, is what you'd call it. Definite charmers."

"But charmers usually break many hearts," Mike said. "And they both left a long trail behind them, so that could be motive."

"And they both received a picture," Raleigh added, absentmindedly considering all the connections the two had made and how that did not lead to narrowing down to one suspect.

"Have we learned more about the pictures?" Max asked.

"They won't divulge what the pictures are of, but we get the idea that it involves past embarrassing situations," Madison said, crossing her legs and reaching for a carrot stick.

"There's only implied blackmail," Raleigh added. "As if it is more about someone letting them know that they have the power to hurt or ruin them. For instance, Frank is gay, but he hasn't told his family yet. The picture reveals that someone else knows besides the few he trusts to have told."

"This way sparks more fear though," Mike said. "The receivers don't know exactly what this person knows and what they will do with this information. Fear and manipulation working together."

Max nodded, his eyes faraway as he absorbed all of this, processing it. "So, nothing to warrant an investigation for blackmail or extortion charges, but plenty of fear going around as to what will happen with this information."

"Exactly," Raleigh said. "They all have one reason or another to believe it is a certain person. After listening to them, I narrow it down, but then the next person changes my mind. Right now I'm at Patrick or Lauren for very different reasons."

"So you believe it is a contestant doing it, not an outsider?" Max asked, beginning a new branch on the oversized paper.

"I think an outsider would have blackmailed them for something," Mike said, "A contestant gets to watch the reaction and see the drama of the blame game going on."

"And are we positive that Deon and Aryanna both received photos?" Max asked, giving them their own branch on the developing messy tree.

"That was the word," Madison said, "but they were real secretive. When someone received a photo, they didn't want to talk about it because, of course, they didn't want to reveal the content of the photos. Usually, we discovered the issue during a confrontation because, as you know, they liked the drama."

"Deon confronted Clara and Lauren, and Aryanna confronted Kimberly." Raleigh added.

Max jotted these down.

"Are we sure it isn't just a wild animal running around out of control?" Sheri asked, picking up a chicken drumette. "I guess I don't want to believe someone would use an animal to kill with. It just sounds terrible."

Max offered Raleigh a reassuring smile. "Well, for Deon's crime scene there was the footprint, of course," Max said. "But for Aryanna's crime scene, small details didn't add up. Now maybe they can be explained away, but a few items had fallen out of her purse over the blood spatter on the grass. I believe it happened after she was attacked. An animal doesn't search someone's purse, not without leaving evidence at least."

Mike ran his fingers through his hair. Raleigh sipped her wine, thinking about the implications. She herself had wanted it just to be an animal or at least an owner who'd lost control of a pet. But this sounded more sinister. More intentional.

"But why?" Sheri asked. "Sure, she was acting strange when I spoke to her, but if she would have had something important, I think she would have already done something with it. She sounded…" Sheri searched for a word, "determined."

A knock pounded on the door, and everyone looked toward the doorway expectantly. Waiting for someone to open the door was only for strangers in Barbeaux Bayou. A moment later, heavy boots clomped in the hall.

"Nobody get up," Joey called, his boots echoing down the hall.

"Hey Joe," Madison said with a smile. "Working late tonight?"

Joey's uniform appeared wrinkled and dark circles stretched down into his cheeks. "Volunteered to take care of some business I think we'd rather keep quiet for now."

"Hmm?" Raleigh puzzled over Joey who now stood in the doorway. Even with the bulky navy blue jacket, the developing stoop to Joey's shoulders was visible. Paw said that no one worked harder than Joey.

"Well, now," Joey said, "A subpoena needed to be served, and since I knew Madison was here tonight, I figured I could do it without a scene. Always the best way."

Joey retrieved an envelope from an inside jacket pocket, walked over, and handed the thick packet to Madison who took it without a trace of emotion on her face.

"Is Deon or Aryanna's family suing the show?" Sheri asked, alarmed.

Madison opened the envelope with one swift jab of her finger. Within moments the papers were unfolded, and she was skimming through them.

Placing them in her lap, she closed her eyes and pressed her lips tightly together. From the death grip on the papers and the lighter shade of her face, Raleigh could tell it was bad.

"It's Jeffrey, isn't it?" Raleigh asked, her heartbeat quickening.

Madison nodded. "He's suing for a paternity test with intentions of seeking custody."

"Custody?" Raleigh asked. "As in, taking him away from you?"

"It doesn't really say much. I suppose I will have to get a lawyer."

"I can recommend my ex-wife's attorney," Max said. "He sure knew how to work the system."

Madison nodded. "At least I don't have to wait for it anymore. I knew this was inevitable as soon as Raleigh moved back into town. He never paid much attention to me until then."

Raleigh jerked back as if slapped, even though Madison's words had no malice in them at all.

"Jeffrey Zedeaux always had this strange fascination with Raleigh," Mike said, shrugging. "But I am surprised you managed this long without him figuring it out. Barbeaux Bayou isn't known for keeping quiet, and Mason resembles Jeffrey in his appearance."

"All the same," Joey said, sinking into an armchair. "You may want to break the news to Me'Maw gently. Let her tell Paw."

Madison nodded. "I will when I figure out how this news and gentle can be achieved at the same time."

"With such a small town," Max said, "It always surprises me that there are any secrets left."

"The key is to never tell anyone," Madison said. "Most people here talk. They tell someone and that someone tells someone else. Nothing stays secret if you don't first confide it in someone else."

Max considered her words for a moment as he looked at the chart. "So did Deon or Aryanna keep secrets? Were they good at keeping secrets, I mean?"

"Deon, no," Sheri said. "When he wanted attention, he'd tell anyone his entire life history, and since he lived for attention, you get the idea."

"Aryanna wasn't open," Madison said. "Discreet is more like it. She shared what she wanted, but she kept quiet about anything that would stain her good girl reputation."

Max added these details to his chart.

"Nice way to work a case," Joey said, peering at the notes intently. "You know ol' Luther walked that stretch of road every night. He drank at Doug's bar until two most mornings and then began his walk. I've picked him up a time or two on my rounds. He sleeps in this old tire-less, rusted Volkswagen near his mom's property."

"So this would have been his routine?" Max asked.

"Yep," Joey said. "That stretch isn't lit by any streetlights. Dark as can be at that time of night, and even the tall pines block out the moonlight. He's lucky that Justin could find him, even with Raleigh's instructions."

"That's a thought," Max said, staring at the chart paper. "Doesn't that dark stretch connect to the back of the station?"

Mike nodded. "Wooded, marsh area. No roads or anything. It's a couple of miles though."

"But dark enough for a dangerous animal to hide." Max said, jotting down something illegible.

"We still need to tie the animal to a human," Raleigh added.

Everyone sat quietly considering the possibilities.

"Would it be possible to check out Elmer's cameras?" Mike asked.

Raleigh nodded. "Maybe with a warrant? I can't believe they weren't real, and they could give us a clue as to the animal and if a human is actually with the animal."

"What are we talking about here?" Max asked, glancing from one to the other.

"Old man Elmer's cameras are certainly real," Joey added. "He used them to bust his brother for stealing his chickens last year. Not a pretty family squabble there."

The lines on Max's forehead crinkled together as he attempted to catch up with the conversation.

"The chicken story," Raleigh said. "He told us the cameras didn't work, but they looked real to us. Maybe the video can give us something."

Max nodded, catching up. He jotted this on the board, but she could see the idea working through his tight stance.

"So Raleigh, did you give my proposal some thought?" Joey asked.

"What proposal, Raleigh?" Sheri asked.

"Working some cold cases with Joey," Raleigh said. "Using my family inheritance for something other than to drive me insane."

"So you're in then?" Joey said grinning.

"Wait," Max said, stepping closer to her, "are you going to be working at the department?"

"Ah, no," Joey said, grinning. "She's only consulting for me, keeping it under the table."

"Won't that cause trouble, Raleigh?" Max asked. "The sheriff's head might explode."

"It'll be alright," Raleigh said, "I may not even be able to… uh… get it to work that way, but if it does, Joey can use some help."

Max frowned and turned toward the notepad.

Mike grinned. "I can imagine the stories that this will drag up. Has to be more interesting than the council meetings."

Max glanced back, and Raleigh could see that he wanted to say something, but he refrained as their eyes met.

She didn't know if it was a sign that he'd accepted her career or if they would be arguing about it later on. The world had tilted today, and she was feeling uneasy about the new stance.

Chapter Twenty-Five

Raleigh stuck the needle back into the tomato shaped pincushion and released a deep breath, hoping to feel its relaxation effects. The taut tension still clenched her shoulders from the surrounding chaos. Kimberly's fingers felt along the seam of the blue sapphire beaded gown where the ravel had been only moments ago.

"Crisis diverted," she said, smiling, her false eyelashes brushing against her eyelids. "Now, let's see how much trouble I can cause."

Raleigh tilted her head, forcing her eyes not to roll. "Try to at least wait until after the crowning so we can get some decent video."

"Relax, it's not me you have to worry about," Kimberly said, sashaying toward the exit, the gown tapping against itself. "Wait until you see what Lauren has planned."

Raleigh groaned. Time to find Lauren and delay, delay, delay. Whatever the plan may be couldn't be good considering how the night was running so far.

Winter strolled in with a red, body-hugging number and stilettos that elongated her legs for miles. The woman already reached nearly six feet, so the added height made an enormous impact, only enhanced by her angular cheekbones and platinum blonde locks tumbling from the top of her head.

"Just who I needed to find," Winter said, a frown playing at her lips. "Madison says my nipples can't show on television. Something about ratings and censors and a bunch of mumbo jumbo that she rattled on about as she ran about in a tizzy."

Raleigh reached into the emergency bag of supplies, which should be called the cover their asses bag, and handed Winter some self-adhesive pads. Many of these girls had never worn beaded gowns and had not realized that the fabric beneath was pretty sheer. After handing out four packages tonight, Raleigh wished they had thought to give each girl a care package with these items if only to spare herself these conversations. The panty line conversations had caused her more than a faint blush.

"Come on now," Winter said, smiling as she ran her fingers over the plastic packaging. "You aren't going to put them on for me?"

Winter winked, saving Raleigh from a response. Earlier, Helena had been unable to figure out how to follow the three step directions, which had caused quite a bit of uncomfortable laughter as several had helped her attach them after she'd unzipped in the middle of the open room.

"Seriously though," Winter said, "I feel like something is going to happen tonight. The tension in the room is unreal."

"How so?" Raleigh asked, fiddling with scissors, pens, fabric tape, and other items as she repacked them back into the bag.

"Plenty of whispers making their way around," Winter said, patting down her flat tummy. "I'm waiting for it to get to me. I'll let you know what's up when it does, but everyone seems on edge."

"Thanks for the heads-up." Raleigh followed her out of the prep room and into tonight's grand ballroom, which on a regular day served as the town hall. The massive, open room had been transformed with gaudy Mardi Gras decorations, all courtesy of the local Mardi Gras shop. Ms. Betty had outdone herself with the gold flourishes and the white backdrops. Mountains of papier-mâché had been used to recreate a casino theme with a Louisiana crawfish and fleur-de-lis twist. Giant dice, cards, and blackjack wheels towered from every corner. Massive fleur-de-lis signs sat on each side of the band, and thousands of balloons arched over individual booths with gaming activities. However, since a real gaming license wasn't a part of tonight's events, the guests played for fun.

Some of the guests had already claimed tables and gathered in small cliques for animated discussions, while others milled about, mingling with all the who's who of Barbeaux Bayou. The mayor dazzled with a red sequined tie, and Councilman Stephens had an eggplant purple tux on reminiscent of Barney episodes that Madison tried getting Mason to watch. He showed no interest. Raleigh recognized the sheriff out of uniform and even Mimi Blanch made her rounds. If Barbeaux had an event of the year, this was it.

Spotting Madison with the show's bigwigs, Raleigh headed toward Mike instead. Hobnobbing with the bosses wasn't Raleigh's idea of fun. Sipping from a beer bottle, Mike directed the camera guys to get shots of the contestants weaving in and out of the dance floor and trying their luck at the game tables. Until the final selection of the queen and king, tonight's goal was a montage of camera shots. A parade segment would be added as the ending of the show on Sunday at the last minute before it aired that night. A tight schedule, to be sure, but local, small-town reality shows didn't have the advantage of months of taping like national television. With their budget, they felt lucky to have pulled off all they had.

"Do we get to drink tonight?" Raleigh asked, nipping a glass of champagne from a passing server.

Mike grinned, his cheek dimpling. "Well, I didn't volunteer for this job. All hands on deck means I'm going to enjoy what I can."

Raleigh glanced around, noticing Lauren speaking with Jeffrey Zedeaux. In his black tux jacket and slicked back hair, he looked sharp, but not enthralled by whatever Lauren went on about. He glanced around the room several times as the two spoke, not paying much attention to her. When he and Raleigh's eyes met during one of his scans, he nodded once with a steely look in his eyes.

"Something's going on tonight," Raleigh said from behind her glass. "Have you heard anything?"

Mike scanned the room. "Lots of whispering."

Raleigh sipped at the harsh bubbles in her glass. Not sweet enough or chocolate enough. Shouldn't chocolate be a mandatory staple at celebrations?

"Max isn't here yet," Raleigh said, sweeping the room again. "He texted earlier that he was on to something, and they had a search warrant to serve."

"Did he give specifics?"

Raleigh shook her head. "No, but he said to be careful that the trail was leading back to the contestants. I figured he got a look at Elmer's video footage."

Mike took a swig from his bottle and used the opportunity to look around the ballroom. "Everyone's present, so someone in here is our culprit."

"At least wild animals weren't invited." Raleigh shuddered as she recalled the condition of Deon and Aryanna's body.

Madison's arm linked around Raleigh's waist. "Tell me why Lauren would be talking to Jeffrey. That's a strange connection."

Raleigh observed the flustered expression on Madison's face. As Barbeaux royalty and a contributor to the Laissez les Bon Temps parade, Jeffrey's invitation wasn't a choice, but Madison seemed especially put out tonight. After the subpoena for a DNA test, Raleigh would imagine that proximity to Jeffery made the ordeal awkward.

"She's up to something," Raleigh said, noticing that Lauren leaned in closer and clutched Jeffrey's arm now.

"Every time I've seen her tonight, she's off whispering to someone. They stop as soon as I approach." Madison's red dress accentuated every curve, in all the right places, but it also drew attention to her. Attention that Raleigh thought she'd been trying to steer away from herself with her new career plans. Frederico Taylor approached with two glasses of champagne and offered her one.

As the son of a wealthy shipyard owner, Frederico Taylor was quite the catch. His quintessential tall, dark, and handsome looks were an added bonus to his bank account. Typically, he flirted and had a fair staple of women on speed dial to keep him busy. Raleigh wasn't sure when he'd noticed that Madison existed as the two certainly traveled in different circles.

"You throw a lovely soirée, Ms. Cheramie," Frederico said, raising his glass to her. "Our balls of the past have never been quite this elegant."

Madison smiled her phony, charming expression. "Just a little something for the cameras. Appearances count for so much these days."

"That they do." He gazed into her eyes, and Raleigh became uncomfortable standing this close to them, feeling as if the two should have privacy.

"I do hope you are enjoying it, and the cameras aren't so bothersome," Madison said, raising the glass to her lips.

"Not at all," he said. "After all, I am not in the limelight tonight. However, I would hope that you would save me a dance after the crowning of our king and queen."

"I'm sure I can make room in my dance card," Madison said.

"Until then." He raised his glass to her and walked off.

Raleigh pulled her sister in. "What was that about?"

"I have no idea," Madison said before chugging the champagne down. "I've never even met him in person before. David had to do all the talking to the parade board to get this event approved. As a member of the board, David said it was too sensitive for anyone to talk to Frederico Taylor but himself."

"Don't look," Mike said, "but if Jeffery could shoot laser beams from his eyes, we'd have holes in us."

"Hmm," Madison said, snuggling in closer to Raleigh. "The two do own rival companies."

"Interesting," Raleigh said, watching as Frederico stopped to talk to a pretty blonde that Raleigh recognized as Barbeaux socialite Tiffani Boudreaux. Young, wealthy, and a college student, she didn't work, but she could be seen around town in her black Mercedes. She was the typical woman Frederico strung around on his arm. "I think you need to see where this leads and what is going on."

Madison nodded. "I'm with you, sister. Something we can finally agree on."

Lauren turned away from Jeffery, but he caught her by the arm. Raleigh watched as he walked with her toward the dance floor, a smile beaming across her face as though she'd just achieved all her dreams. Clearly, Jeffery had deduced more from the introduction than was there, but did that mean he was jealous, or was something else going on?

"Y'all follow them to the dance floor," Madison said.

"What?" Raleigh asked alarmed.

"You two go dance and watch her," Madison said, taking Raleigh's champagne glass. "I want to know what's going on there."

Mike set his beer bottle down on a nearby table. "I usually prefer to ask my partner to dance, but I think we need to stay on her. Something isn't feeling right."

Raleigh nodded, watching Madison drain her glass. It was a good thing that their job involved socializing and taking care of the contestants tonight. The Mardi Gras club was in charge of hosting duties, after Madison had Madified the carnival club's original plans, of course. Having never attended the carnival club ball, the typical décor wasn't her firsthand knowledge, but according to the members, Madison had raised the bar high for future balls.

Raleigh followed Mike to the dance floor, the strappy heels tapping flimsily against the confetti-covered linoleum floor. She preferred good solid boots, but evening gowns and killer heels apparently made a statement, at least according to Madison. As usual, her sister's advice when choosing a dress had been to pick one that Max couldn't ignore, even though she had to add she still couldn't understand why she wanted him in the first place. With this green cross beading detail, Raleigh wasn't sure what statement Max would understand nor would it count if he didn't arrive to see her in it.

She glanced around the ballroom, yet again, as Mike swept her up into his arms. Her body relaxed against his chest, inhaling his ocean fresh scent. Must be a new body wash.

"Looking for Max?" Mike asked, his eyes penetrating hers.

She shrugged. "He's always late or a no-show."

"But last night he made an effort to turn things around," Mike said, adding a half-smile. "Does that change things between you two?"

Raleigh sighed. "Truthfully, I don't know."

Raleigh moved her head against his chest so she could get a view of Lauren and Jeffery swaying as Lauren laughed at something he'd said. It was an overdramatic laugh, something to show him that she was into him and thought everything he said was funny. Raleigh cringed.

"Raleigh," Mike said, his thumbs pressing into her waist. "I've been waiting to tell you something."

Raleigh looked back up at him, noticing the crinkles on his forehead indicating his seriousness. Something was up. She'd noticed it recently, and maybe now he'd decided to share with her.

"I figured I'd wait until things fizzled out with Max, but it's like watching a roller coaster that I'm not sure is ever going to come to a stop." He cringed, biting down on his lips. "I mean, I don't want to keep waiting and not tell you."

Raleigh's heart began to pound, blood pumping into her ear. Did Mike know something about Max that he'd withheld from her? What was it? How could Mike keep something from her? Her thoughts raced over the possibilities.

Raleigh swallowed hard, trying to keep her dizzying thoughts at bay. "Tell me what?"

"I want a chance, Raleigh Lynn," Mike said, sucking in air so sharply it whistled. "I've wanted a chance with you since I screwed up that kiss in college."

"Oh," Raleigh uttered, staring up at him, all thoughts deserting her brain. His words sounded foreign, like a translation in a French class.

"I know you will think this is crazy." He laughed, rolling his eyes. His bottom lip twitched. "That we will lose this close friendship we have, but I can't think about any one else these days. I've tried to date other women while waiting, but what's the point? I don't want any of them."

Raleigh opened her mouth, hoping words would form, but they didn't. She continued to gape at him.

"I want your crazy Twix addiction and your knowing all my stories since we were three years old. I want to chase down leads with you and sit at Me'Maw's table and really be part of your family. I want to be there for you when the dead visit so that we can give them closure together. And I don't want to feel like I get kicked in the teeth every time I have to watch him hold you and it's not me."

Panic gripped her in its grasp. Had the world tipped today? Tons of emotions swirled inside, causing an ache in her head.

To avoid his expectant gaze, Raleigh turned toward Lauren and Jeffery. She watched as Lauren slipped a photograph into Jeffrey's jacket pocket without him noticing. Stopping mid-sway with Mike, she watched as it snagged a bit on the pocket hem, and Lauren leaned in closer, planting a kiss near his lips as she pushed it in further.

Unaware of the picture, Jeffrey twirled her out and pulled her back into him. Raleigh noticed he didn't return the kiss.

"Mike," Raleigh said, "Lauren is the blackmailer. I just saw her put a picture in Jeffrey's pocket."

A frown tugged at the corner of Mike's lips as his eyes hardened. "What about what I've said?"

Her fingers pushed into the smooth indention of her scar. "I need time to process this. I'm not saying I haven't thought about you in that way, but what if it goes wrong? I don't know what I would do without you."

He nodded, tilting his head, his eyes warming. "What if it goes right though?"

"Come on," she said, yanking him by the arm off the dance floor toward Madison. She needed to stall this conversation so she could collect her thoughts.

Speaking to three of the office secretaries, Madison watched them approach and stepped away to meet them.

"What's happened?" Madison asked, scanning the room with her piercing eyes. Her sister was on a mission. Those court orders had set a kindling under her, and it was building steam.

Winter sashayed their way, the slinking fabric accentuating her hips, causing more than a few heads to turn. She hooked Madison around the waist, maintaining a beauty pageant smile on her face as she closed their circle in. "I just heard something that you need to know ASAP."

Raleigh waited, the feeling of waiting for something to happen constricting her throat.

"Lauren has told everyone today that you are losing your son to Jeffery Zedeaux and that he has proof that you are a horrible mother and has enlisted her services to expedite the process."

"What?" Raleigh gasped, her gaze immediately going to the two on the dance floor. Madison may be selfish and stubborn, but she was family.

Besides, she'd always done the best she could for Mason.

"She's his lawyer?" Madison said through clenched teeth, the coldness of her green eyes revealing her anger. "Her name isn't on the papers."

"It's probably her law firm representing him," Mike added.

"What good will this do except to embarrass Madison?" Raleigh asked, confused. "The votes have already been calculated for the winner, so she can't change the outcome today."

Winter's smile continued, although her eyes flamed as she scanned the room. "But it gives her social clout in a room of Barbeaux's high society. Everyone is now associating her name as Jeffery Zedeaux's attorney, and we all know the elite flock together."

"She's the blackmailer," Raleigh said. "Or at least the one with the pictures who isn't really blackmailing. It all feels ridiculous, but I just saw her slip a picture into Jeffery's jacket pocket without his knowledge."

"Could you see the picture?" Madison asked, watching as the two walked off the dance floor at the conclusion of the tune, his arm draped around her.

"No," Raleigh said. "I couldn't make it out from our standpoint, but he doesn't know it's there. He probably won't discover it until later."

"Which leaves the question," Mike said, his forehead wrinkled in puzzled thought, "why would she be wanting to scare her own client?"

Clara approached, looking stunning in a yellow, beaded chiffon number. Diamond earrings sparkled on her ears, drawing attention to her blond, curled locks. She couldn't pull off the sexy goddess of Winter, but with all the glam, she certainly had an ethereal inner beauty.

"Madison, Mr. Lebasque told me to let you know that it's time," Clara said, nervously standing behind Madison.

"Thanks, Clara," Madison said, exchanging glances with Raleigh before walking toward the stage. A sense of foreboding overcame Raleigh, and she almost called her sister back, but she dismissed it as simply a result of all the drama of the moment.

"Are you ready?" Raleigh asked, feeling a need to busy her mind and end Clara's awkward, silent staring.

Clara shrugged. "I'm ready to get this over with."

"Me too, Sweetie." Winter smiled. "Then I'm going to kill Lauren for sending me that picture. Her pretty face won't be so attractive after a good bar fight."

Clara's face paled under the layers of makeup, creating a ghastly effect. "Lauren is the one blackmailing everyone?"

Winter nodded. "I'd love to know how she got ahold of those pictures, but the gossip will reveal all since this is Barbeaux Bayou. Well, good luck, Clara. We could all use a little these days."

Winter sashayed toward the court lineup where others had begun to gather for the ceremony.

"Do you think Winter is serious?" Clara asked, concern in her eyes.

Raleigh laughed, thinking of Winter's reputation. Typically, she danced on tops of bars with Madison, but they both appeared to be growing up these days. But one didn't really get too far from their roots, or bar tops in the case of these two. "Winter isn't one to play around, but Madison might beat her to it this time. Lauren should have thought twice before she became involved with something like this."

"Especially as a lawyer," Mike added, crossing his arms as he watched the group form in front of the stage. "I still don't understand what she's getting out of it."

Clara shook her head. "I think I need to go line up now. I just can't believe it's her. She always seemed so nice."

Mike and Raleigh were alone again in a room full of people. An awkward moment of silence passed between them, with the words he'd said standing in the chasm. How would life be if they were together together instead of just friends? His blond hair and angular jaw certainly offered an enticing package, not to mention she knew what his chest looked like from hours helping Nick in construction. With all her fantasies about him lately, she couldn't pretend it wasn't a notion. But an idea only, really. What would happen if they fought? Who would she confide in then? He was her best friend.

"Remember in fourth grade when Molly decided that no girls could talk to boys?" Raleigh asked.

Mike grinned. "Yep, and you broke the rule."

"Yes, but before I broke the rule."

Mike frowned. "It was a long two months. I'd watch you on the playground swinging with the others but ignoring them at the same time. Nate even said that he missed you as our fourth for touch football for recess."

"What I remember is how lonely I was," Raleigh said, looking up at him, hoping he'd understand what she was saying.

He nodded. "I don't…"

Max walked up at that moment, clutching his pinstripe tie in his hand."Did I miss anything?"

Raleigh looked away so she wouldn't see the innocent expectation in his eyes. "Lauren is behind the pictures."

"How do you know?" Max asked, pulling the tie around his neck.

Mike cleared his throat and filled him in on what had transpired since the ball began. Raleigh watched as Madison took center stage with a microphone in her hand while the contestants milled about, some huddling together whispering. None of them lining up waiting for the procession as they should. Raleigh couldn't tell if any of them were even in the right order since their lines looked more like zigzags.

"I'm going to go help Madison out," Raleigh said, touching Mike on his arm as she left the two of them discussing a seemingly nonexistent motive.

Raleigh walked around crowds of people, smiling as people glanced her way. Her sleek green and black dress accented every curve in her body. When Madison had showed up with the designer gown, her first instinct had been to refuse it, her second to ask whom she'd stolen it from. Not a straight stick like Madison, Raleigh's curves didn't fit into some designer's idea of a perfect body, but she had to admit that it pinched and sucked in all the right places with the added benefit of setting off the green of her eyes. But now that people ogled her, she'd prefer a frumpy frock.

Arriving near the contestants, they glanced her way once before shuffling into their places. Apparently, she'd become the sheepdog, and the sheep didn't move unless she rounded them up. When that had happened, she was unsure.

Several were missing, including Clara and Lauren, who from her vantage point, Raleigh had just watched walk in this direction. She began to scan the dance floor.

She caught Patrick's attention and motioned him over. He clapped some young gentleman on the back and headed over with a smile. Looking miffed, Lauren and Clara entered from the back doors, which led to an outdoor pavilion. Lauren approached Kimberly and asked her about her lipstick, while Clara walked to her spot and stood sullen, glaring at the room.

Ben continued talking to his group until Raleigh tapped him on the shoulder and motioned to the lineup. He continued a moment until she began tapping her foot, crossing her arms across her chest. The couple became uncomfortable, glancing at her instead of listening intently to his hunting camp story.

Finally, he waved to his friends and headed for his spot. Counting them off, she verified everyone was in their place before giving Madison a thumbs up, signaling for the DJ to stop the music.

As Madison made nice with her sultry voice to the cameras, Raleigh straightened ties and adjusted collars before moving onto girls' hems not falling right.

Couples were summoned center stage and Raleigh faced Clara.

"Everything alright?" Raleigh asked as Clara showed her teeth to check for anything marring their perfect gleam.

Clara's eyes glistened with unshed tears. "You know Deon warned me not to do this show. I should have listened to him, but it's too late now."

Raleigh smiled, patting her on the arm. "It will all be over in forty-eight hours, and it will just be memories. Not all of them bad, I'm sure."

Clara clamped her lips down hard, and Raleigh hoped those tears didn't spill and mess up her make up. At least not until after the camera got footage. In her head, she knew that she'd had a Madison thought.

Raleigh stepped aside as Clara and Patrick, the shocking pair, joined the procession to the center arch.

"Ladies and gentlemen, I present this year's Laisez Les Bon Temps Royal Court," Madison said, her voice echoing in the building. A resounding applause swept the room, and the cameras did a panorama shot of the crowd.

When the camera returned back to the contestants, Francois's head bobbed from behind the viewfinder and his face was a gasp.

"Now, for the presentation of this year's king and queen…" Madison trailed off as an uproar went through the crowd. Several women let out high-pitched screams. A silence then befell the room.

Raleigh turned to see a giant wolf-like animal blocking the doorway to the pavilion, standing only twenty feet from her.

She backed up slowly, conscious of the click-clack every step her stilettos made against the floor. If she'd worn boots, she could have eased away from certain attack without the glaring announcement of each step.

The creature inched forward, sniffing the floor. Raleigh held her breath as she took another step back, hoping to not draw attention to herself.

The wolf lurched forward in one giant leap and stood inches from her. Raleigh froze, her legs trembling.

"Someone do something," Lauren screeched.

Ben hissed. "Shut up. You'll get its attention."

"I don't want to die like the others," Lauren sobbed.

"This is all your fault," Clara muttered, her face ashen.

"How?" Lauren screeched. "I don't have control over some wild animal."

"It's you," Clara said. "You sent all those pictures."

"No," Lauren stuttered.

"Don't lie," Winter said. "We watched you slip one to Jeffery Zedeaux earlier."

Lauren stomped her foot. "I didn't do anything wrong."

Raleigh exhaled as the wolf creature stepped away from her, but the relief was short-lived as it stepped towards the huddled contestants. Raleigh turned to watch as it eyed them down.

"You." Clara clinched her fists. "You sent that picture to Deon. You told him that I loved him. That letter was private."

"You should be thanking me," Lauren spit out, her face in a grimace. "I did what you didn't have the courage to do."

"Only he didn't love me." Clara choked on a laugh. "He said I was only ever going to be a sister to him. As if I'm not an adult! Like I didn't know he warned everyone to stay away from me. So you would think that would mean he wants me. But no. I was so angry."

Clara glanced at the wolf, which was studying her now, his head tilted, ears pointed up.

"But at least it isn't a secret anymore," Lauren said, tilting her head, aware that the entire ballroom now stared at them, listening. "He died knowing. You can't regret that."

"You don't get it." Clara waved her arms in front of her and the wolf growled, a deep long rumble.

"Ladies," Raleigh said, "I'm not sure that now is the time."

"What don't I get?" Lauren hissed, her voice lower. "That you experienced unrequited love? A broken heart? Big deal. We all have. Life goes on. The show must go on, as they say. We have bigger problems right now in case you didn't notice."

"It's not his fault." Clara gestured toward the wolf. "All Sheeloo knew was that I was angry. He thought Deon hurt me."

Raleigh glanced from the wolf to Clara, understanding clicking.

"You have a name for that thing?" Lauren flung out, disgust in her voice.

In one bound, the wolf sprung towards Lauren, landing right in front of her. She sobbed, tears streaking through her makeup, shoulders trembling.

Raleigh moved in quickly, motioning for the other contestants to merge into the crowd.

"Clara," Raleigh said calmly, with more control of her voice than she thought she could manage. "You need to call him off."

"He won't listen to me anymore," she replied angrily.

"You need to try." Raleigh gritted her teeth, feeling the heat from the wolf's body near her.

"Why?" Clara asked, narrowing her eyes at Lauren. "Hasn't she caused enough pain? And like she said, it's all legal, so it will all be okay. Who cares how many lives she has destroyed? She gets to walk away. If Sheeloo allows her to."

"I'm sorry, okay?" Lauren cried out as the wolf sniffed her hands and growled. "I didn't know things would turn out like this."

"You can't even muster a decent apology!" Clara yelled.

As the wolf snapped at Lauren, Raleigh grabbed her by the shoulder and yanked her to the side. The wolf growled at Raleigh and howled, the sound echoing through the metal building. Several more screams went up around the room.

In an attack pose, the wolf lowered its gaze at Raleigh and prepared to pounce. Lauren clung to her back, shielding herself with Raleigh's body. Raleigh jumped as a hand squeezed hers and looked up into Mike's concerned green eyes. In her peripheral vision, she caught Max moving to the side with his sidearm drawn.

"Clara," Raleigh said, gripping Mike's hand. "This is Sheeloo's last chance."

"I told you, he doesn't listen to me anymore," Clara cried, sobs rattling through her body.

In one majestic leap, the wolf lunged for them, flying through the air. Raleigh swung her head into Mike's chest, momentarily catching Max hesitate to take the shot as he watched the animal come down on Mike.

Raleigh screamed as she pulled Mike towards her, losing her balance with Lauren clinging from behind, all three tumbling over with the impact of the wolf's body colliding with them.

Through the growling, a shot pierced through the commotion. The wolf squealed and then was silent.

Raleigh pushed herself up off the floor. Mike covered his hand with his other hand, and Raleigh saw escaping blood and smelled warm iron. Raleigh searched around them for something to absorb the blood, but came up empty.

Winter bent down and pulled the pad from inside her dress and clamped it over his hand. Red stains came through, but Raleigh held it down tightly against his skin.

Max towered over them, kicked the unmoving wolf, and shouldered his weapon. "Call for a medic." He called out to another officer at the edge of the crowd.

His eyes swept over Raleigh, and then he walked over to Clara and had her turn around to cuff her.

Lauren sat down on the floor and sobbed. "I can't believe this is happening."

Madison walked up behind her as well as Jeffery Zedeaux. He reached into his pocket and handed Madison the picture. She gripped it in both hands, a look of concentration across her forehead.

"You may not suffer any legal consequences, Ms. Lauren," Jeffery said, with one hand on his hip, wrinkling his black tuxedo jacket. "But professionally, you are done. Blackmailing your own clients is not acceptable behavior for an attorney."

"I swear I didn't do anything wrong," Lauren said, sobbing harder. "It wasn't me."

"I watched you do it, Lauren," Raleigh said softly. "But why Lauren?"

The tears ceased, and her eyes were cold. "Because everyone in this town has a secret."

Her eyes gave away something else. Something she wasn't saying. Her interrogation would be fascinating as Raleigh glimpsed something almost psychotic about it.

Max motioned to Officer Nick, who had stepped up behind them in uniform. "Take Lauren in for questioning, too."

Her tears returned as Nick pulled her up and half-dragged her toward the exit.

Madison handed the picture to Raleigh. It was a much younger Madison, teenage looking, less put together, cuddling with a much more relaxed Jeffery Zedeaux. She'd been caught mid-laugh and him with a love-sick grin; they exuded happiness. But clearly in Madison's stick figure, a telltale bump rested below her nonchalantly placed hand.

Interesting. Had Jeffery been oblivious to this when they were together, or did he think something else had happened to Mason? Now wasn't the time to ask, though, and give Jeffery any fuel to use against Madison in court. She and her sister would be having this conversation later though.

"You need to get that bite checked out," Raleigh said, glancing down at Mike's hand again. The white padding now completely blood stained.

Mike grinned, but it turned into a grimace as he moved his hand. "I want hazard pay for tonight. No one said anything about wild animals when I was roped into wearing a tux and being all social."

Madison laughed. "I didn't invite the wild animals, but I will buy you a gift as your hazard pay."

"Ask for a receipt," Raleigh said.

"Yes, because Lord knows Madison will probably just shop her own closet," Winter said, laughing.

Chapter Twenty-Six

"It's coming Nanan!" Mason shouted as he ran around with a giant inflatable baseball bat Mike had purchased off a traveling shopping cart loaded down with parade trinkets.

Raleigh glanced up the highway and saw the police cars signaling the beginning of the parade. Stuffing her hands in the pockets of her jacket, she walked over to Madison, who was in heated talks with Francois.

"Let's get into positions for the toasting," Raleigh said, interrupting the argument.

"Whatever," Francois said, huffing off.

"What was that about?" Raleigh asked.

"He wants me to help him get a raise," Madison said, looping her arm through Raleigh's for the warmth. "He should have been more cooperative when we were trying to work together. Luckily for me, Austin Lebasque is much more cooperative and is still willing to invest in my business venture even after this horrendous mess."

Raleigh kept quiet. He probably deserved a raise after working with Madison. Who didn't? But Madison had a point as well. Francois couldn't have honestly believed that the boss he'd picked a fight with on a weekly basis would recommend him for a pay raise. Hopefully, Lebasque had plenty of patience.

"So you never got around to explaining that picture to me," Raleigh said as the two walked toward the platform. "Did Jeffery know you were pregnant?"

Madison nodded. "When I told him, he was excited. Then he told his parents."

"And?"

"Well, his father told him that he could be a father right now or he could be in the family business, but he wasn't going to have both."

"I guess he chose the family business," Raleigh said. "But that doesn't explain why he didn't know about Mason."

"Well, he gave me the money to have an abortion," Madison said, glancing down at her red pea coat, studying the big buttons down the front. "I didn't know what to do at first, but then his father sent him away to run their Georgia shipyard, so he wasn't here to see if I followed through."

"So you hid your pregnancy from him," Raleigh said in awe. "You might be the only person in Barbeaux Bayou to keep a secret, especially one that huge."

Barbeaux Bayou was small town, but its population was big enough to have circles of people. The Cheramies didn't travel in the same social planet as the Zedeauxs. But gossip traveled, so that had been risky.

"Well, I went to school for a bit in the city and took some business classes. When I came back with a baby, I kind of spread it that the baby was yours." At this, Madison gave Raleigh a contrite smile. "But after awhile, everyone just thought of him as mine, so it was okay. His parents would have heard it was yours and that's all that mattered."

"Oh," Raleigh said, digesting that bit of information. She supposed it didn't really matter. The town had spread enough rumors about her while she was gone. What was one more for Mason's sake? "So what was Lauren trying to accomplish then? This wouldn't help her case."

"I suppose," Madison said as they reached the steps for the platform. "She wanted to remind him that he didn't want Mason from the beginning."

"I don't like the guy," Raleigh said and then shuddered, unable to believe what she was about to say. "But he does seem to love you. Even I can tell how he looks at you."

"I know," Madison said, nibbling on her lip. "But sometimes it's just not enough. All the grand gestures can't erase my memories of not being chosen.

And I may not be mother of the year, but I've always wanted Mason, and I just can't forget that he didn't. Love may not be easy, Raleigh, but you have to start in the same place. He and I just aren't in the same place."

Raleigh nodded. "I think I know what you mean."

"I know you do," Madison said, squeezing her arm. "Now wish me luck. After this toast, we are done."

"I can certainly toast to that," Raleigh said, feeling the anticipation of a normal life around the corner. Well, as normal as traiteur to the dead can get.

Raleigh watched as Madison made it up to the platform with the mayor and the parish president before walking back toward Sheri and Mike and her family.

In his navy jacket, Max stood talking to Sheri. Dressed in a purple tutu, green tights, and a gold sweater, Sheri had applied her eye shadow to match her attire. With a thermosed drink in hand, the stress of the last few weeks had evaporated from Sheri's countenance. Shawn having someone besides her to blame and that daiquiri had taken years off her face.

"Raleigh," Sheri exclaimed, "Max was just explaining to me how Clara lost control of her 'pet'." Sheri added air quotes around pet.

"Wolves, even when it's a hybrid dog, aren't meant to be pets." Paw scowled. "At three years old, they become their own master. That girl was foolish."

Max nodded. "Clara could no longer control the animal, but it still sensed when she was upset. As a pack animal, it thought it was protecting her. We believe Luther was an accident. Sheeloo, the wolf, had expanded the territory it hunted, and Luther wandered into it too inebriated to defend himself. She's looking at a few charges there though."

"At least her motive is clear." Mike kicked at the gravel. "I just don't understand what Lauren was getting out of the pictures. I could have understood blackmail, but just sending them?"

Max shrugged. "The contestants tested the waters for Lauren. Ultimately, her plans were much more elaborate. In interrogation, she divulged that Jeffery Zedeaux was going to be her first mark." Max shuddered. "The woman was unhinged. She had serious plans to have control of everyone who was anyone in this town."

"Did she say how she obtained the pictures?" Mike asked.

"Through the years she has been able to steal them as she's come across them. She's been planning this for a long time. Madison isn't the only one who can keep a secret in this town."

Raleigh remained quiet. Even though Madison may have to come out with the full secret all during a custody trial, it was her sister's secret to tell. Clara had taught them this at least.

"At least we were able to use old fashion detective work with this one," Max said, looking at Raleigh "Not too hard for you with death for this one."

Me'Maw chuckled. "Life and death follow. Raleigh can't escape who she is."

Me'Maw winked at Raleigh from her portable, plastic rocker, and Raleigh smiled. Others would consider the comment odd, out of place. But the woman always saw into Raleigh. Straight through. No hiding anything.

The sirens stopped in front of them, and the volume filled their ears, blocking out any sort of response.

Raleigh tugged Max's arm and motioned for him to follow her to the back parking area where they could be alone and speak without yelling and miming.

Near the station building, the noise remained loud but not ear shattering. Crowds of people waited by the road as the King and Queen float stopped in front of the viewing stands. As tradition, they would be toasted by the mayor and all the officials, which meant the float could be stopped before them for ten minutes.

"Max," Raleigh began, hoping the right words came to her and she didn't screw this up. "I think we need a break."

"What?" Max asked, his eyes narrowing, as he pulled back from her. "A break from what?"

"This relationship," Raleigh said, remembering Madison's words from earlier. "I can't change who I am, and I don't think you want all the parts of me."

"I thought we went over this," Max said, reaching out and touching her arms with his soft hands. She felt the thickness of his fingers curl around her forearm. "I told you I would try."

"But I can't forget that you don't really like who I am," Raleigh said. "Those pieces of me won't change, and I feel like they have to so that this relationship works. It's not fair to either of us to keep fighting about something that we can't fix or change, especially since I don't want to change who I am."

"So that's it?" Max asked, an air of formality back to his voice, coldness in his eyes.

"I think it has to be," she replied, hoping that this was the right decision. Giving up wasn't easy since she didn't like to fail.

He nodded curtly, staring down at her, emotionless. She wasn't fooled though. As a good detective, Max knew how to hide his feelings.

With trepidation, she walked back toward her family, back toward her Paw. She could be reassured she'd made the right choice when she spoke to the family rock.

Paw's heavy coat was rough against her hand as she brushed against him. She leaned against his side, head against his arm. She felt the stoic strength of the man, as well as inhaled his bacon breakfast.

"Where's Max?" He asked.

"It's over," she said, forcing herself not to look back to see if he were still standing near the building. He probably wasn't, but she didn't want the image. "I guess this is where you say something like, when one door closes, another one opens."

He chuckled. "Raleigh Lynn, you've been having a door swaying in the wind for a very long time with that one over there." He gestured toward Mike, who was waiting on the side of the road with Mason. "Maybe closing a few doors might do you some good."

Raleigh frowned. "Mike's my best friend. I don't want to ruin anything between us."

"Ah," Paw said, his eyes twinkling. "I've been married to my best friend for sixty-two years. What if you don't ruin it, what if you just make it better?"

"Sometimes the old man knows what he's talking about," Me'Maw called from her chair. "This might be one of those times, Raleigh Lynn."

"You two are disgustingly sappy today," Raleigh said, frowning. "I thought you might be worried about all the trouble the two of us could get into."

"Y'all going to get into trouble anyway." Paw grinned. "This way y'all don't drag any other innocent into y'all hell."

Me'Maw laughed. "Make up your own mind, love. Just make sure you follow your heart."

"Raleigh," Mike called, gesturing for her to come to the road. "You're going to miss Winter. She's calling for you."

Raleigh shook her head at both her grandparents, and walked to the front to wave to Queen Winter and King Patrick on their float. After the votes had been tallied, the official winner was Lauren, but she was declared to be officially kicked off the show after the incident. As first runner up, Winter had been thrilled to step up and take the position. She wore the tiara well and looked magnificent in her white beaded gown. Patrick looked exactly like the nerd who was gloating that he was deemed the winner.

At the front, Mason darted back and forth near the float, waving to the children attendants that he apparently knew from school. Sheri gossiped with a lady who needed her hair done and had forgotten to call for an appointment, and she and Mike stood side-by-side waving at Winter and Patrick. What could she say? She loved her crazy, mixed-up family of friends and true family. Six months ago, she'd have called someone psycho if they would have told her she'd be back home living here, happy at that. She'd avoided this town like the plague.

Life had happened though; it would keep happening. All of it, not just death.

She reached down and took Mike's hand, the unbandaged one. She felt his larger fingers between hers, and it didn't feel the same as the fingers that had stuck mud in hers the day they'd made those mud pies. It was different somehow. He looked down at her and smiled, his cheek dimpling.

Acknowledgments

Though this story takes place in a fictional world, it is a conglomerate of the places of my childhood memories. I consult the people around me continuously to keep the perspective of South Louisiana. I also want to thank those who offered stories and help along the way in keeping the folklore authentic.

ALSO by JESSICA TASTET

The Raleigh Cheramie Series

THE CUSTOS SAGA

UPCOMING
Book #2 VINDICA

JESSICA TASTET is the author of four novels and a children's story. She's worked as an English teacher for eighteen years and an editor for five years. She lives in Louisiana with her family.

For updates visit:
www.jessicatastet.com